THE KINSMEN BOOK 2

THE INFINITE DARKNESS

Pete Cruickshank

For Catherine

Acknowledgements

This is my second novel, and I feel it only fair to thank all those who helped me complete the first. Everything I learnt, all the mistakes I made and rectified throughout the first Kinsmen book, taught me what to do, and, more importantly, what not to do when publishing this one. Also, thanks to all those who reviewed the aforementioned book.

Concerning Book 2, I'd like to thank
Steff Madawi. My first port of call for critiquing.
My editor Steph Dagg for being with me every step of the way.
My second proof readers — Adam and Catherine.
And finally any and all those who've supported me through social media.

Cast of Characters

James Tennel — Meta-human who works for Garianne and husband of Korina Tennel.

Cieshella Garianne Phulum — Head of the Galacien Observation Agency for planet Earth.

Lytpniuph — An Amelerian veteran of the Nacuerian/Galacien war.

Chnar — An Amelerian. Lytpniuph's first officer.

Jonas — Human super-sentient.

Al (Alex Lethbridge) — Human super-sentient (Earth^2).

Alicia Elde — Human super-sentient.

Cerise — A woman Alex sees in his dreams.

Alex Lethbridge — Human super-sentient.

General Alexander Lethbridge — Human super-sentient (Earth ^{3}).

Princess Victoria — Princess royal of the House of Hanover (Earth ^{3}).

Queen Marina — Monarch of the British Empire (Earth ^{3}).

Korina Tennel — A meta-human (wife of James Tennel).

Belanar Krrikant — Galacien general.

Kursis Orpemantus — Galacien council member.

Yosar — Galacien council member.

Mentoria 'Min' Kendeisa — Veteran of the Nacuerian/Galacien war.

Kallon Ghomn — Galacien citizen. Min's lover.

Talmhon — Galacien council enforcer.

Ruth — Alex's implant.

Alek (Aleksandr Lethbridge) — Human super-sentient (Earth ^{4}).

Nicola — Mercenary (Earth ^{4}).

Nemulous Handerrel — Galacien citizen, human president of Lorusia.

The Adversary / Rhea-hotut — A malevolent god-like being.

ONE. THE CHOICE 1

TWO. TERRA 8

THREE. THE PHI-VIRUS 23

FOUR. ALICIA...34

FIVE. ABDUCTION...42

SIX. DENSARI...54

SEVEN. KRRIKANT 63

EIGHT. THE MARTIANS...70

NINE. GALACIEN PRIME..81

TEN. REUNION 93

ELEVEN. REVELATIONS 105

TWELVE. DISCOVERED..121

THIRTEEN. NICOLA 133

FOURTEEN. KALLON 144

FIFTEEN. INTERSECTIONS IN TIME 160

SIXTEEN. TEA AND SYMPATHY 168

SEVENTEEN. THE TRANS-GALACTIC JUMP 176

EIGHTEEN. LORUSIA 186

NINETEEN. TREN-DOS 193

TWENTY. RUTH 203

TWENTY-ONE. ATONEMENT.................... 209

TWENTY-TWO. DISLOCATION...................... 221

TWENTY-THREE. THE ENTROPHIER........................... 234

TWENTY-FOUR. BATTLE................................ 240

TWENTY-FIVE. CLOSURE 260

TWENTY-SIX. COUNTER-STRIKE 271

TWENTY-SEVEN. DARK ENCOUNTER 286

TWENTY-EIGHT. THE END 300

TWENTY-NINE. CONFRONTATION 308

THIRTY. GALACIEN48 321

THIRTY-ONE. GARIANNE............................... 334

THIRTY-TWO. THE GAME.............................. 347

THIRTY-THREE. ASSEMBLY........................... 359

There are many universes
Some are almost identical to your own
Others are completely different

For the most part they exist as self-contained islands
Never affecting one another
Or aware of each other's existence

universes are born and die every day, yet the
multiverse continues
However, at some point throughout all of eternity,
even the multiverse must face a threat

One. The Choice

The Antarctic, Earth, ten years ago

A lone figure slowly staggered across the desolate white landscape. James Tennel was slowly freezing to death. He had long ago stopped thinking rational thoughts and moved purely on a survival instinct to live. The agony in his limbs was a scream his mind had become almost accustomed to. To stop now would mean to collapse and he knew he would never get up if he fell, for he had pushed his body too hard and for too long.

Ahead of him loomed a huge cliff of ice. *A possible shelter from the wind or maybe just a different place to lie down and die*, he thought. The latter wouldn't be long now. *Funny in a way, but when you live out your life, you never think about how, where and when it's all going to end.* James certainly hadn't thought his visit to the remote scientific outpost on Antarctica would end in disaster.

At last he reached the wall of ice and snow. So large, it seemed to almost have a sentient presence about it in this lonely place. He began to make his way along it hoping for an opening, an escape from the merciless wind that was sapping his life away. It was not long before he found one large enough to squeeze inside.

The crevice was only several feet wide but rose and zigzagged much farther than James could see. For what must have been the first time in hours, the wind no longer beat on James, as he collapsed from exhaustion onto the ice floor of the cavern. Grunting with effort he eventually managed to prop himself up against the wall and reluctantly checked himself over. He could not bring himself to take off his gloves or his boots to check his extremities: he knew the sorry state he was in. James also knew there was nothing he carried with him that was any help in his situation. He was, for all intents and purposes, subject to the mercy of God, and God didn't seem to be paying much attention.

Now that James was no longer pushing his body, the flood of exhaustion was like a physical battering. His head lolled as consciousness started to slip away.

"No," he said aloud. *If I fall asleep, that will be it.* But there was nothing else to do. He would never move again and help would never find him. He laughed; what were the chances of that?

None.

The only thing left to do was die. Again James' head slowly sank down and his heavy eyelids closed.

Moments passed then his eyes sprang open. He slowly lifted his head to see a women sitting cross-legged against the opposite wall. James was so shocked to see another person here that his heartbeat raced and he started breathing heavily.

Was he hallucinating? He stared dumbly at her, convinced that she couldn't be real.

Nevertheless he spoke. "Who are you?" James croaked.

"My name is Garianne," replied the woman in the most mellifluous voice he had ever heard.

James found Garianne odd for a number of reasons. Firstly, she wore an impeccable black business suit of jacket and trousers with a white blouse. She should surely freeze to death almost as quickly as James, yet she seemed quite comfortable. Secondly, she was smiling at him.

"Are you really here?" James exclaimed. It seemed to him a silly question, but he couldn't help thinking that his body had been claimed by the cold and now his mind was following.

Garianne's smile broadened as she reached out and put her hand against his cheek. The heat from her hand was so startling it reminded him just how cold his body had become during its numbness. Like a carcass in a meat locker. That's how he must have looked too.

"Do not be afraid, James. Though you are very close to death, it will not be painful, and it may not happen at all. I am here to offer you an alternative."

James tried to move but found he couldn't.

"Help…" he whimpered.

"I can, but you must first understand what you are asking. You see, to put it simply, I am not from your world. I, and others like me, have been here for some time now and we observe the Earth. We do not interfere. This is your planet. You must rise and fall on your own. You evolve and you survive; if you don't evolve then… well?" she said, implying the obvious. "Yours is just one of many species throughout the galaxy. The ones which have transcended somewhat and now move between the stars are called the 'Galacien': a conglomerate of many space-faring races. I am the Galacien's Chief Observation Agent for the Earth. I have made it a habit to have humans work for me in my post here. I want you to work for me, James Tennel."

James decided he was not hallucinating. He was now more afraid than ever about his new conclusions concerning this woman.

"A deal with the devil to escape death, is that it?" he croaked. "When the end draws near and there's no other way out, I hold out my hand to you? Sell my soul?"

"No, James, that's not it at all," said Garianne.

"You can't expect me to believe that, surely?"

Garianne slowly leaned forward, calmly whispering, "This is the way it usually is. They don't believe me, so I show them."

This time James did move but it was only a shuffle as he tried to move away from her.

Something flashed in his eyes and suddenly he was back at his parents' house. He could see his mother and father back home in Cambridge having tea and biscuits. His father, as usual, was tapping away vigorously at the keyboard on the computer, while he saw his mother leave the room and pick up the phone to talk to her brother. He seemed to sit between the two of them, the sights and the sounds all too real, but it could not distract him completely from the biting cold he felt from his true location. If anything, it seemed worse, for his mind seemed to sense how alien such temperatures should be in the place he saw before him.

"I'm showing you this because, if you do decide to come with me, this is what you must give up. You can never have contact with them again for you will be officially dead," said Garianne.

The illusion faded and he found himself back in his tomb of ice.

"Why can't you just help me live? I don't want to be a part of your Galacien."

"I'm sorry, that's not an option." A deep sadness crossed her face, making it even more beautiful. "We can't interfere and our existence must remain a secret. Direct contact with a species such as yours in the past has proven to be disastrous."

James was finding it hard to stay conscious. His head dropped, eyes staring at the ground. The ice particles glistened like stars. He did not have much time now.

His words came out slow and slurry. "If... I... refuse?"

Garianne moved close to him. He could feel heat radiating from her body, in complete contradiction to her surroundings. "I do not want you to die, James. I would much rather you lived. However, if this is your wish I will respect it and leave you in peace."

Moments passed and James thought that there were no more words, but suddenly he managed to say, "And... if... I... agree?"

"I will take you away from here, enhance your body and mind to reach a potential you've never dreamt of. You will work for me and, in return, I will promise to do my utmost to ensure your family, friends — in fact, your very species — is taken care of. You will experience things beyond the limits of your imagination. Your achievements will exceed those of all humanity." She paused and by some monumental effort James managed to lift his head and look into those incredible eyes barely a foot away "James, I offer you a life truly worth living."

That face, those eyes — the most genuine, gentlest, kindest.

He gave the subtlest of nods and then fell into Garianne's strong arms. James was by no means a small man, yet she lifted him as easily as she would a child. Garianne considered him for a moment, and then, in the blink of an eye, they were gone.

Two. Terra

The Terra system, present day

Lytpniuph looked upon the blue-green planet which sat against the sea of stars. The vessel's viewer encompassed the entire 180 degrees of the front of the ship, giving the illusion that the front section of the bridge was completely exposed to the hard vacuum of space. For many this might have been an uncomfortable thing to experience. Lytpniuph and his crew, however, being seasoned veterans of space travel on a Galacien ship, were quite at ease with the sight which presented itself before them.

Lytpniuph sat back from all fours onto his two back legs, stroking the short soft brown hair on his head and neck. Hair covered his entire body, barring the pads of his paws and, to a lesser extent, his face. He scrutinized the planet before him with deep curiosity.

"Captain, we've been sitting here for over an hour now. When do we go planet-side?" asked Lytpniuph's first officer, Chnar.

"You know the warning as well as I do, Chnar, and I don't take it lightly. Neither should you. Every ship which has entered orbit or attempted to land on Terra has disappeared: every one. I don't intend to add this ship to the list."

"He knows you, though, you were with him during the war. Surely he'll let you in? If not, we can defend ourselves."

Lytpniuph regarded him. "You are young Chnar, you believe a little too blindly in Galacien superiority. Don't make the mistake all too many before you have and underestimate him: he cannot be easily quantified. Remember, he evolved from a mere primitive barbarian into something more than we were, perhaps more than we are now," said Lytpniuph, looking at the planet hanging there silently. "I cannot imagine what he has become since then."

"If he has evolved so much then he must have received your message. He must know that you are out here and that it is imperative that he meets you."

"Must he? If you had ever met him, you'd realise that he feels he 'must' do nothing. He can't be forced."

"What about taking a closer look at Terra? Passive scans may give us some idea of what's going on down there. He may not even be there anymore. It may only be the planet's automated system that was responsible for those disappearing ships."

Lytpniuph didn't think Galacien citizens would be so rash if it was possible for them to die. As was tradition, they had all downloaded copies of their minds before leaving Galacien Prime. If the worst came to pass, they would wake up in a rehabilitation centre with no memory of these events. Even severe trauma was difficult to come by these days. The Galacien could easily shut off pain or use their cerebral implants to commit instant painless suicide if they ever found themselves in a situation which warranted it.

"We cannot make such assumptions, Chnar. Waiting is our only option, so we wait," said Lytpniuph.

Chnar knew that was the end of the discussion and nodded in resignation.

Lytpniuph so wanted to use the ship's delicate sensors to take a look at Terra. No-one had for over two thousand years. The Galacien had their innumerable eyes covering every conceivable spot of the galaxy yet the planet called Terra remained a dark spot, a complete unknown.

When the planet's first and only inhabitant took up residence there well over two thousand years ago, it was not so hidden. He could be observed, though only from a distance, limiting them to some degree. They could not use many of their sensors: they could only watch. He seemed to spend the first year doing nothing at all, much like those whose primitive planet he'd originated from. Over a decade more was spent exploring his new, quiet, empty world. He wandered its vast plains of grasslands, its deserts and snowy peaks. He swam its oceans from shore to shore; he never tired. In time he returned to the small primitive home he had built for himself.

Finally, four hundred years after the planet had been given its name by its new and sole occupant, all light leaving it was recognized by the Galacien's sensors to be the same. This was also true with all other wavelengths of the electromagnetic spectrum. Lytpniuph's ship waited at a distance only a little farther out than where the invisible phenomenon encompassing Terra enacted this strange influence. They saw Terra and anything in close proximity as it was two thousand years ago. This did not seem all that obvious to the average sentient being, yet the sentient ship and its sensors could see the tiny asteroids which appeared trapped in time and feel the inconsistency of the planet sitting like unreality in a freeze frame of the solar wind. Affected by nothing and affecting nothing, caught there like a fly in amber.

How Jonas had accomplished this, nobody knew.

Lytpniuph wondered what it really looked like 'now', beyond that all-encompassing barrier. Was it much the same? He hoped not. Yes, the universe and the Galacien Conglomerate of Worlds still presented their wonders and, even on rare occasions, a little magic. But not like this. Not like 'him'.

Lytpniuph sat down at his place on the bridge of the ship, quite content to wait. He believed that legends should not be rushed, especially when they were such an unknown quantity, and as potentially volatile as this one.

It happened when he least expected it. His mind had finally wandered to completely unrelated matters. He heard it through his implant, a low rumble of a voice from long ago, though now with more depth than he remembered. Still, it was unmistakable.

What is it, Lytpniuph?

He could not help but smile. It immediately brought back memories of those days from the war, those terrible, yet extra-ordinary days. Despite his mind being elsewhere, he was ready.

We need to talk, thought Lytpniuph through his implant.

Neither the ship nor the crew were aware of this conversation.

Then talk, rumbled the voice.

I'd prefer to come to you in person, if you'd allow it?

I am sure you would. That same archaic way of speaking, Lytpniuph noticed. Had he changed?

There was silence. Lytpniuph hoped he was thinking it over.

Come alone or not at all then, said the voice.

Agreed, said Lytpniuph, standing up.

Chnar and the crew looked at him as one. "Contact has been established. I'll be leaving immediately."

Like a wound on the belly of a great sea beast, the underneath of the ship's hull split apart, releasing a shaft of white light into the blackness of space. Silently a pale humanoid shape dropped gracefully from the aperture. Its rough configuration was unmistakably Amelerian. The major limbs were distinguishable, though not the individual digits that extended from those limbs. Lytpniuph was completely integrated, although in an unconventional sense, with the Sentient Integrated Bio-tech All-Purpose Tool, known more commonly as SIBAT. Usually one's mind would be downloaded into the SIBAT to avoid any physical limitations the body might impose. However, the current circumstances required Lytpniuph's personal presence.

He stretched out his limbs and broke away from the vessel which had brought him here. Superimposed on the upper left side of his vision he could see the ship receding away from him, the opening underneath closing and sealing itself up perfectly, until it looked as smooth and featureless as the rest of its underside. Ahead lay Terra looking as it had for two millennia.

Lytpniuph gave a mental command and the SIBAT accelerated to a tenth of the speed of light. These latest models were capable of so much more since the Galacien/Nacuerian war. He still found it hard to believe that something so small was capable of Hyperspace travel: its range could reach that of the satellite galaxies, if one was prepared for such isolation from the rest of civilization once one came out from the stasis required.

Like all Galacien citizens, Lytpniuph could live as long as he wished. He naturally moved with the times and technology as they all did, yet they were all a product of their first generation. Those who were born more recent simply accepted such technological feats, but to him, having his own first-generation memories of how things once were, he still found it incredible. He wondered how Garianne, being so long-lived, considered such things, and what the Galacien Conglomerate of Worlds had been like in those early years when she was in her first generation. Garianne was much like Jonas in that there was no-one quite like her. They were both unique in their own way, whereas most people he knew seemed much the same as any other citizen of the GCW.

Approaching the cloaking field, thought Lytpniuph to the ship and its crew. He knew it wasn't a cloaking field in the typical sense, yet it did hide what lay inside. *And what would that be?* This last thought he kept to himself.

If you don't hear from me in one standard day, you are to contact Galacien Prime and await instructions. Let them decide what to do next. Don't come in after me, are we clear?

After a brief pause he heard Chnar in his mind. *Understood.*

Lytpniuph reduced his velocity to a mere one hundred metres per second. Again the excitement built as he wondered what he would see beyond the field. Perhaps a planet similar to others in the GCW with a surface covered in technology and swarming with sentient life.

No. That was not Jonas' way.

Perhaps, as a grandiose experiment, he had expanded outwards, developing nanotech on an advanced enough level for self-replicating machines to control their own evolution into who knew what.

Lytpniuph reached the field and passed through to the other side.

His mouth hung open in astonishment.

Terra hadn't changed at all. Lytpniuph checked his sensors and instructed his implant to run a self-diagnostic, as well as checking his own physiology for abnormalities. He had to be sure. It was confirmed — everything was normal.

He checked visually, sliding through the magnification. It was true: Terra was as it had seemed over two thousand years ago.

There were subtle differences that told him that he was observing Terra as it was now. Asteroids that had been burned into Galacien sensors for eons were now gone, and the solar wind, amongst other things, was reading as active and normal. Yet the planet itself looked very much the same with none of the signs of technological progress he had expected. Lytpniuph tried to think of something he might have missed, but he already knew his first assumption was the truth. He felt angry and cheated; nothing had been accomplished here. No wonders, no miracles. Exactly what had Jonas been doing here for the last two millennia?

As he'd suspected it would, communication with the ship had now ceased. Bringing up the aft display in his vision showed him it sitting there waiting. He could see them yet they couldn't see him, not now he had passed through the barrier. Disheartened and with frustration burning inside him, he continued towards the planet. His sensors impassively regarded Jonas' humble abode as he approached.

Primitive, Lytpniuph thought. *After everything we taught him, after everything he learnt. To wallow in seclusion like this is a crime against sentient life, against evolution. How ironic: we refer to him as super-sentient but he's as unmoving in time as his barrier illustrates, yet how could he achieve even that?* Lytpniuph let loose the full capabilities of the SIBAT's sensors. Again he was confused as there was nothing on Terra which could be generating the barrier. Where was its power source? Something of that magnitude must need an enormous amount of power.

The SIBAT quickly entered the planet's atmosphere and landed softly only a hundred metres from Jonas' simple house of wood and stone.

"I can only rationalize that there is some incredibly important reason for you to come here. You may know me, but that does not give you the right to come here stated a voice plainly, its source emanating from the dwelling "Now, tell me why?"

"Gladly," said Lytpniuph, "but please, could we discuss it inside?"

"If we must," the voice said.

The door opened and Lytpniuph walked into the house, which comprised one small room. Jonas stood facing the fire, his hands gripped against the ancient gnarled wooden mantelpiece, his back to Lytpniuph.

"Do you know how long it has been since anyone but myself has set foot through that door?" asked Jonas.

"Far too long," replied Lytpniuph.

His SIBAT quickly flowed from his body, reconstituting itself into its original form. It stood immobile in the corner of the room.

"I trust Garianne's handiwork still protects your privacy from the prying eyes of the Galacien?"

"Of course, no one will hear what you say here," replied Jonas, still keeping his back to the Amelerian.

Lytpniuph was worried. He could not tell if Jonas was simply brooding or if he was keeping his anger in check.

"It is good to see you again, Jonas. I know that may not mean much to you, but it is," said Lytpniuph.

Jonas grunted then turned to face Lytpniuph. He seemed about to say something offensive but then thought better of it.

"Perhaps… it is good to see you too. It has been so long since I have spoken in person to... anyone," said Jonas.

Lytpniuph smiled. "You did state that you wished no other living sentient being to be within a light year of this planet — hardly within chatting distance of your nearest neighbours, are you?"

Jonas smiled momentarily and then, naturally, was sombre again.

"I prefer to be alone."

"Still?" asked Lytpniuph.

Jonas looked thoughtfully into the fire. "It is time for you to tell me why you came here," he demanded.

"I thought you should know," Lytpniuph began, moving uncertainly around the room, "the Galacien are planning to *allow* the extinction of the human race on Earth. The Council has been discussing it on and off for some time now."

Lytpniuph looked closely at Jonas for a reaction, for some kind of an emotional response. There was none.

"How long until the extinction event?" asked Jonas.

"A little under one Earth year," replied Lytpniuph.

Jonas looked at him and nodded slowly, sighing.

"Perhaps it is for the best," said Jonas as he sat down in his chair by the fire.

Lytpniuph also sat, though, to his disappointment, since there was no other furniture, on the floor on the other side of the fire; cross-legged like a human, his long back straight and his even longer arms laying limply by his side.

"Over seven billion sentient human lives, Jonas," Lytpniuph emphasized. "Do you really mean that? I know you do not want to have anything to do with them anymore, but they are your kin."

"No! They *were* my kin," Jonas replied sharply. "I feel kinship towards no-one now, except perhaps the meta-humans on Galacien Prime. It is they who are the only future of the human race. Not that planet of..." Jonas faltered. He could not find the words. "I watch them from time to time, you know, every few decades or so. I don't know why." Jonas shook his head, his face contorted in revulsion. "I've witnessed senseless mass genocides, the likes of which make me..."

"You have access to the Earth Simulation?" interrupted Lytpniuph.

Jonas nodded. "Resources, belief, corruption for power and money. They destroy that which they do not understand, that which is different. I could go on. Put simply, the human race is sick."

"Every one of them?" asked Lytpniuph, "Are there no decent humans on Earth?

"As I said before, the meta-humans, having been chosen and trained by the Galacien. I feel they at least are enlightened enough to survive what is to come," said Jonas.

Lytpniuph looked about the room "What have you been doing all this time?"

"Studying, reflecting," shrugged Jonas. "Digesting. I've studied the flora and fauna of this world. I've been watching their behaviour, how they go about their business unaware of the larger universe out there. The life cycle — those first moments of birth to that last moment of death."

"You've been watching plants and animals for over two thousand years?" Lytpniuph rubbed his forehead furiously. "You learnt the secrets of the universe in mere days, so what kind of progression have you made since then? None. How can you not see your potential, your capacity for further evolution? You have become stagnant, merely existing."

Jonas gave Lytpniuph a chilled look. "It is you and the Galacien who have succumbed to stagnation."

"What?" exclaimed Lytpniuph in disbelief.

"Study your history and see for yourself. The progression of the Galacien and the other space-faring species over the last few millennia has slowed to almost a standstill. Perhaps you have not noticed and are impressed with your most recent innovations? I, however, am not, and I despair."

"How can you speak of stagnation? Look at yourself! I can tell that you have evolved somewhat in a spiritual sense. You are in control of your emotions and seem quite at peace with yourself and your environment, though perhaps that is understandable since it is one of your making. But to accuse *us* of lack of progression? From one such as yourself this is the height of hypocrisy."

"You do not understand. The lack of evolution on your part is the real problem, the implications of which I do not think you fully grasp. You have nothing to compare yourselves with, nothing to challenge your authority, for you are at the top of the evolutionary ladder in this part of the universe," accused Jonas.

"What about the Nacuerians?" replied Lytpniuph.

"That was over two thousand years ago. You have no reason to believe they still exist. For a short time after that, I believed the Galacien Conglomerate of Worlds would go through a possible renaissance, but you had me to win that war for you. Psychologically the GCW never felt that self-belief from winning the war themselves," said Jonas.

Lytpniuph looked down at the floor. "My home world was destroyed during that war. My people died by the millions fighting the Nacuerians. Please don't tell me they didn't do their part. Even if it was infinitesimally small in comparison to what you did," whispered Lytpniuph.

Jonas was silent, studying the Amelerian. The fire crackled.

"Forgive me. My social skills are somewhat... blunted, shall we say," apologised Jonas.

"They never were exquisite," said Lytpniuph.

"Being on my own does not help."

Lytpniuph felt it was time. "The GCW want you to go to Galacien Prime to give your word that you won't interfere with the Earth situation."

Jonas leaned back in his old chair. "I already told you I would not. If they want my word then there, you have it: take it to them." Jonas nodded to the door.

"In person," insisted Lytpniuph.

"Again, why?" Jonas asked, shaking his head, puzzled.

"Circumstances on Earth have changed. Garianne strongly opposes the decision, and they are concerned you will be heavily influenced by her views."

"Garianne..." Jonas stood, turning his back to Lytpniuph.

The Amelerian waited patiently, knowing that she was the only one who could affect his decision.

Jonas finally turned to face Lytpniuph, his brow furrowed in thought. "When do we leave?"

Three. The Phi-virus

London, Earth[2]

It was twenty-six days since the first reported case of the Phi-virus. Al knew this because he hadn't slept since the outbreak. In those first few days, the victims were counted in their hundreds, but not long after that the numbers rose shockingly at an exponential rate.

Two things were clear by the second week: the virus was still untreatable and it was global. Everyone had it — everyone but him. Al suspected that the reason why he had not contracted the virus could only be the same reason why he was unusually resistant to heat and cold, pain and injury. As a child he had once placed his hand on a hot ring on the hob at home to no effect, other than a slight tingling sensation. He'd never told anyone. He'd never been physically hurt in his life. Once he'd fallen from a branch high on a tree. His friends had rushed to him, thinking he'd broken some bones or, even worse, been killed. He'd merely got up and brushed himself down. They'd said he was lucky. Even back then he knew better but never told anyone.

Even more significant was his ability to move unusually fast. The first couple of times it was merely a reaction. On the third occasion he caught a fly in mid-air and knew this wasn't natural. At school, where they were always testing you, he was noted for being the quickest, the strongest and the brightest. Nothing seemed challenging or insurmountable. It concerned him that he may be noticed as being too different and, at first, he was. But he wanted to be like everyone else, so he would fake weakness or confusion from time to time so as to appear normal. Nonetheless it was obvious Al was gifted and he had many friends because of it. People wanted to be in his presence, for he gave off a vibrancy, an ease, which rubbed off on those around him.

He lay there thinking of the good times with all his friends and family. Was it really him who lit up their lives whenever he was around them, or was it the other way around? Now that they were all gone, he felt empty.

Al hadn't moved for days now. The Sun rose slowly in the sky and the shadows slid across his vision. The only sound was the melodic song of the birds. At one time he'd found the sound of the breeze blowing gently through the trees a relaxing one. Now he hated it. It was far too common and prominent. The sound of the trees were now a constant reminder to him that they were all dead, and he was utterly and hopelessly alone. In his mind he could hear the long-gone echoes of a plane overhead, the children playing in the garden next door, a dog barking in the distance. Cars coming and going, the slamming of their doors. All part of life's symphony.

He would give anything to hear it again — to have them all back. But they were all gone and he wanted to go too. He'd tried many different ways to end it, but to no avail. The human race was destined to die but he, apparently, was destined to live and suffer. Was this hell? If not it had competition, right here in this place. He couldn't live and he couldn't die. His last attempt had been substantially higher than a tree: he had broken in and worked his way to the top of the Shard in London. Finally getting out onto the ledge of a window so very far up, he had begun to lose his nerve; so hard when every fibre of your being is telling you this is wrong. He couldn't remember if despair made him let go or if the strong winds had blown him from its structure, only the terror of realizing that he'd crossed the point of no return and he was falling. As the ground rushed up to meet him he found himself landing softly on his own bed at home. Had madness finally claimed him? He felt unsure of anything anymore. Yet some part of him knew he was responsible. He'd seen the image of his bedroom and, for an insignificant amount of time, travelled there. Al knew he could move fast, but to be so fast as to be instantaneous?

What did it matter, though? What did any of it matter? They were all dead, Al could feel it. In the depths of his soul he had felt the last of them slip away into darkness. He knew he was the last human on Earth. From that moment he had just stopped, and for these last few days had not moved, slept, become thirsty or hungry, only lain there as immobile as a rock on the grass, existing.

With a jolt, he felt it. Like being startled when you thought you were alone in a room. Adrenaline flushed through his system and he was upright. The world looked strange; Al hadn't been vertical in such a long time. Someone was here — here in London. He wasn't alone anymore. He focused and, in an instant, he was there too. Al looked around desperately for what he had sensed. Strange, now he was closer he discovered he couldn't quite feel exactly where she (and he knew it was a she) was.

"Please," said Al. His voice sounded unfamiliar and hoarse through non-use. "Please, I won't hurt you." He bit back the tears which threatened to overwhelm him. "Please."

It was too much, silent tears streamed down his face.

"Please, help me."

He heard her walking from out of the shadow of a ruined doorway.

"I am here," said a voice so beautiful it could not be real.

Then she emerged. If this was madness then it was wondrous. The woman wore a blood-red dress which hugged her tall, perfect form. Her smooth dark hair cascading down her back looked unnaturally clean and perfect, as did her complexion, in contrast to her environment. She had full lips and a firm, smooth jaw-line. Yet it was her eyes which drew Al in more than anything else about this extraordinary vision of perfection. Her dark eyes shone with a depth of knowing he found he could not comprehend. There was something almost supernatural about her.

"How is this possible? How are you alive?" asked Al.

Even the horror of the world melted away as she smiled at him. As she approached Al, his heart quickened and his breath became a little shaky. How had she remained so unaffected physically and, apparently, psychologically? Al was suddenly all too aware of how dirty and shabby he must look and that he hadn't showered for many days now.

"I... I thought I was the last one," he said.

"You are."

"I don't understand."

She walked over to a bench and sat, back straight, legs crossed.

"I'm not from around here. In fact, I'm not from your universe. I've come here from another Earth to ask for your help."

A laugh of disbelief escaped from Al's lips. "What? You have to be kidding me?"

The woman's expression didn't change. "No. Look at me. Really look at me. I know about your abilities. I know you can sense things others can't. What are those senses telling you now? Am I telling the truth?"

Al looked at her. What else could he sense? Many things eluded him, somehow, like locked doors in an enormous house, though some of the rooms he could easily peer into. She was old, very old, despite her appearance. Extremely capable. Physically and intellectually she was beyond anything he could imagine.

"Who… what are you?" Al stammered.

"Am I telling the truth?" she insisted.

There was something else about her… yes, there. No, she was indeed not of this Earth. Not even, as she had admitted, of this universe.

"Yes. A parallel Earth?" said Al. "And you want my help? What about me? Look at what happened here, everyone's dead. The Phi-virus killed everyone on the planet.

The woman looked about the place as if she was only now just considering her surroundings as significant.

"If I help you, will you help me?"

Al thought only for a moment and nodded. What else did he have to live for?

The woman stood up in one fluid movement and held out her hand. "My name is Garianne."

"Alex, but everyone calls me Al. Everyone used to..." He broke off as he clasped her cool, smooth hand, its grip sure, and for a brief moment he felt like his old self.

She walked towards one of the houses in the street.

"Well, Al, let's see what happened here."

The front door was already open. Al followed her into the hallway and upstairs into a first-floor bedroom.

A house this size in this part of London would have cost a fortune, he thought. Now, it didn't mean anything. None of it mattered. Whether you were rich and famous, clever or beautiful, where you lived, or what you did, the Phi-virus got you. It didn't matter if you were the Queen of England or the poorest man in the world. Where you'd been, or what you'd done. What was worse was the thought that none of human history mattered any more. Mr Einstein and Mr Shakespeare may as well have never existed. With the prospect of no future, what did any of the past matter now?

He knew there were bodies here, he could smell them in the bedrooms. Garianne glimpsed into the children's room.

"Please," Al said. "I don't want to go in there."

Garianne gave him a mournful half-smile and nodded, closing the door gently, as if not to disturb them. She walked across the landing into another bedroom where a woman's corpse in pyjamas lay on the bed. Only a few days old, one of the last to die, yet the smell was still too much for Al to get any closer than just inside the room. Garianne seemed unaffected. She clapped her hands together and then slowly pulled them apart. Between them materialised a glowing white box, as if she were magically pulling a drawer from out of her hand. Taking her hands away, the box remained in the air.

Al's eyes went wide, "What's that?" he exclaimed"It's what you might call a portable all-purpose toolbox. I'm configuring it for an autopsy."

Light danced across its surface and Al could see the box's internal structure changing.

"They performed loads of autopsies, when this thing hit."

"Not like this," observed Garianne.

From its top, the glowing box produced a small ball of light. It slowly descended onto the dead woman and, upon contact, dispersed itself over her body, enveloping it in a soft light. Another ball of light came from the box. It hung above the bed a moment before suddenly expanding, producing a vision of an alien world.

"What am I looking at?" gasped Al.

"A holographic image of the woman's dead cells. I'm searching for your Phi-virus," replied Garianne.

The scene continued to shift viewpoints.

"How are you doing this?"

Garianne said, "There is what we call an implant in my head, very small. Through it I can control the toolbox using mental commands."

"You're controlling this thing, just by thinking. That's... incredible," said Al.

Garianne considered Al. "Yes, but in no way insightful for you. I'll switch to vocal." She looked again at the body and at the holographics being played out before them. "Ah, there it is. Extrapolate a simple simulation from existing data."

Numbers flickered into view running backwards at rapid speed. The holographic cells whipped back to life and the attacking virus seemed to leave the scene. What remained appeared to be a healthy microscopic world.

"Now run simulation, times ten speed. Let's see what we're dealing with here." Garianne watched, completely focused on the decimation of the woman's cells. The various defences her body threw at the Phi-virus all became just another victim, until all that was left was a dead landscape.

Al's short moment of wonder faded as he began to sense that all-too-familiar dread of despair beginning to permeate his being. He sat down in a chair, his head in his hands.

"Two things, Al. Firstly this virus isn't natural: it has been manufactured," said Garianne.

Alex looked at her in horror. "I always thought it might be something the government created that somehow got out of control. A lot of people thought that."

"No. That's the second thing. It's extra-terrestrial in origin."

"What do you mean?" said Al.

The holographic image and the original ball of light whipped back into the box, which Garianne then clasped between her hands. When she opened them, there was nothing there.

She walked out of the bedroom and down the stairs. Al jumped from the chair and quickly followed. Outside Garianne looked up at the sky.

"Nothing up there... yet."

Al approached her, puzzled.

"I can only speculate," she told him, "but I believe the human race has been the victim of an alien attack."

Al's knees went weak as he sat in the middle of the street.

"What?"

She spoke as if the human race was a matter of small consequence.

"I can't believe it."

"Densari, to be specific." Again she made a gesture and holographic images snapped to life, illustrating a solar system and strange bulky creatures which looked like humanoid barnacles. Al looked up from his sitting position, holding his knees close to his chest. Garianne gestured at the holographics. "They must have launched a projectile from their home system, hundreds of light years away, jumped it through hyperspace, and introduced the virus into the Earth's atmosphere. It appears to only affect humans."

"Why? Why would they do this?"

"Perhaps they want the Earth for themselves and merely saw you as an infestation. Although there are a number of other possible scenarios. Al, it would be..." Garianne paused and stared towards the horizon.

"What is it?" he cried.

"They're here."

Four. Alicia

London, Earth

Alicia Eld awoke on her bed in the darkness of her room, disturbed by the rare fact that she had just been dreaming. A dream which was already now beginning to fade from memory. Again unusual and rare. She never forgot anything. Alicia tried in vain to recall the events. A big brooding man speaking to a creature which was definitely intelligent but not human in a small, fire lit room.

What was this? Frustration came upon her yet she held it back and calmed herself.

They were watching, always watching.

She could not remember exactly how long it had been since she last dreamt or, indeed, slept. Thirteen years? Certainly she had stopped sleeping by the age of two when, to the astonishment of her elders, her language skills were as accomplished as a child twice her age. It could also not be denied that her other intellectual faculties and her coordination were similarly on a par with those older than her.

In retrospect, her only mistake, considering what she now knew, was to openly acknowledge her abilities. Her brief exposure to the media now made her shudder, not only because it appeared self-indulgent for one who had not yet reached her third birthday, but also because, not long afterward, she quickly became aware of this feeling of being observed by some unknown and unseen entity. Alicia now felt as if it had always been this way. Shortly after that feeling began, she first sensed specific points in her surroundings which she concluded must be the source of said observations. Even at a young age, Alicia had already learned to trust her instincts, and what they told her was not to acknowledge their existence, for they would become immediately aware of these highly developed abilities that she herself did not fully understand.

Who 'they' were, she did not know. However, she did know they were watching her more intently than the people around her. At first she considered the hypothesis that it only appeared this way. That they were, in fact, clustered around her locale. This deeply disturbed her. It meant the game was up and she was only kidding herself that she was deceiving them. However, as her senses developed, growing ever stronger, she realised this was not the case. These 'eyes' covered every point on the globe. They were watching everyone and everything. From the busiest streets in Shanghai, to the most remote areas of Antarctica. From the edges of Earth's atmosphere, to the darkest depths of the world's oceans. No one and nothing escaped their notice.

Alicia reacted to none of this and never told a soul. It was her deepest, darkest secret. As time went by, she continued to accumulate knowledge about them, while they seemed oblivious to her more unnatural abilities. How she had learnt to read the emotions and minds of others. How she could sense her surroundings with far greater sensitivity than was deemed normal. How she could do these things was still a mystery to her.

The only time she thought she'd been noticed was when her mind had first left her physical form. Alicia was seven when, after going to bed, as was expected, despite her not needing sleep, she found herself alighting from her body. Despite this unusual turn of events, she quickly calmed herself and adjusted, as was her way. Alicia recently learned of the great machine minds behind the 'eyes', tirelessly monitoring every conceivable physiological and behavioural response of every human being on the planet, could easily notice a reaction in one of their subjects. As yet she'd not discovered their purpose, but she was sure someone as different as she was would attract attention and then, in all probability, intervention. A smart person would make every effort to ensure that didn't happen, and she was a very smart person.

She learnt how to adapt in this metaphysical form as easily as in her physical one. In this state she could move about at the speed of thought to any location on Earth. The physical world became of no consequence as she passed through it as sand passes through a sieve. Most importantly, she could not be seen or detected by anyone or anything, including the machine minds. She was completely free to watch while not being watched herself.

Lying there in the darkness of her room, she once again shed her physical form and its limitations, leaving it there apparently asleep, as she had done almost every night for the last seven years. She moved up through the attic of her parents' house and high into London's night sky. Alicia led two lives: her day life, where she appeared to be a normal if exceptionally gifted young girl, and her night life. During the day she found life constricting and was always careful how she behaved in case the machines became suspicious of just how much her intellect had grown since those early years. She pretended to be as slow and blinkered as those around her. At night she felt free. She could be herself, free of the, until now, all-seeing machines. Yet she was still limited, for she could not affect the material world around her. Like an ethereal ghost she could only observe. In a way, therefore, she was never completely free. For different reasons, she felt she could do nothing of consequence in either of the lives she led.

Alicia began what she thought of as her rounds for the night, high above the streets of London. The night sky held only a few wisps of clouds here and there against a backdrop of stars. Below the snaking Thames reflected the full moon and the lights of the city from both sides of its banks. Alicia knew London from this vantage point better than anyone, so frequent now were her excursions across this legendary city.

She didn't know for sure why the source of the machines' 'eyes' resided here, in a building, rather than in any other city on Earth. The fact that the only other supernatural being, besides herself, happened to also live in this very city was an astronomical coincidence, and this had not escaped Alicia's notice. As part of her routine she would pay a visit to the machines and their human companions, whom she had discovered referred to themselves as belonging to something called the Galacien, and continue to learn from them. For tonight, though, she would check in on the aforementioned supernatural being with whom she shared so many of her unexplained and amazing abilities — Mr Alex Lethbridge.

She remembered when she first encountered him. It was a chance passing on the street only six months ago. Her mother insisted they go shopping in the city, and he was with his friends. She sensed something as he approached, but could not pinpoint it until he drew closer. When he did pass her, she was so surprised to discover there was another like her that she nearly lost all of her usual composure. She only glanced at him but was able to get a sense of him for the rest of the day, so that when she did retire to bed early, feigning illness, she was able to observe him in her ethereal form, without the machines, in turn, watching her.

Alex, apparently, was not as fully aware of his abilities as she was. She wanted to make contact but the machines saw everything and, like the others, he was not aware of her in her other form. Surprising, for she was certain he was capable of it.

Alicia found Alex at the University, asleep in front of the computer. Even though he was four years her senior, in some ways she felt older than him, for her intellect reached far beyond her fourteen years and he seemed oblivious of his full potential. Tonight would be different: things would change. Alicia was confident she'd finally find a way to converse with him in her present form, without anyone else being privy.

She took in the scene in an instant and realised there was nothing here which could provide her with further insight or knowledge. She focused on his thoughts instead. Patterns slowly began to emerge before her. Thoughts and emotions were relatively easy to read in her physical form, and in her night-time state it was child's play. People's minds were open books for her. Nothing could be hidden from her. The machines may be able to deduce almost anything from physiology and behaviour, but they couldn't look into the depths of the soul as she could. She knew things about people that they themselves were unaware of.

Alex's current dream took shape before her. Again he was with the woman who was represented as a blur. Why Alicia could not visualise this person she did not know. His surroundings of a grassy cliff top and a setting sun were crystal clear, yet she could not seem to make a lucid representation of the focal point of his dream. Alicia found she could not focus on their discussion either, for she sensed something outside the dream which disturbed her. Reluctantly she turned away and the dream before her dissipated.

Confused, Alicia looked about her. It took a moment for her to believe what she couldn't see. The machine 'eye' in Alex's room was gone.

Impossible.

They were always there, never malfunctioning or absent. Wherever or whatever she was doing, there had always been the machines, watching. It should have comforted her that they were gone.

It didn't.

She sensed that within kilometres of her current location there were no 'eyes'. Alex was at the epicentre of this absence. What was happening? Then she was abruptly aware of a number of people popping into existence, surrounding the University grounds and moving towards their position. With a thought she was beside the closest one. He was moving fast and seemed to be using some kind of stealth technology which rendered him invisible in the physical world. Alicia peered into his mind and immediately found defences similar to those in the agents of the Galacien she'd encountered. The source of these defences seemed to come from a small implant in the man's brain.

She cursed. Minds were easy in this form but technology was a problem. She could observe its structure, but she could not ascertain its functions or influence them in any way. But even though she could not read their thoughts, their intentions were apparent. Alicia could feel their steely resolve to capture or kill Alex. She was not sure which yet.

Alex was awake now and was also aware of their presence.

She moved to him.

Five. Abduction

London, Earth

Alex sat on the grass, the cool breeze blowing through the hair on his skin, gently lifting away the warmth of the setting sun which was sinking behind the horizon of the calm ocean. He closed his eyes, and a slow, content smile spread across his lips as he sensed her approach from behind.

"How can a dream feel this real?" asked Alex as he felt the wind picking up again.

"You always say that," replied the woman.

Alex stood up and kissed her obligingly on the cheek.

"So, what is it tonight then?" he asked. "Weapons training, battle strategy? Or something less violent? There are still a few languages I can't speak yet. Or shall we dance the Tango?"

The woman's mouth broke into a grin. Rolling her eyes, she shook her head in dismay. Her smile went as soon as it appeared and was replaced with a look of concern.

"No, I came to say goodbye. I'm going away for a while."

Alex mirrored her expression. "Why, what's going on?"

Her frown deepened and it began to worry him.

"Everything will change. It will all become clear soon enough." She smiled, again shaking her head. "You won't remember any of this when you wake up — you never do — but one day you will. When it matters most."

"That's a lot to remember," said Alex.

"Indeed it is."

Alex went to her and held her for as long as he could. He was average height for an eighteen year old here, the same as in the waking world, yet she still towered almost a foot above him. She kissed him on the forehead as they broke away, looking him sternly in the eye.

"Goodbye Alex. Remember, when it's time, when we meet in person — and we will, one day — do exactly as I say."

He nodded slowly. "I will, Cerise."

"Now you must awaken. Trouble's coming."

Alex woke with a start. He was sitting down with his head on his arms, the faint hum of the computer next to him, and the screen blaring an image of a statue of Aristotle into his tired eyes. The many history books scattered on his desk were like a mass of overgrown leaves. The time on the clock, too late. He'd stayed on to catch up on his work at the University. The few remaining students who had been in the room were long gone. The whole building was probably empty by now. He looked at the text on the screen. He shook his head: it was too late to get back into it now, better to start tomorrow.

He looked around, confused. He'd been dreaming of something, but he couldn't remember what. He tried to recall something of it, but the harder he tried the more futile it became. Already it had slipped away like something on a fast-flowing stream which was quickly out of sight. Yet something remained.

"Trouble's coming," he whispered, and the certainty of that fact was like that of his own name.

He started to quickly pack up his bag and shut down the computer, suddenly stopping when he heard something.

Alex, listen to me. You are in danger, came a girl's voice.

Alex spun round, but there was no one there.

You can't see me. I'm speaking directly to your mind.

Telepathy? Alex thought back.

If you like. Now, you have to do exactly as I say. You have to trust me. I know you have no reason to, but those who are coming for you do not have your best interests at heart.

No, this isn't real. I'm just talking to myself, internal dialogue.

Not so, and you know it, said the girl.

Who are you?

The power went out. The room was plunged into darkness, the relatively poor light of the city outside bleeding in a little.

He heard another voice, clear this time. *He's in computer lab two, third floor.*

"Who's there?" Alex said, the sound of his voice seeming like a guilty plea in the awful silence which followed. "This isn't good," he murmured.

Alex instantly regretted saying anything at all. His instincts were telling him he was in trouble. He needed to be quiet: he needed to get away.

Working our way to him now. Still no sign of detection.

Detection? They were coming down the corridor, he could tell, though he did not know how. Alex moved silently into the adjoining lab.

He's moved to lab one.

How do they know that? thought Alex.

Alex. It was the girl's voice. *You need to teleport out of there now. I know you can do it.*

Alex could feel his heart pounding and his breath quicken as he backed through the next lab, bumping into chairs. How did she know who he was? Who were these people?

Alex, I'm trying to help you.

They were getting closer. It was a warm autumnal evening and all the doors were open so they simply walked through, silent, invisible, yet he knew they were there about to come into the room.

No, I've got to get out, he thought.

He ran. He did not think of exactly where he was going, he just grabbed his bag and ran as fast as he could, away from where he knew they were.

He's on the move, running north west. Tracking?

Yes, we have him.

Alex, you can't get away by running. You have to teleport, now!

Alex wasn't listening. He felt his pursuers behind him break into a sprint, heard their pace quicken at a frightening rate, pounding upon the floor, reverberating around the corridor. In seconds they would be on him. His mind screamed as if he was in a nightmare. Fear tore away at any strength he had in his legs as his pursuers appeared around the corner. He perceived them as barely visible, light seemingly moulded around their bulk. Alex could then see them all too clearly as he abruptly sank through floor, screaming.

Different rooms flashed by as his scream was muffled in the floors between them. Puzzlement overcame horror for an instant as he hit the ground, hard. He was breathing fast and there was a dim light down here.

"What the hell was that!" he exclaimed, looking around at the broken concrete floor, dust everywhere.

Again he heard the voices, now very clearly. It was almost as if he'd become attuned to it.

He's gone! He must have teleported.

No. He can't leave, we've set up too much interference.

He disappeared through the floor.

Alex, I didn't know you could do that. It was the girl.

Yeah well, neither did I. Whatever 'that' was.

It's a shame you can't teleport — well, not far at least.

Who are you?

Later. Suffice it to say I probably know a lot more about your capabilities than you. Perhaps together we can get you through this and exchange pleasantries later.

He's in the basement, not moving. He heard the voices of his pursuers in his mind. *I think he saw us... somehow. Permission to teleport — we need to finish this quick, before we're detected by the Galacien.*

No, if you teleport they'll know immediately. They'll already be suspicious that they can't 'see' this area. Get down there as quickly as you can.

Alex heard a deep thundering noise, then again and again. Each time it was a little louder.

They're coming, he thought.

Again he ran. Through the basement into a narrow corridor with numerous pipes just above his head, he came to the only door, a large white double fire door with a glowing green 'Exit' sign plastered across it.

You can't run. You're going to have to stand and fight.

He pushed the bar hard and opened the door a few centimetres until it hit something big and heavy on the other side. He could tell that it was massive and he would never move it. He felt insanely angry at the idiot who had barred the door. As he backed away, the ceiling behind him fell in with a resounding crash and something large and invisible filled the corridor. He could see the pipes above bent and the walls on either side destroyed. The thing reached with its arms and something extended out towards him. Still filled with anger and frustration, Alex instinctively raised his hands and a loud roar like the sea filled his ears.

Alex looked up to see that everything was distorted and that he was untouched and unharmed. It was like looking through water: everything was constantly shifting. He could almost see what approached him. All sounds were dulled, yet he still heard the other break through the fire exit behind him. They had him on both sides. He extended a hand out to this one too. He could feel the energies around him. He was the source — somehow he knew it, could feel it. He also knew they were trying to get through this barrier he controlled.

Cool! The girl's voice. *I mean, excellent. You've erected a force-field.*

He could feel them pushing against it with giant hands, applying some kind of energy to it themselves. He could feel heat leaking through. It began to build. He knew how to apply more of himself to the barrier, but it was so difficult, like learning to swim for the very first time. He felt like he was putting so much effort in, but his energy just wasn't being applied efficiently.

Don't give up Alex. You can hold them. I can sense the potential within you. Dig deep.

That's easy for you to say, you're not stuck in the middle of these freaking things.

He could feel her in his mind, spurring him on, but he was now on his knees. The creatures on either side of him were getting closer, pushing harder, wearing him down. The heat was like nothing he'd experienced before. He was sure it would not be long until he fainted. He was trapped: there was no way out. But he needed a way out... it was too hot... he needed to get out!

He looked up and felt a queer sensation of suddenly being sucked in and then spat out. He hit the floor, yet it wasn't the floor. Alex found himself outside in the dark standing on the roof of the University building.

"How did I get out here?" exclaimed Alex.

He's disappeared. Now on the roof. They'll know now. If he teleports again, we'll have to follow. He cannot be allowed to escape.

Alex ran to the edge of the roof, his shoes crunching on the gravel. Putting his hands against the wall he looked over the brightly-lit city. Sounds drifted up from its streets, oblivious to his peril. Something unseen reared up from the edge of the roof. Alex yelped and moved quickly back, stumbled and fell.

I can't do anything to stop him, Alex, it's up to you.

What should I do?

It has to be instinctive. Use your will.

He sees me! Al's assailant realised.

Alex continued shuffling back, scattering stones as he scrambled to his feet.

"Yeah, I see you and hear you. What the hell do you want?"

"You." The invisible shape came at him then suddenly disappeared.

They're here, we have to...

The voice was cut off. Alex stood there on the roof, the silence stretching out as the cold wind blew around him. The voices had departed, the sense of being 'prey', gone.

Then another presence, there, behind him. A plain-looking middle-aged man wearing a dark suit sat casually on the edge of the roof.

"Sorry about that, it seems like we've made a bit of a mess of things. We came as fast as we could, but to tell you the truth, they caught us completely off-guard." He laughed at some irony which Alex obviously wasn't privy to.

"What the hell just happened? Who are you?"

"My name is James, which is the easier of your two questions to answer. The first, however... Those beings who came for you tonight are generally known as meta-humans."

"Meta? Doesn't that mean 'more than' or something?" questioned Alex.

"Yes, 'more than' or 'beyond' human, in this case, achieved by advanced technology," explained James.

"How advanced?" said Alex.

"Significantly. Thousands of years in advance of us. Alien technology, to be blunt." James waited, expectant of Alex's reaction.

"Alien!" gasped Alex in disbelief.

He gazed about the rooftop as if looking for proof of such a claim.

"Yes. Bestowed upon them — and myself, I might add," said James.

"So you're one of these meta-humans as well. Why should I trust you then?" asked Alex warily.

"Different agendas. They came here from Galacien Prime; that's an alien world, in case you were wondering. They came here to kidnap you. My agenda, however, is to keep you quite safe and help you any way I can."

"Help me, eh?" Alex found himself relaxing as his shoulders sank and he regarded the city. "Why me?"

James smiled. "Because you're different, Alex. Because you are very, very rare. You are what we refer to as a super-sentient being."

The obvious emphasis wasn't lost on Alex, nor the undercurrent of reverence.

"I'm super-sentient? What does that mean?"

"It means you are the stuff of legends. That you can do the impossible," James smiled. "You, like so few things these days, are not understood."

"What do you mean?" asked Alex.

"How did you know they were coming for you? How did you teleport yourself to the roof?" questioned James.

"Teleport? I don't know. I could hear them, sense them. I don't know how I did it," admitted Alex.

James laughed, shaking his head, "That's what makes it miraculous: nobody does. Despite how advanced Galacien culture is, no one knows how a super-sentient works."

"Galacien... those are the aliens, right?" posed Alex.

"Right," replied James.

"So how did you know I was in trouble?" asked Alex.

"That would be easier to show you, I think. Perhaps tomorrow, after I've spoken to Garianne. You're the first super-sentient we've seen in over two thousand years, Alex, so we want to do this right. I'm sure I'll be getting in a bit of trouble for telling you as much as I have without consulting her, and in turn, the entire Galacien Conglomerate of Worlds Council." His head cocked to one side, as if listening to something. He nodded, "Yes, they're calling me in."

All Alex could do was stand there dumbfounded. Strangely, this was the first time James had seemed crazy to him.

James rose from the edge of the roof and walked over to Alex. "I'm sure you have a lot of questions." He took out a business card and handed it to Alex. "Go to this address at 5pm tomorrow and all of them will be answered," he smiled at that, "and then some."

Alex gasped and almost fell over again when the man who had called himself James promptly vanished from sight.

Six. Densari

Earth^2

Over a dozen dark shapes in the sky descended upon Al and Garianne. For a moment, Al couldn't move. He was frozen to the spot by the extraordinary sight. His heart hammered hard against his chest, instinct burning in him to do one thing: run.

"We have to go," he said to Garianne.

She calmly regarded the roaring vessels approaching them. "No, we stay."

"Are you mad! If what you've said is true, then these Densari won't have any qualms about killing the two of us. Listen, I can sense them. They're landing all over the planet."

"Calm yourself. Look at what they've done to your world, your people. You can't run away, Al. You must confront them."

Al was shaking "I can't. I know I've got these incredible abilities, but there are millions of them out there. I can feel them."

The wind was whipping up now as the enormous vessels hung directly above them.

"Remember what I said before, Al? If you help me, I will help you. I can't do it all by myself, however. You must take responsibility."

Garianne clasped Al by the arms and his shaking subsided. Their eyes locked and her grip tightened. Al felt something he hadn't felt for weeks.

"Remember how it used to be," she shouted above the roar of the Densari ships' engines, "when it seemed as if you could do no wrong — when nothing was impossible. Despite everything that's happened, you are still that person. Have faith in yourself and follow my lead."

Hundreds of armoured figures dropped from the vessels above and, despite the height of the fall, landed softly on the ground around them. Al noticed they had four arms, yet seemed basically humanoid apart from their unusual bulk. Some of them gestured towards Garianne and Al, uttering strange guttural sounds Al could not make sense of. The streets were a calamity of these alien figures, with dust and rubbish blowing around them due to the turbulence being caused by the ships' engines.

Cutting through the noise came Garianne's voice. "I am Garianne, you are Densari. State your purpose."

The soldiers stopped. All of them, even the ones about to enter the houses. They all turned to look at Al and Garianne. Al was sure she had not spoken English and yet this is what he had heard. He had witnessed her advanced technology before. Was this another example — some kind of automatic translator?

The Densari looked at one another, eventually moving aside as one stepped forward mere feet away from Garianne, towering above her. Al sensed the lethality of this alien warrior who stood so imposingly before her. He could only stare. He didn't know what else to do.

"You speak Leecham," stated the Densari, its voice deep and slightly muffled from the helmet it wore.

"Yes," said Garianne, looking about as the Densari soldiers approached them.

"How is this so? You are human. How are you alive?" The Densari leaned closer, its visor almost touching her nose.

Garianne did not flinch: her confidence was unshakable.

"I don't have time for this," Garianne said frankly. "Are you listening to me, all of you? All you Densari in your little ships?" She looked up. "I want your Emperor here. Now."

The lead Densari moved back for the briefest of moments and then launched himself at Garianne. Al barely saw what happened next, it was so fast. Garianne spun past him in one fluid motion. Light encased her form, extending from her right hand into a lethal blade. The Densari's body fell to the floor, its head tumbling some distance away from it. The seasoned Densari soldiers lifted their weapons in unison and the world exploded around Al and Garianne. The street was ripped up before him, a phone box and bus shelter torn away into pieces from the backlash of energy unleashed upon them. The ships surged closer, looming menacingly less than a hundred feet above. The world was a mass of dust and debris and through it, Al saw Garianne take down one Densari then the next, her personal shield-cum-weapon deflecting any assault.

Al felt something strike him hard. Before he could make sense of what had happened, he was hit three more times. Lying on the ground, he looked up to see a Densari soldier reaching down to grab him. Al couldn't give him a chance to finish him off. As soon as the soldier touched him, Al teleported them hundreds of kilometres away above the French Alps. He caught only a glimpse of the mountains spread out far below them, then he teleported himself back to his previous location.

Garianne brought down another soldier. When she caught sight of Al teleporting back, she smiled briefly, before running towards the last of the Densari soldiers.

It was over in minutes.

. The dust began to settle on the armoured alien bodies strewn over the street. Al stood there in stunned silence.

Garianne addressed the ships above. "I repeat, the emperor here, now!"

Al approached her slowly. Garianne turned to him and her face softened. "You have nothing to fear from me, Alex Lethbridge." Al merely nodded. "Thank you for the help, by the way," she smiled.

A laugh escaped from Al. "I believe you did most of the work."

"Be ready for the next round. Remember, this is for all those who have suffered and died. This is your world, your family, your friends. You cannot let them do this," said Garianne.

"But they're all dead. What does any of it matter now?"

Garianne's face hardened and, for some reason, he felt ashamed. "It matters. Otherwise, all of your lives, everything humanity ever did, everything you ever were, will be for nothing. You're fighting for nothing less than thousands of years of human history. Millions of years of evolution."

There was a low whine and then a sound like a locomotive screeching to a halt, a flash of light and then abrupt silence. In front of them stood a figure in a giant polished gold and jade-green suit of armour, holding a long golden spear. Behind him, more Densari soldiers.

"Ah, at last the Densari emperor," Garianne remarked to Al.

She approached the impassive figure. "I invoke trial by combat for the possession of this planet, which you have so arrogantly presumed was yours by right of superior technology."

"With you?" growled the emperor.

Garianne shook her head and then looked slowly over to Al.

"What! You've got to be kidding? Why should I agree to this?" balked Al.

"Because you must," said Garianne. "This is your world, you must fight for it."

The Densari emperor scrutinised Al, readying himself for battle without delay.

"This is crazy. Why should I do what you say? I don't know you..."

"But you trust me," said Garianne, walking over to him.

It was true: he'd only just met her, but somehow there was something about her. Only...

"I'm scared," he whispered to her, his voice a-quiver.

"I know you think this is too big for you. I know you find it hard to believe that you can beat him, but this creature, this Densari emperor, is just a bully. He needs putting in his place."

Garianne moved back, folding her arms, and before Al could say another word the Densari emperor struck him with something he didn't even see.

Al hit the ground hard and looked up at her, confused. Until the Densari had arrived, Al had never been in a fight before in his life. Because of his unnatural strength, he had made sure to stay out of trouble for fear of hurting someone. The emperor was on him and what followed was nothing short of an ugly, brutal attack. Al's head was kicked against the floor, the clothes torn from his body. He stumbled and fell like a fool. The emperor lifted him by his hair and repeatedly pounded his armoured fist in Al's stomach. Finally, the emperor flung him against a nearby car.

Al looked in astonishment as the twisted metal of the car came easily away in his hands, crumpling like tin foil. The emperor came at him again, a little slower this time, a strange look in his alien eyes. Tiny projectiles flew from the emperor's hands and suddenly Al's world erupted into fire. The emperor and his soldiers stood fast against the blast.

The Densari emperor turned from the carnage, satisfied.

Inside the inferno, Al stood at the epicentre of a small crater. The car was a mass of melting plastic and rubber, the chassis a broken shell. He considered the fire dancing on his hands, causing him no pain or discomfort, and, for the first time in so long, felt as he once had. When the world seemed a brighter, happier place and nothing he set his mind to was impossible.

Al strode purposefully from the fire towards the emperor.

"Hey, you forgot something!" he shouted.

The emperor turned, taking a step back as he saw his foe advancing on him. He brandished his spear, crackling with energy, and thrust it at him.

Al's face was now contorted with anger. He didn't miss a step as he knocked the spear aside, and, in a blur of movement, had his hands about the emperor's armour, pulling it apart piece by piece. The emperor's attempts to stop Al didn't even slow him down, and, in moments, the alien struggled with Al's hands as they choked him.

Al looked at Garianne. She seemed sad and all the anger flooded from him.

The emperor dropped to the ground.

"Leave my world, before I change my mind," Al growled.

The Densari was repeating something over and over, and Al could sense that thousands more vessels were approaching.

Al felt a sense of dread, like the world had suddenly become dark. The stakes had just risen considerably, yet he knew instinctively that the most dangerous person amongst all these players was Garianne.

"I don't think you heard him correctly," she said to the emperor.

Without warning, the ships around them started dropping from the sky. The Densari emperor and his soldiers looked up in disbelief. As the first ship crashed, Garianne turned to Al. "When they are able, they will leave and not return."

"Everyone's dead though, there's no way..."

"There is always a way and I will find it," declared Garianne. It was surely impossible, but he believed her. "Now, will you help me?"

Al nodded. "What do I need to do?"

Seven. Krrikant

The depths of space

Korina Tennel sat quietly contemplating in the simulation of the Parisian Café. Preferring the shade from the hot sun, she requested a regular breeze through her implant. The crowds passed by, going about their business. The busy waiter brought over the drinks, disappearing as fast as he'd come. Korina sipped her latté nervously. It wouldn't take them long to realise that this part of the ship wasn't being monitored.

James finally appeared quietly from behind, kissing her gently on the cheek.

"Happy anniversary, darling. Sorry I'm late; Garianne's been away and I'm taking up the slack. I promise I'll make it all up to you when I see you."

"Three years since I decided you needed looking after — you were doing such a terrible job," she commented.

"I thought the Galacien did a fine job looking after me?" he replied, faking confusion.

James had been with them ten years now, though he seemed to have not aged a day, due to the modifications they'd made. Korina was much older, originally born in the Victorian era. She had lived two full lives before being copied into this current body. *And a very nice body it was too*, thought James.

She shook her head. "Oh, you poor thing. That's what I mean. A life without love isn't worth living."

"And I thought I had it all."

"An easy mistake to make, dear. Like I said, it's a good job you've got me to set you straight."

"I guess the Galacien aren't the be all and end all they're made out to be, are they?"

Korina's mouth smiled, but her eyes didn't.

"What is it?" asked James, suddenly concerned.

"Something's happening. Something's not right," frowned Korina.

"What do you mean?"

"You're not getting the whole story of what's going on out here, James. There's been a lot of fighting in the outer systems between some of the younger space-faring races — the Nagoad and Fenarari being the most notable.

James couldn't quite fathom what he was hearing.

"But why? The Galacien Conglomerate of Worlds... it works, we've seen it. I don't understand."

"Apparently information came to light about the feuds of the past — information which has been falsified. Heinous acts of genocide involving both parties from long ago. Old grudges. The violence started small and escalated. Only a minority, but it's enough."

James allowed himself a moment to think while he took a sip of his drink. Back on Earth the simulation interface was doing an excellent job of making him believe that he was actually drinking coffee. "What are the Galacien doing about it?"

"I'm on a ship right now with Galacien General Krrikant. We were heading over to Nagoad space." She took James' hand. "There's a problem, though. For some unexplained reason, we've altered course for Earth. I thought you should know. I thought Garianne should know."

James looked at Korina. "This is too much of a coincidence."

"What do you mean?" she said.

"We've just discovered a super-sentient here on Earth," said James.

Korina gasped.

"It's not widely known as yet," James continued. "Obviously Krrikant knows. It's the only reason for the change of course."

Korina slowly put down her cup, "Another super-sentient, after all this time, and on Earth. Who..?"

"His name is Alex Lethbridge. Eighteen years old and, among other abilities, he seems to have a knack for teleportation."

"Do you have any idea of his potential?"

James leant closer to her and there was a gleam in his eye. "It's too early to say yet. But you never know, he could be multiversal."

Korina slowly shook her head at the implications. "With training he could go anywhere in the multiverse. Incredible."

"We don't know for sure yet, but yes, it's a possibility."

"What does Garianne plan to do?"

James said, "We're meeting with him tomorrow for his orientation."

Korina remembered hers. "Well, that's going to be an eye-opener. I wonder how he'll take it. Better than you I hope."

"Hey! Garianne exaggerated." Said James, "I wasn't that bad."

Korina smiled, but it quickly faded. "There's something else going on here, James. Things haven't been right for years, but I can't put my finger on it. People in positions of authority, council members I've known for years, making foolish decisions or resigning for no credible reason. Friends acting strangely. I'd usually put it out of mind but Garianne once told me to trust my instincts, and right now they are telling me there is something very wrong with the people on this ship. It's getting worse. Someone I accidently bumped into in the corridor looked as if he were about to swing for me. He tried to cover it with a smile, but…"

"That hardly sounds like someone who is supposed to be part of a highly enlightened society," agreed James, now deeply concerned.

"They're acting like an immature species."

James gave a quick laugh, but there was not much humour in it. "Like we were before we were enlightened."

"James, I'm scared. Whatever this is, I think it's spreading on the ship." Korina's implant then informed her she had guests requesting to enter her quarters. "I must go, but we'll speak again soon. I love you."

"Love you too. Be careful."

Korina gasped as the simulation was abruptly stripped away, leaving her sitting in her quarters. General Krrikant stood there, flanked by two aides.

"Was I interrupting?" enquired Krrikant, "I'm sorry. Only, it seems you have some concerns. Please let me help."

Korina stirred uneasily in her seat. The General had never addressed her directly, and she was suddenly aware of how alone she felt, being the only meta-human on board. With whatever was happening here, would she be perceived as a threat? The GCW were peaceful, yet recent events had made her feel not quite as secure as she once had.

"Why have we changed course?" she asked, unsure of herself.

The Galacien had enhanced her in every way conceivable, yet the imposing figure of the Galacien General made her feel like a child again.

"New orders, direct from the council. We are to collect the super-sentient, recently discovered on your home planet. Here, see for yourself." Krrikant sent the information to her implant.

For a moment Korina was speechless. They knew about the super-sentient on Earth, and so soon? Her mind raced with a hundred questions, yet strangely she couldn't keep hold of a single one. In fact, she was finding it hard to concentrate at all.

"I feel strange, dizzy. Something's not right."

"It's all right, Mrs Tennel," said Krrikant. "The feeling will pass soon."

Korina felt something cold and alien in her mind. There was that mild sense of duality she had felt briefly when she first started using the implant. Now, though, she was all too aware of something else — another will quickly taking precedence over her own. A small part of her mind screamed and fled from the new nightmare into a deep, dark corner. Korina shook her head and everything seemed as it should be.

"How strange," she remarked.

"How do you feel?" asked Krrikant.

"Oh, fine. Sorry about that, I don't know what came over me. Please, what were we talking about?"

"We are on course for Earth to collect the super-sentient. There may be some trouble when we arrive. We need you to help by convincing your husband to side with our cause."

"Of course. I'm surprised we don't have someone there on the inside already."

Krrikant found it hard to hide his irritation. "We have been trying for years. Garianne's operations on Earth are very hard to penetrate. Those that work for her are extremely loyal and she watches them closely. Even the AI systems do not divulge information about what goes on in her own little empire, and when they do, I have my suspicions as to the authenticity of their contents. She's hiding a great many things."

"That shouldn't be a problem if you can get me in there; I'll make sure we can infect the others," said Korina.

Krrikant nodded. "Above all, we must have possession of Garianne and the super-sentient. Do not underestimate her."

Korina gave a contemptuous laugh. "She can't resist us, nothing can. They'll all be ours soon enough."

Eight. The Martians

London Earth[3]

General Alexander Lethbridge swore profusely, spilling his Cognac over his uniform as the war-room lurched to a halt. He rose from his ornate red leather chair, and pulled the polished brass horn from the wall.

"Report. Why have we stopped?" he barked into it.

"General, the way is barred by rubble. There's no way round," resounded a muffled voice through the mesh.

Alexander cursed himself, scratching at the scar on his left cheek, a habit he'd tried to break on more than one occasion. He should have been paying more attention to his surroundings. Taking a deep breath, he closed his eyes and reached out — sensing the streets around him, hearing the sounds of battle kilometres off in the distance.

"There is no alternative route. We must proceed on foot; everyone disembark. I'll secure the princess, and keep it quiet, we don't want to draw any attention."

Alexander promptly disappeared and then reappeared outside the royal quarters. The ᵣtwo guards, startled, instinctively reached for their weapons — one his pistol, the other preferring the knives hanging by his sides.

Both lowered them as they saw it was the general.

"At ease, gentlemen."

They both stepped aside as Alexander adjusted his collar and straightened his tunic. Clearing his throat, he gave the door the gentlest of knocks.

"Enter General," said a small voice from the other side.

Alexander suppressed a smirk and opened the door. Inside sat a small, teenage girl wearing an immaculate blue and white dress, quite inappropriate attire for the war zone called London, which they must now traverse.

"General, are we leaving the *Vanguard* so soon?" she asked, moving elegantly from the chaise longue.

"I'm afraid so, Your Majesty. We must make our way on foot from here, if we are to meet with your mother at Kings Cross. It is not safe here."

The little princess did not appear afraid, however, she could not fool the General. He could sense her fear permeating the room.

"Are they here... the Martians?"

She had a wild look in her eye which disturbed him. Did she not realise the danger they were in? Had she no idea that the human race was fighting for its very survival? He envied her naivety, if indeed that's what it was. For he believed that his race was mere weeks away from possible extinction unless he could come up with something miraculous.

"Princess..."

"Victoria," she interrupted. "Call me Victoria, as you have done before."

She was named after her legendary grandmother whose influence had continued long after she herself had died, seemingly eternal, until the invasion. This Victoria seemed just as headstrong as her namesake.

A distant rumble reverberated around the room ever so subtly. Alexander knew the *Vanguard* would deaden any such shockwaves, and his own senses were telling him that the fighting was heading their way.

Alexander went to her on one knee. "It is inappropriate, Your Majesty, but if it will get us on our way. 'Victoria', we must make haste."

Before Alexander could stop her, she threw her arms around him. He reddened.

"Please, your...Victoria."

Victoria released him. Before she could make another move, he took her hand and led her from the room and into the corridor, the guards falling in behind them. As they hurried through the innards of the armoured transport, the noises of battle became louder. On emerging from the Dreadnaught class armoured vehicle known as the *Vanguard*, the sounds seemed almost on top of them.

Alexander strode purposefully through the deserted dark streets of London, surrounded by an attaché of men protecting the Princess. Alexander stuck to quiet side streets when he could, so as not to be too exposed, but his options were limited: so many routes were cut off by debris. Luckily, he could sense what was coming kilometres in advance so he knew the perfect route to the station. He could also sense the all-too-familiar Martians, some of whom were unnervingly closing on their location.

"We must quicken our pace," he rasped at the others.

Turning a corner the rats scattered at their presence. Victoria squealed at the sight of them.

Alexander quickly calculated and tried an alternative, less direct route to the station away from the Martians. But he already knew in his heart the final outcome.

"Captain," Alexander whispered, looking around them. "We're not going to make it. I'm sorry..."

"You just go, sir."

"No," said Victoria, shaking her head "We stick together."

"We can't, Your Majesty. He can't take all of us. It's you who's important," replied the captain.

"No, please," she implored Alexander.

"Just go, General," insisted the captain, grasping Alexander by the shoulder.

The men around him simply nodded, their rifles ready for a fight they couldn't possibly win. The princess threw her arms around Alexander again, sobbing this time.

He could hear the Martian machine approaching now. Alexander found it hard to breathe, to swallow.

"It's been an honour, gentlemen," said Alexander.

"Please, don't leave them," spluttered Victoria into his tunic. "Please, don't."

Alexander knew he should go now, but before him stood men who represented everything an individual should aspire to be. They were the noblest parts of humanity. If they were to lose that, what was the point of anything?

"Everyone grab onto me!" he bellowed over the approaching din of the Martian machine.

The soldiers looked at one another, uncertain.

"Now! That's an order."

They all obeyed.

The captain, the last to hold reluctantly onto a spare part of his arm, whispered, "You can't do this. I know your limitations."

"Watch me," Alexander growled.

The Martian machine turned the corner, towering above them, as Alexander's mind reached out for the station and attempted with all his strength to teleport them all across. He felt the connection, but the captain was right — there were too many of them. Alexander dug deep; he was so close. The Martian's lights were upon them, and he felt them tense, gripping onto him for all they were worth. He heard the familiar click of its guns about to open up when the captain looked at him, nodded, and let go.

Suddenly they found themselves on one of the platforms of Kings Cross station.

Alexander fell to the ground, his strength all but gone.

"No," he croaked.

He felt himself being carried by the men he'd saved onto the waiting train, steam emitting from its underside as if eager to be away from this place. Darkness slowly enveloped him as he heard the great locomotive ever so slowly break away from the station.

Alexander woke to the comforting, rhythmic sound of the train. No longer could he hear the distant sounds of battle, or that dreadful squeal of the Martian guns. He remembered, with bitterness, the hand which let go, allowing them to escape.

"How do you feel?" asked a voice.

Alexander quickly rubbed his eyes and immediately took in his luxurious surroundings. He was in the royal carriage and it was still dark outside the ornate, stained-glass windows. There in front of him stood Princess Victoria, Queen Marina herself, and a strikingly beautiful woman he had never seen before. He jumped up and stood to attention, ignoring the smirking Victoria from the corner of his eye.

"Do you intend to answer the question, General, or must I ask a third time?" said the Queen.

"I... I'm fine. Thank you, Your Majesty."

His eyes flickered to the other woman who stood taller than the queen, and in some ways appeared even more regal. There was something very strange about her, and not just in the way she dressed. Was she foreign? She could do to cover up a little, it was a little inappropriate, especially in royal company.

"At ease, General, you're making me anxious."

"Yes, Your Majesty. Sorry, Your Majesty."

Victoria broke into fits of giggles.

The unnamed woman remained impassive.

"Victoria!" exclaimed the queen. "As you have no doubt realised, General, I am not quite as strict as my late mother. However, Victoria here could do with some fine-tuning in her education of manners and general etiquette, wouldn't you agree?"

"Indeed, Your Majesty."

"Yes, well, speaking of manners, I would do well to introduce our guest. This is the Lady Garianne."

"An honour," replied Garianne, in a voice like velvet.

"A pleasure to make your acquaintance," said Alexander automatically.

"Good. Now Alexander, would you please give us a little intelligence on our current surroundings?" asked the Queen, gesturing with a wave of her hand.

Alexander nodded and reached out with his senses. The train thundered through the dark English countryside. He stretched out further, until he encountered the first alien shape of a Martian war machine.

"We are quite safe, Your Majesty. The nearest Martian is about seventy kilometres west of here, nothing ahead," said Alexander.

"Thank you. Lady Garianne has some important news for us."

Alexander looked at Garianne. This seductive-looking woman with her silky smooth voice, whom he had never heard of before, seemed so comfortable in the queen's presence. How had she acquired the queen's ear so easily?

"My pardon, Your Majesty, but may I enquire as to who exactly Lady Garianne is?" He instantly wondered whether he had overstepped the mark.

The queen raised her eyebrows, as Victoria suddenly burst forth. "She saved Mamma's life, and the train was broken beyond repair, or so the engineer said, but Lady Garianne managed to fix it." She seemed quite pleased with this.

The queen nodded. "Lady Garianne has earned our trust and, if you had seen what I have, possibly more. Now, if you would?"

The queen inclined her head towards Lady Garianne, who regarded them each in turn.

"First, I must ask that what I am about to tell you will not leave this room."

"Your Majesty, are you sure Princess Victoria should be present?" asked Alexander.

"Yes. Since my mother died I have held no secrets from her. There are things she must know should she unexpectedly have to take the throne."

Alexander realised what she was implying, and considered the young future queen. Victoria looked at him with a confidence he had never seen before, seemingly all too suddenly twice her real age. He could see the queen had made sure she was quite prepared. This little girl who, with luck, would survive to become a young woman, knew as much as he did, perhaps more, about the state of their great empire.

"That will not happen prematurely, I will make sure of it," Alexander assured the queen.

"I know you will," said the queen.

"I can give you that opportunity, Alexander," said Lady Garianne.

She clenched her fist and faced them. Alexander tensed slightly, his senses telling him there was something unusual about this woman. Lady Garianne's hand abruptly opened and light sprang forth, taking shape in the room all around. He saw a vast sphere, with shapes upon its surface. He recognised them from hundreds of mission briefings. This was the Earth. On the other side of the room lay another sphere. Was this Mars? Thousands of stars surrounded them, creating a feeling that they were standing in a space far larger than the carriage they presently occupied. Like fireflies, Alexander could see specks of light leaving the Martian surface and streaming towards the Earth, and, like an infestation, he could see hundreds of lights spread upon the surface of his own planet. Lady Garianne presented an overview of the grim situation they found themselves in.

"How are you doing this?" asked Alexander.

"Technology many years in advance of your own and of the Martians. I am from another Earth, a parallel universe. This is proof of that claim. If you are still unsure, Alexander, I suggest you use those extraordinary senses of yours. If you focus, they will tell you this is not my natural environment."

Alexander did as she asked. It was true: she stood out from anything else here and not because of her unnatural confidence and her awe-inspiring presence, beside which even the queen herself seemed to pale in comparison. It was as if the world was washed in one particular colour and she another. No, it was more akin to an instrument, whose pitch was different from all those around it.

"You are unique in this world and my instincts tell me you speak the truth."

"Is that the Earth?" said the young princess.

Lady Garianne looked down and smiled, momentarily taking Alexander's breath away. "Yes, this is a tactical analysis of the war. Not good. Within three months the Martians will have overrun the Earth and the human race will be no more."

The princess held tightly onto the queen's hand.

Alexander felt his jaw clenching. "There must be a way."

"I can help to prevent this from happening, and in return I ask that you help me, Alexander, to save this." Garianne gestured again and the entire scene, stars and all, reduced to a bright speck which she held between two fingers. Letting go of it, other specks appeared around it, spreading out until it felt as if the royal carriage, their very world, would drown in these points of light.

"It's beautiful," said the young princess, mesmerised.

"Your universe is only one of a great many others," said Garianne. "Each one is represented here by a point of light. Something evil threatens this part of reality that we share. I can help save your world, if you will help me save this. In doing so you will save your world twice over. Firstly, from these so-called Martians, and secondly from an even greater threat."

Alexander already knew his answer, but found he was dumbstruck as he watched each point of light blinking out of existence.

Nine. Galacien Prime

Galacien Prime, The Galacien System

Jonas was teleported into one of the council's inner receiving stations on Galacien Prime. They were different from how he remembered them, certainly more advanced. Galacien technology had developed so far that any indication of the workings of their machines was hardly noticeable. Two thousand years ago a teleportation station such as this would have been unmistakable; now the only perceptible fact that it existed at all was a faint, fading glow on the reflective surface of the floor. Jonas wondered how far they might progress given another two thousand years. He didn't think they'd even need to install machines in their structures by that time — a portable device may be feasible to teleport a person anywhere on Galacien Prime. Unfortunately, they should have reached that stage long ago.

The Galacien council member Kursis Orpemantus stood waiting for him, a smile plastered on his face.

"You honour us with your presence here today, Jonas. It has been too long since the hero of the Galacien/Nacuerian war has visited any of us," he said.

Jonas stepped away from the teleporter. "My seclusion may seem odd to others, though it is my way, and I expect that to be respected. I hope this will not take too long."

Not waiting for a reply, he briskly set off towards the council chamber.

Kursis hurried alongside him. "Naturally we will make this as quick as possible." He continued to grin, which brought a frown to Jonas' face. He'd only just met this Kursis, and already he was finding him irritating to the point of nausea.

"You will find the whole area quite devoid of its usual life. We wouldn't want to distress you with the usual crowds."

Jonas could sense that Kursis wasn't exaggerating: the whole place was eerily quiet. He could sense fewer than a hundred people for kilometres around. Was that normal, even under these circumstances?

On the way they passed an enormous viewing area. The super-dense, transparent material seemed to almost grow out of the side of the building and stretch out to show an elaborate vista.

Galacien Prime was a giant, artificial shell on a cosmic scale, which encompassed the Galacien star. It had been created by a multitude of super-sentients thousands of years ago, during an era the Galacien referred to as 'The Golden Age'. It harnessed the full energy output of the Galacien sun and contained the equivalent surface area (on which most of the Galacien citizens lived) of millions of planets: space was something that was in abundance. Even those who had lived here for many years still found some of the concepts difficult to grasp, for this had been created long before even their technology was capable of such a feat. Indeed, it might be perhaps tens of thousands more years in the future before the Galacien themselves could replicate this incredible accomplishment, without the help of super-sentients.

Jonas gazed out across a view that seemed to stretch on forever: where buildings larger than any city on Earth sat in the solitude of vast natural-looking landscapes — from flat plains of grass with no other discernible features for thousands of kilometres in all directions, to oceans which could easily swallow most planets. Yet all were Galacien-cultivated. He felt sure that even though the Galacien were well informed of their environment, they could never be as fully aware of it as he was now.

Jonas sensed Kursis approaching from behind.

"Jonas, they're waiting."

Jonas turned, scrutinising this one for a moment. It seemed only a moment to Kursis, but it was enough. Jonas set off again, leading the way.

They passed the elite SIBAT guards, stern and a little more tense than he would have expected, standing by the entrance to the council chambers. No physical beings existed inside those suits. Tens of thousands of years ago the Galacien, like many other species, had still used armour to protect their soldiers. As sophisticated as it was and whatever enhancements it provided the wearer, there still existed a body within, no matter the species, which was never as strong as the technology behind the armour. Soldiers were still being killed.

As the centuries rolled on, the armour, which acted for a warrior's attack and defence, continued to evolve into ever more devastatingly advanced and precise weapons. Energy shields added to the wearer's defensive capabilities. The armour itself advanced on a more fundamental level, namely those elements which controlled the technology itself. Galacien technology, even in this area, was far superior to that of other species in the galaxy. Their assault programs could infiltrate their enemies' systems and shut them down, or even take control of them, in a matter of seconds or even nanoseconds, depending on the sophistication of their opponent's technology.

Many more centuries passed until the Galacien approached the idea of using artificial warriors. An earlier attempt was abandoned, for controlling soldiers remotely had proved problematic. The signal susceptible to infiltration and disruption, whether naturally occurring or intentional, always proved to be the weak link in an otherwise very strong, practicably unbreakable chain. In short, it could not be counted on as a certainty and Galacien technology was becoming so elegant and refined, there was no place for such unreliability. The Galacien had highly trained warriors and the technology, but how to combine the two? The solution — to download a copy of the warrior's mind into the soulless machine. This led to the greatest success. It was possible to destroy the body of the warrior, but never kill him, for his mind remained safely stored someplace else. The Galacien had used this technique ever since.

Inside the large circular chamber waited a dozen or so council members, with twice as many guards. Jonas felt the same sense of unease as he had felt outside, though now it was stronger. He sensed nothing from the council members except what he could read from their non-verbal communication, for they were all holograms. Again, here was an example of Galacien technological evolution. When he'd first made contact with them, their holograms were distinguishable from their real presence, albeit subtly. Now, if it were not for his extraordinary senses, he would find it impossible to tell if they were really here or not: the illusion was perfect. The guards, on the other hand, were very real and their minds nervous, for Galaciens.

Jonas shook his head in annoyance. "What is this about, Kursis? You have nothing to fear from me."

"We are not so sure of that," said a female Galacien council member, her holographic self walking gracefully towards him. Jonas's implant identified her as Yosar. "You know the fate that awaits Earth, I'm sure. We will not interfere."

"I know."

"This is the way it has been for millennia, and will always be," added Kursis.

"I am not arguing with you," affirmed Jonas, "yet still I can see in your eyes you are not sure."

"We know you do not hold any particular affection for your kind, but you are still one of them. It is the world that birthed you and your ancestors. Are you sure you can accept what is to come, even though Garianne has spoken out openly about opposing the Galacien's non-interference concerning this matter?"

Jonas slowly regarded the gathered council members. "I have been asking myself that question for over two thousand years now, and I have still not found a satisfactory answer. Does any species deserve to die for a possible threat they may pose in the future?"

Yosar looked sadly at him. "We deal in certainties, not probabilities. We cannot risk the lives of innocents. We tried it before, a long time ago, and the cost was too high. That is why this has to be the only way."

Jonas nodded, deep in thought.

"What will be will be, and we ask you not to oppose us in this," she said.

Jonas sighed. "What do you want of me?"

Kursis turned to face him. "Your assurance, your word, that when the time comes you will not interfere. You are happy with the arrangement you yourself made all those years ago?"

"Yes," said Jonas, as confident now as he had been back then.

"As are we: let's not disturb the waters. Offer us your assurance that you will not interfere, and go home. That is all we ask. Forget about the humans. It is a great tragedy when an entire planet's population must die, of that there is no doubt," sympathised Yosar.

Kursis approached Jonas from the other side. "There are still the meta-humans here, and yourself. The history of Earth will be 'stored' so the loss will not be a complete one. Return home to Terra, Jonas, and be at peace."

They all looked expectantly at him. Light years away, he felt the full weight of those so like him, yet so unlike him, weighing upon his conscience. He could feel the council's overwhelming anticipation, and, as he maintained his silence, he felt his decision turn sour in his mind, into something else.

Kursis looked sternly at Jonas. "Enough of this. We cannot be sure. I'm sorry Jonas, but you must be detained until the event has passed."

All the guards in the chamber snapped to attention in perfect unison.

"What? After what I did... what I had to do to an entire species so that you could survive?"

"That was a long time ago," said Kursis.

"The passing of time does not give it any less meaning. If not for my intervention, none of you would even be here," Jonas emphasized, glaring at the guards.

"I'm sorry, Jonas," said Yosar. "Guards, detain him."

"Hold!" bellowed Jonas. The command was given with such determined authority that the guards, as well trained as they were, could not help but falter. "Don't do this — you have a choice. I cannot be responsible for what will happen if you continue."

They all considered this a moment: a warning from a super-sentient being who had been responsible for the destruction of a Nacuerian force, whose number beggared imagination, and had destroyed the very pinnacle of Phalinon intellect. But the Galacien had grown arrogant over time; arrogant and powerful.

"Too late, Jonas," Kursis smirked, "too late."

Several things happened at once. Jonas sensed a dampening field descend, covering thousands of kilometres in every direction and preventing him from teleporting away, as well as a very powerful force-field surrounding the entire chamber. The council members disappeared and the guards immediately attacked him.

It was over in just a few moments. Within a fraction of a second they fired concussion projectiles from their shoulders. These weapons didn't need aiming but fired as soon as the warrior's mental instructions told them to do so. A hundredth of a second after they'd fired, their energy matrices received their target allocation; by this time they were already a quarter of the distance between their gun ports and Jonas. The projectiles corrected their courses an instant later and erupted less than a metre from their target. Jonas suddenly felt as if his whole body was being brutally beaten from every conceivable direction.

The following second a different kind of projectile reached him. This one was far more powerful, which accounted for its late arrival. It had taken the guard assigned with this task a little over a second to bring his weapon to bear and for it to reach to within a metre of Jonas's contorting body. When it did it blossomed into a perfect translucent sphere. It shimmered with bright blues and violets, surrounding its prisoner. Even slower than the containment field projectile, other much smaller objects of matter flew towards him. They stuck onto the surface of the spherical containment field. Thousands of microscopic needles broke through the surface in unison, and each expelled something unseen inside the field. The Nano-machines were in him, even as he was knocked back by the last of the concussion projectiles.

Jonas tried to stand up on the surface of the containment field beneath him but his legs buckled and he fell to his knees. More guards jumped down from the higher levels above, their suits taking the fall easily and gracefully. They moved in closer to Jonas as he fought to stand up.

Kursis and Yosar's holograms appeared high above, watching.

"I expected more from him," commented Kursis.

"I can't believe it's come to this," sighed Yosar. "It doesn't feel right."

"Perhaps not, but it is necessary," said Kursis sternly.

"You're right, though. I too expected more. The super-sentients that came before were far more capable and powerful. Look at him, he can barely stand after our initial assault. Perhaps his part in the war was exaggerated? Garianne may have been far more instrumental than we had previously believed."

"Perhaps. He may be super-sentient, but he is still human; still one of them. He does not possess the capacity to fully realise his potential. That is why he has fallen so easily," Kursis asserted.

"What a waste," said Yosar.

"Yes. To think of what we could have accomplished if he hadn't chosen this self-indulgent exile of his."

Kursis turned away from Jonas. "It appears we won't be needing the guardian-class SIBATs or our forces in orbit after all. I'll order them to stand down."

"It does seem a little overkill now, doesn't it?" Yosar said, looking at the figure of Jonas, who was down on one knee, his hands together as if in prayer.

"Better to err on the side of caution, Yosar, than to underestimate him..."

Kursis stopped as he saw on her face an expression of confusion.

Kursis spun around. Jonas was looking directly at them, calm and focused, with his upturned palm outstretched as if offering them a gift.

The guards stood frozen.

Jonas quickly closed his hand halfway as if tightly holding something invisible.

"You did underestimate me," he said, abruptly tightening his hand into a fist.

An overwhelming shockwave burst from the containment field, rendering the ground asunder and disrupting the very air as it spread outwards. The guards stood fast for a fraction of a second, then were blown away like leaves in the wind. The structure of the council chamber fared no better, and the energy matrices containing Kursis' and Yosar's holograms were shattered out of existence. They both found themselves standing where they really were, completely cut off from the council chambers.

Kursis sent out an emergency mental command through his implant. *We have a problem.*

Ten. Reunion

Galacien Prime, the Galacien system

Min surveyed her creation. The holographic vista spread out across the vast hallway before her; every tree, rock and waterway had been carefully worked out. The residents would love it. Most habitats' landscapes were generated by machines, but many people still liked the idea that their environment had been lovingly crafted by a person who did it for their own pleasure and for the inhabitants. She imagined them walking by the rivers and being the first to discover her many waterfalls, or climbing her rocks and mountains. She had taken particular care in making them unique, being an avid climber herself. It would make a fine addition to her ever-growing portfolio. Next time she would work on something a little grander, something different that had never been done before. This time it would be for Galacien Prime. She already had some exciting ideas.

Kallon slipped his arms around her, firmly kissing her on the cheek.

"You've done enough. Send it."

She smiled, reaching up to stroke his face. With a mental command to her implant, the holographic landscape disappeared. She packed it up and sent a copy of it on its way for approval.

It was obvious there was a problem, even before she was aware of the intruder. As Min dropped onto the bed with Kallon, that connection with the rest of the Galacien, that familiarity at the back of her mind, was gone. Her first reaction was shock that something had happened to the grid, for she instinctively knew her implant was fine. Min did not have to run any diagnostics. She sat up from the bed attempting every trick she knew to re-establish a link, only to reaffirm what she already suspected. Something, or someone, was preventing her.

Kallon stood up, looking, listening. "Yours too?" he asked.

Min nodded. This was not good. Scanning the house, she sensed a human only moments before he entered the room, He closed on them quickly, his intentions obvious.

"I don't know you," said Min, backing away, her human heart pounding.

Kallon attempted to intercept the intruder, but was brutally struck down with a quick series of expertly landed blows.

Assessing the situation, Min's training immediately kicked in. For a moment time slowed down for her as her implant combat routines shocked her entire system, and her vast experience automatically governed her response. Min back-flipped onto her bed into a crouch, then sprang into the air as her unknown assailant tried to grab her. Clutching onto the anti-grav light above, she managed to bring herself down onto the other side of the bed and kick out with her foot as the intruder turned to face her. Her kick connected perfectly with a respectable force behind it, as did the blur of her three successive blows, yet he was completely unaffected and seemingly unaware he had been hit at all. Min had a moment to notice an unnerving calm in his eyes before she ran from the bedroom. The man followed.

Locke, to me. I'm under attack! she thought, as the man tackled her to the floor.

Min turned and kicked him in the face, hard. Still, he was unfazed despite the damage she caused. He picked her up by the ankle as if she were a child and flung her casually across the room. Min crashed into the furniture, and momentarily felt pain as she tried to maintain consciousness. Her implant subdued it and informed her of her injuries: a broken arm, some broken ribs, internal bleeding. The man was coming at her again when something big came through ceiling between them. Debris and dust surrounded the hulking SIBAT.

Locke, subdue the intruder. Use any force necessary, thought Min to the machine standing between herself and her assailant.

Coughing violently, she tried to crawl away.

Locke, stop the intruder.

She heard nothing except the scraping of her slow struggle across the floor. Min twisted her neck round to see the man and the SIBAT standing toe-to-toe, immobile.

"Locke, I said stop the intruder, now!" she shouted.

The man put his hand against the SIBAT's chest and pushed. With a great crash the SIBAT toppled over. Purposefully the man came towards her. She fought back the panic and tried to think. Her implant combat routines gave her options which were pathetic at best, but she already knew that. She tried anyway, going for the nerve clusters. He brushed them off as easily as he'd done everything else she'd thrown at him. In response, he slammed her face first into the wall, breaking her nose. A series of punches broke a number of teeth and had her doubled over, coughing blood. She knelt there a moment as she felt her bruised eye begin to swell. She caught a breath, and as fast as she was able, grabbed him by the testicles and squeezed as hard as she could. The man stood there as still and silent as a statue, looking down.

Impossible, thought Min, *even if he cut off the pain, there would be some kind of emotional reaction.*

There was only that dreadful calm as he slowly broke her hand away and lifted her up by her neck.

Immediately, she felt herself choking, and when her feet left the floor he spoke in a terrible, deep, voice.

"Know this. When you die here, it will be for good. There is to be no next life for you — your copies have been destroyed. Your life is at an end."

"*No!*" she tried to scream, but all that came out was a whimper and bloody spittle.

She flailed around, wanting to push her finger into his eye socket but it would do no good. Her own eyes bulged and the pulsating in her head joined the screaming in her mind as everything began to fade away.

Something big hit her and she became aware that she was breathing again in shallow gasps. The hand around her throat had loosened somewhat and she could hear a great commotion all about her.

I'm on the floor, she realised, *that's what hit me.*

Her good arm was free and she reached to the hand about her throat: it had been detached from the body at the forearm. She wrenched it free from her neck and filled her lungs with sweet air. As Min's vision began to clear, she could see that on the house grounds several more men dressed like her attacker were slowly approaching.

Min's assailant was nowhere to be seen, but she could hear fighting in the next room.

Kallon? she thought, trying to reach him using her implant. But there was no response.

The wall opposite her exploded as her assailant broke through it and hit the wall next to her, collapsing onto the floor. Then, through the new hole in the wall, stepped Jonas. For a moment he looked at her, his expression she found impossible to read. He was here in the flesh, after all this time. Before she could say anything, she saw her attacker jump to his feet and turn to her. She saw him about to spring for her when his head left his body and tumbled across the floor. Jonas was there, detracting an energy blade back into his arm.

Jonas turned to her, "I saw Garianne use something similar to this once. It always impressed me how she utilised it."

He reached out to help her up. His hand was cool and reassuringly firm in its grip.

"She's an impressive woman," whispered Min hoarsely, trying to regain her composure. She dragged her eyes from him. "There are more outside."

"It doesn't matter. We're going," stated Jonas, and the next moment they were on the bridge of a starship.

"Wait, Kallon," she gasped.

"It's all right. He's here," said Jonas.

It could have been the bridge of any number of starships, so why did Min find it so familiar? The holographic imaging sprang into life and they were given a tactical display of the Galacien system. Planets reduced to points orbited the star while fleets of ships' trajectories were displayed along with any other significant information. Min had only a moment to realise that their current position wasn't highlighted. Jonas gave the tactical display a brief glance before he lifted her effortlessly into a suspension field. Her body was plunged into the cylinder of warm orange light as she hung weightless a foot from the floor.

"Allow the ship to access your implant and you will be good as new in no time," instructed Jonas.

She merely nodded.

Jonas turned back to the holographic display, studying it, manipulating it.

Min watched him a moment. He had come for her when she needed him most — when no-one else seemed even aware of what was about to happen to her. She shuddered at the memory as she opened up her implant to the ship.

Hello Min, said the ship.

Lom? I thought you were dead, destroyed during the war?

Destroyed, yes. Dead, for the most part no. Jonas was able to save a part of me and reconstruct the rest of my mind.

That's... incredible. How could he possibly do that?

You still lack faith in him.

Min involuntarily rolled her eyes. *It's just.... it seems impossible. I can't see how he could have done it.*

And yet here I am.

You sound a little like him.

I am no longer what I was. That which was destroyed is lost forever. It took him years to recreate me into what I am today. There will always be a part of him in me now.

Min smiled. *It's good to have you back, even if you are somewhat changed.*

We all change, Min. I am sure you yourself are different in many ways to the person I once knew, yet you are still Min. Now, let us see what we can do about those injuries, shall we?

In her mind she saw the report of her physical traumas come in and solutions were quickly supplied. Subtle yet strong force-fields in concert with nano-machines quickly sealed up and regenerated her cells. Again, Min was glad her implant had cut off any pain as she heard her arm and ribs crack when they were forced back into position.

A little while later Min stepped away from the suspension field, flexing her arm and reaching around her ribs. Her implant reported no remaining injuries and that everything was back to normal. It gave her cold comfort as she approached Jonas at the holographics.

"Thank you," said Min hesitantly. He turned to face her. "Really, thank you. If you hadn't come..."

"You would be dead," shrugged Jonas.

"He said he'd destroyed my copies. Had he really?" said Min.

"Yes, I think he… they had," said Jonas.

"Who are they? Why would they want to kill me?"

"I think they were trying to draw me out. Apparently they thought my past affection for you would drive me into attempting to save you."

She could not hold his gaze; it was unwavering. Despite her thousands of years of experience, she felt like a first lifer all over again.

Min laughed. "You did save me." She bit back the tears.

"Best to let it go," whispered Jonas as he looked into her eyes and drew her to him.

She wept quietly, not caring how self-conscious it made her feel.

Eventually, as the tears subsided, she said, "I hate being human, I hate being weak."

"You chose to remain human all this time. Why?"

"I don't know. It's not just being human. I didn't think anything could hurt me. Living on Galacien Prime, the SIBAT, the implant, my training — none of it made any difference. All of our evolution, enhancements and technological superiority, that man stripped it all away and what was left was a pathetic wretched creature. Those last moments... is that what it's like to die?"

"The Galacien have wrapped you up in a psychological security blanket all your life. You were ill-prepared for such an experience. I'm sorry it was because of me."

She stepped away from him, wiping the moisture from her eyes, feeling suddenly very self-conscious in his presence. "It's not your fault."

"No..." He paused, staring out of the view into space. Lines of concern broke across his brow.

"What is it?"

"Lytpniuph. They targeted the two of you simultaneously. I couldn't save you both. They made me choose."

Min felt a flash of relief that it had been her he'd chosen, and then shame. "Is he dead?"

"No, I would have known."

"Then what?"

"I think they're going to change him. The same as the others."

Min looked at him, head shaking, her mouth open.

"When council member Kursis met me prior to entering the council chamber, I sensed something. I decided to check what was really going on. It only seemed a split second to him as I looked him in the eye; however, for me time stretched out into hours as I dived into his mind, and, in turn, his implant. As I suspected, he had been subverted by an alien intelligence, our true enemy."

"Alien in what sense?"

"It was the same intelligence which subverted the Nacuerian species, manipulating it into invading our galaxy over two thousand years ago."

"I knew nothing of this intelligence. You never spoke of it before."

"No, Garianne and I..."

"Garianne? She knew?"

"Yes. The Nacuerians were only the first wave. You must realise the malevolent intelligence behind this — we call it the Adversary — is godlike in its capacity. We barely survived its first attack, will not survive the second."

"What is its plan, and how do you know of this?"

Jonas looked uncomfortable — and something else she had rarely seen in him from those days long ago. She reached out to him, touching his arm. "What is it?"

"I had to destroy them, they left me no choice... There wasn't any time, even for me, to calculate a way of saving them." Jonas shook his head, hands gripped on the holographics table.

Min looked at him, confused.

"Min, the Nacuerians weren't monsters, they were victims. A once-noble race, the Adversary encountered, changed, twisted them physically and mentally into what we fought during the war."

The silence stretched out as Min contemplated his words.

"You had no choice, no time. Don't punish yourself further."

Jonas nodded, yet Min had the feeling this would be something which would haunt him for the rest of his life.

Jonas looked at the holographics display a moment and seemed to refocus, "This time it's different. People are being subverted but only mentally. There is no physical difference and no conventional way to detect the change."

"What is the nature of this change? How does this Adversary manipulate people who are working under its agenda? Is it some kind of link?" asked Min.

"Perhaps not in the way you imagine. When I looked around in Kursis' implant I could detect no outward difference. However, it was connected through a very subtle metaspace link, something beyond Galacien capabilities to accomplish. At the other side of this link resides a creature made of pure energy, which directly controls the host."

"Is this creature the Adversary?"

"No, although similar. I believe within each subverted victim, because of this link, there's an infinitesimally small fraction of the Adversary itself. This time our enemy attacks us with deception and we don't know its identity until it is too late. It will destroy the Galacien Conglomerate of Worlds from within and I believe it has already begun."

Eleven. Revelations

London, Earth

Garianne sat in her office studying the three-dimensional holographic displays suspended above the table where she sat. James entered the room quietly. When he reached the table, he waited patiently.

"What is it?" asked Garianne, not taking her eyes from the holographics.

"It's about Jonas."

"What about him?"

"He's gone rogue."

She looked up, "What do you mean, he's gone rogue? He's all alone on Terra."

"He went to Galacien Prime, where the council asked his assurance that he would not interfere in Earth's... trial."

"And?" pressed Garianne.

"He didn't give them a firm answer. They had no choice but to detain him."

"They tried to force him?"

James nodded.

Garianne shook her head, "Fools. Jonas was never co-operative at the best of times. Do you have their report?"

"Of course."

"Very well. Let me have it," she gestured.

James's implant sent the report to Garianne's in a fraction of a second. It took her only a few moments to review it.

"Suspiciously vague about exactly how he escaped, don't you think?" queried Garianne.

"They underestimated him."

"Obviously."

James thought for a moment. "He must have infiltrated their systems. As unbelievable as it sounds, that may account for the lack of data: he'd cover his tracks, destroy anything they could use against him."

"Have we any idea where he may be now?" asked Garianne.

"They believe he's still in the home system. It seems logical to assume he'll come here. We have our orders direct from the council to detain him if he does."

"They tried that on Galacien Prime and failed, so what makes them think we will fare any better with our limited resources?" said Garianne, doubtfully.

"You, apparently," said James, with a note of finality.

Garianne leaned back into her chair, her hands steepled in thought.

Alex stepped out of the taxi, paid the driver and closed the door. The autumn wind blew the leaves up around his legs, rising and falling with each great breath, and whipping the tips of his hair into his eyes. He casually brushed it aside as his gaze followed the floors up the building to its roof. He knew almost immediately that there was something very different about this building, something strange.

To all intents and purposes it appeared like any other grand stone building of London that was reaching the centenary of its construction. Though it wasn't its exterior where he perceived the anomaly, it was high up — there, on one of those floors, although which one he could not be certain. To him, it seemed that somewhere there was an infinitesimally small crack, yet what was beyond that he could not tell. This was partially what was so odd: Alex could sense everything around him for almost half a mile, yet this seemed like a sliver of nothingness, as if it didn't exist at all. He withdrew his awareness back to his immediate surroundings. The taxi pulled away, leaving him lingering on the pavement as the people on the street went briskly about their business, wrapped up in their own affairs.

What did he have to fear? His imagination grasped for an answer and found nothing concrete. He needed answers and they certainly weren't lying around here on the street. They were in there.

Taking a deep breath, Alex walked through the automatic doors and into a large foyer. He looked around and made his way towards the main reception, though before he'd taken more than a few steps towards it, James intercepted him. Again he wore an impeccable and expensive looking suit. With a relaxed smile, James extended his hand.

"Hello Alex, I'm glad you came."

"Yeah. Me too, I think," said Alex, forcing a smile and allowing James to shake his hand.

Alex then noticed the people around them watching him — subtle glances while they talked to one another or worked on their computers. It made Alex feel more than a little uneasy.

"Something I should know about?"

James smiled, "They're just curious."

"About me?"

"Oh yes."

Alex waved at the people glancing at him, and they quickly pretended to get on with their business.

"If you'd like to follow me, I'll take you to Garianne," said James, turning towards the lift.

Alex followed him in. "Okay, so what is this place?"

"Didn't you notice the six-foot-high letters on the way in?" smiled James, as he pushed the button for the twenty-fourth floor. The lift doors opened and they both entered the lift.

"I was kind of distracted. There's something a little weird about this place. Sorry." Alex felt like he'd just insulted James, though he was reassured when he sensed his only reaction was one of curiosity.

"This is the Galacien Institute for Technological Advancement — GITA for short," said James.

"And what do you do here at GITA?"

"Mainly research. We spearhead new technologies, and we introduce ideas to the people we believe can utilize them. There are some extremely bright people working for us."

"And Garianne's in charge of all of this?"

"Yes," said James, as the lift doors opened.

Alex followed James down to the end of the corridor, where large, wooden double doors waited.

Alex knew *she* was in there.

James made to open the doors.

"Aren't you going to knock?" Alex whispered.

Alex smiled. "She knows we're here; she wants us to enter."

Before Alex could question James' judgement, he effortlessly pushed the heavy double doors open to reveal a large office. The style of the office mirrored that of the building itself, a perfect melding of the old and the new. Wood-panelled walls and wooden floorboards sat in idealised harmony with stone, marble, glass, and the necessary addition of modern technology. In any other circumstances, Alex would have easily been transfixed by the many fascinating details which leapt to his senses from within the room. Yet no-one's attention could stray for more than a moment from the figure who faced them.

In front of the large window, on the far side of the room, stood a woman who was smiling pleasantly. The depth of her shining eyes swallowed his soul, making him feel both anxious and elated. She blinked twice and suddenly she appeared far less strange, though he could sense that she was far more than what people would consider ordinary.

He realised that he had frozen a few feet inside the door; that he was staring at her. James had stopped between them, and politely cleared his throat.

"Alex?" said James.

"It's all right, James," Garianne assured him. Her words were like a perfect melody which seemed to resonate around the room. "He's adjusting, aren't you, Alex?"

Alex stared a moment longer then slowly nodded. She was unlike anyone he had encountered before. In a way he couldn't quite grasp what he was sensing from her.

She gave Alex a sympathetic look. "Would you care for some tea?"

Alex simply nodded again; it seemed a bizarre question, in light of the current situation.

"What about you, James?" she enquired.

James immediately jumped into action. "Let me. I insist."

"No," said Garianne, "allow me."

James stopped as if his feet were glued to the floor and seemed quite unsettled by this turn of events. He looked at Alex and then back to Garianne.

"I insist," she continued, giving Alex a wry smile.

Alex tried not to chuckle at James' continuing discomfort as Garianne so very patiently made the tea, her movements fluid and precise as if she were practicing a mime. Soon she returned with three steaming cups of tea. Her sudden proximity startled Alex a little, as if she hadn't seemed quite real until that moment.

"Milk no sugar, right?" said Garianne.

Alex nodded, taking the cup, not asking how she had known.

Garianne gestured for Alex to sit on an old fashioned leather sofa and joined him there.

It was only then that Alex noticed another figure standing against the left wall of the room. He'd mistaken it for a statue as it stood completely unmoving except for its eyes. Alex thought of it as an 'it' because he couldn't sense whether it was male or female. It appeared to scowl at him from behind the mask of static features; he could certainly sense its distaste for him.

Garianne noticed the non-verbal exchange.

"This is Talmhon," she said.

She was unfazed by the way Talmhon looked at Alex, continuing as if it was of no consequence. Despite her presence and the situation, Alex could still feel its eyes burrowing into his skull.

"I'm sure you have many questions. I'll try my best to answer them," said Garianne.

"All right," said Alex putting down his tea, "you could start by telling me who you are — who you *really* are. Something's not right here. You're, well..." he struggled.

Garianne looked at him, intrigued.

"Who do you think we are?" asked Garianne.

Alex didn't want to say what he thought, what he felt.

"Do not skirt around the obvious. Forget what you've been taught to think. What do you *feel*?"

Alex shook his head. "The unbelievable. That the only person that's human in this room apart from myself is him," said Alex, indicating James "And he's not quite..."

"What of us?" Garianne said, indicating herself and Talmhon.

The question hung there in silence.

Alex looked from one to another. He felt he was a long way from home.

Slowly he said, "You are not from this planet."

"No," replied Garianne simply.

"How long have your kind been here, on Earth?"

"We've had a permanent presence here for well over two thousand years."

"Okay," replied Alex, blinking in astonishment. He tried to take in the gravity of this admission, which he knew to be true. He could feel that she wasn't lying, and also, he was relieved to find that her intentions seemed benevolent. Garianne took another sip of tea, as relaxed as if they were discussing the weather.

"Anything else?" prompted Garianne.

"Are you kidding? How long have you got?"

"All day. I've cleared my schedule for this."

"What about you? What are you?" asked Alex.

Garianne looked wistfully away for a moment and then back into his soul. "You know, I've changed species so many times in the past — becoming them, living entire lifetimes as them — that I can't remember which species I started out as. Sometimes I feel I've been around forever, or come full circle. I'm over six thousand years old. I know what you're thinking: I don't look a day over a thousand!"

Alex couldn't help but laugh. "And now you're human?"

"Yes," stated Garianne, again in her matter-of-fact manner. "At the moment."

Alex paused for a second, unsure whether he would like the answer to his next question. "So what do you want from me?"

"It's as much *what you are* that interests the Galacien Conglomerate of Worlds, as what we want," said James.

"What am I then?"

Garianne leaned closer to him. Her eyes, her hair, her physical presence somehow seemed to almost overwhelm him. His heartbeat increased in direct connection with her proximity. Why was that?

"You are what we refer to as a super-sentient being," said Garianne. "Unlike any other creature in the known universe, you possess extraordinary abilities that the Galacien still cannot comprehend."

"Do not be so sure, Garianne," said Talmhon , its voice deep and guttural. Alex jumped; he had almost forgotten its presence. "Galacien science is breaching frontiers even you are unaware of."

Alex felt worried. He looked at the creature and then at Garianne.

"I'm sure they are. However, none of us have ever been able to explain him. You are a mystery, Alex," she said smiling, and suddenly it was as if Talmhon had vanished. Alex could not help but smile back, and share whatever it was she was feeling. "I for one am glad you are here. The universe is a far more interesting place with you in it."

"Thanks," Alex said. "Are there others like me?"

"Super-sentients are a one in ten billion occurrence. Due to the vast population of the galaxy and its multitude of species, this meant that there were hundreds or even thousands alive at any one time within the Galacien Conglomerate of Worlds."

"You mentioned that conglomerate before. What is it?"

"The Galacien are the most advanced species in the galaxy. A long time ago, they managed to congregate the other space-faring races into a union of peace for the betterment of the whole: the more advanced species guided the less advanced ones."

"How come we humans didn't know anything about this?" asked Alex.

Talmhon stirred. "Because you are inferior, immature, and unworthy."

Alex looked at Talmhon, his teeth and fists visibly clenched.

"Keep a leash on that dog of yours, Garianne, in case I see fit to discipline him," boomed Talmhon.

Garianne's eyes glazed over as she turned to Talmhon, who suddenly disappeared from the room.

"What did you do?" whispered Alex, worry spread across his face.

"Merely sent him on his way," replied Garianne, with a casual wave of her hand.

"They won't take kindly to this," observed James.

"What was that thing?" said Alex.

"It's not a 'thing', Alex. Its name is Talmhon, and it was here at the Galacien council's request. They wished to oversee this meeting."

James rubbed his chin, his hand spreading up his face to his forehead.

"It's not that bad, James, they can still see what transpires here. That is essentially what they want."

"You've got cameras in here?" asked Alex.

Garianne and James both looked at one another.

"In a manner, yes. Molecular-sized wormholes cover every nook and cranny of this planet, allowing us to see everything. Nothing transpires without our and the GCW's knowing."

"Still, you know what will happen," insisted James.

"I'll hear no more of this. We both know what is coming."

"What do you mean?" questioned Alex.

"Nothing. I'm sure you have far more important questions to ask me. For example, would you like to know what happened to the others like yourself?"

Alex didn't want to let it go, but it would have to wait until later. He felt as if he could go off in a hundred different directions if he blurted out every question popping into his head. *One thing at a time*, he thought.

"All right," he conceded.

As the sun made its slow progress across the window and James brought more tea, Garianne continued to calmly tell Alex of the Galacien 'Golden Age' when the super-sentients made incredible accomplishments until, inexplicably, their birth-rate declined to nothing, and the remaining ones eventually died. Many years later, another super-sentient named Jonas was discovered during the Nacuerian/Galacien war, right here on Earth over two thousand years ago. She went on to tell Alex how Jonas saved them all and then lived in isolation all that time, his activities unknown.

"Why now?" frowned Alex. "I don't understand why you've left him alone all this time until now?"

"Perhaps those in power feel like it is time he worked for them in the same way the super-sentients of the past did. Perhaps they wish to create a new Golden Age. And now with your appearance, perhaps they feel there are more to come soon," said Garianne.

"Are there?"

Garianne shrugged. "Perhaps, perhaps not."

"Those 'in power', are they watching us now?" Alex looked around nervously.

"You get used to it in time, but yes, we're all being watched, Alex."

"Jonas wasn't," said James.

The room fell silent as Garianne considered Alex a moment "Would you like something to eat?" she suggested.

The day seemed to have passed a little too quickly. As Alex realised how hungry he was, he could see out of the large window the clouds starting to change colour to their evening purples and oranges. However, the slight chill he felt owed nothing to the slow setting of the sun before him.

"Yes, thank you." He shifted on the sofa, feeling uncomfortable. "Listen, I'm grateful for the help last night, especially from James and the girl, but what is it you want?"

Garianne frowned. "What girl?"

"The one who spoke to me in my head," said Alex.

Garianne looked to James, who shrugged.

"I'm not crazy. When I was attacked last night, I heard a voice — a girl's voice."

Garianne's eyes narrowed as she scrutinised him. "What did she say?"

"She seemed to know exactly what was going on, and she knew about my abilities, better than I do. She was trying to help me. I'd like to thank her."

"We know nothing of this," admitted Garianne.

"Then who was she?" asked Alex.

Garianne moved slightly closer to him and again felt his heart quicken. He had truly never been in the presence of anyone such as her. It seemed as if everyone he had ever met was a faded watercolour, while she was animated and vibrant in comparison. How did she convey herself in such a manner? She was by far the most attractive woman he'd met, yet at the same time she could seem almost more motherly than his true mother. It was as compelling as it was confusing. She was fascinating. The graceful way she moved, her poise, it was relaxed yet he felt almost a little scared because his senses noticed those little things which others could not. He knew she was lethal. He could see it in her physique and in her eyes, as if she were ready for anything.

"She spoke English? What kind of accent did she have? How old would you guess she was?" queried Garianne.

"She spoke very eloquently. I believe she's from London. Her age was difficult to place, but her voice sounded like a teenager. However, the way she spoke, the things she said, maybe older. She seemed very intelligent."

"I think I should look into this personally. Anything anomalous last night, James?" Garianne took a sip of tea and then looked over her shoulder for a moment as James considered it and Alex had more tea himself.

"You mean except for the meta-human incursion? No."

"What happened there?" asked Alex

"Hmmm... Oh, don't concern yourself with them, Alex. They are merely humans residing on Galacien Prime who obviously had ideas above their station. I assure you they will be punished for their attack on you."

"Punished?"

Garianne chuckled, "Oh, dear. Nothing quite as severe as you probably imagine. We're more humane than you are, ironically enough. Being citizens of the Galacien, they have access to freedoms and technologies undreamt of by humankind. They will be deprived of some of these for a short amount of time, relatively speaking. They'll probably be living lives far better than any human here on Earth, but they'll feel badly done to because they're not used to it."

"Not much of a punishment, if you ask me," muttered James.

"Maybe not. But they won't be allowed to leave Galacien Prime anytime soon or take part in any private communication, you can be sure of that. In short, Alex, you need not worry about them. There are far larger issues which require our attention," said Garianne.

"Such as?"

"The imminent destruction of your planet."

Twelve. Discovered

London, Earth

Alicia's eyes shot open. She attempted to calm her rapid breathing as quickly as possible. Her years of vigilance nearly ruined in a careless moment, so carried away was she by revelation after revelation from the woman who called herself Garianne. She had been caught completely unprepared. Alicia ran it over in her mind: Garianne had quite subtly, though very definitely, turned and looked right at her. How had she known she was there? She was undetectable, wasn't she? The others in the room, James and Alex, didn't even notice, and Alicia was quite sure that's exactly what Garianne wanted. Alicia felt a slight tightness to her chest as she considered that this Garianne was her superior in every way, and, more than that, had a terrible feeling that she was simply playing games with her.

She needed to get away from the house. If there was even a small chance they were coming for her...

Not here, she thought.

She quickly crossed her bedroom and grabbed her jacket. She opened the door and bounded down three flights of stairs.

"Are you okay, sweetheart?" she heard from the adjoining room.

"Yes, Daddy. Just going out for a walk."

"Well, be back soon. Dinner will be ready in about thirty minutes."

She glanced round the corner into the kitchen watching him expertly chopping vegetables, and felt something she hadn't felt for a long time. A foreboding, an uncertainty about her immediate future. Would she see either of her parents again? Anger rose in her; they had taken away her freedom all her life. To hell with it, she would not keep it locked away. Let them watch.

"I love you, Daddy," she whispered, her voice shaking.

Then she was gone, oblivious to those she passed on the street rubbing their temples in pain.

So now she knew what it was all about. Alien beings, alien technology. They had been here for some time now since that great war thousands of years ago. Then there were these 'super-sentients'. Alex was one of them, and so was this Jonas of whom they spoke. What about her? But perhaps most significant was the as yet unknown threat to the entire planet. She wished she had learnt more. Yet when Garianne began questioning Alex about her, making startlingly accurate predictions, she knew she was in trouble. Perhaps she should have left earlier before Garianne sensed her presence? Somehow, though, Alicia was convinced Garianne knew she was there all along. The way she casually turned around at the moment of her choosing. There was nothing surprising in those eyes. She *had* known all along. Alicia wasn't sure whether they would come for her or what they'd do. One thing she was sure of — this Garianne was a very dangerous woman.

The street lights were coming on as she progressed closer towards the City of London. The nights were beginning to draw in a little, now they were into the back end of autumn. Alicia kicked up the leaves as she walked briskly along the pavement. The wind blew up her hair. She sensed those around her and something caught her mind: two men, following her and keeping pace. She decided to make a few turns on the streets and the men followed. Were these men agents of the Galacien? Why not simply teleport her somewhere secure and have it out, there? She saw a narrow deserted lane and made for it.

The men closed the gap.

In the street, where no-one could see except the ever-present machines, the men caught up with her and tapped her on the shoulder.

"Excuse me miss, police. May we ask you some questions?" said the thick-set man all in black.

"Really? You look more like bouncers," observed Alicia.

"Just a few questions," said the other man.

Then, without warning, the machine eyes went away, and Alicia's heart began pounding. As much as she hated them, not having their eyes watching was unnerving. No witnesses.

"I think I should go," said Alicia.

"No, you stay," growled the first man, grabbing her jacket and slamming her against the railings.

Her fear vanished, turning to something else. All her life she had been hiding. All her life she had been scared of the machines and what lay behind them. No more. She was tired. Enough was enough.

Alicia checked the street. Still no-one.

She looked at the second man, who suddenly stepped forward and punched his colleague hard on the chin. The first man let go of Alicia immediately and retaliated. Alicia watched them slug it out for a moment while she slowly straightened her jacket.

"Stop," she ordered and they did so. She walked over to the first man. "Don't move, either of you." They obeyed as she laid her hand on the first one's head.

Her brow furrowed in confusion: there was something foreign in his brain, very small.

"It's called an implant," said a voice.

Alicia spun round to see Garianne across the street. She was sitting on a wooden bench, one leg crossed over the other, with her hands together on her lap. Her relaxed yet poised figure was illuminated by an old Victorian street lamp above.

It took all of Alicia's control to maintain her composure.

"I'm sure you think of me as your enemy, Alicia, but I can assure you that couldn't be further from the truth," said Garianne.

Alicia held her silence, holding the other woman's gaze, though she found it difficult. There was something different about this one — different from all of them.

Garianne smiled and Alicia could feel the power of it poking away at her defences.

"Interesting how you were able to circumnavigate the implant's defences. I'm guessing you've only just learnt how to do that."

Alicia said nothing.

"You have to admit this is nice, just the two of us? Although they hate to have this blank space in their records, especially after the other night."

"Are you referring to the machines?" said Alicia.

It was pointless maintaining her silence. Now they knew who, and possibly what, she was, they would be busy scrutinising her entire life. Still, they didn't know everything. Perhaps it was foolish to interfere with the two men who still stood there, as if trapped in time, but she was so tired of hiding. Things had to change; she could not go on being... inconsequential.

"Machines?" Garianne laughed. "I think they might find that primitive reference rather offensive." She leaned forward, feigning secrecy. "Although, essentially, that's what they are."

Alicia glanced at the two men and walked over to where Garianne sat. She considered looking into her mind.

"I wouldn't do that, if I were you," warned Garianne.

Alicia felt an unfamiliar rush of heat to her face. "How did you know?"

"When you get to my age, it's pretty easy to read people. Please sit, Alicia, there are matters to discuss."

Alicia paused for just a moment and then did so.

"Believe it or not, there are few moments in my life which are truly significant. This is one of them. You won't understand why now, but sometime in the future you will. As you have no doubt guessed, you are super-sentient. However, even for a super-sentient you are very special, Alicia. I have spoken to many others about the dark days ahead, but for someone such as yourself there is a quicker, more efficient way of communicating the current state of affairs."

Garianne's eyes seemed to flash for the briefest of moments, then Alicia felt the world around her stop and slip away. In its place she saw another Alex from an Earth ravaged by a world-wide epidemic which only he survived. Another Earth, invaded by Martians and the holograph of reality. Before Alicia could ponder her own significance in all of this, she saw Garianne speaking to the Alex of her own Earth and the picture was complete.

Alicia gasped and held on to the end of the bench for support.

"Give yourself a moment to adjust," said Garianne.

Slowly the world around her came back into focus and she was herself again — except, everything had changed.

"What was that?" asked Alicia.

"I transferred some of my recent memories, using my implant."

"But I don't have an implant."

Garianne smiled. "No, you don't need one. Usually the receiver must 'read' these memories in real-time, whether at the time they occur or at a later date. However, because of your unique abilities, you are able to assimilate the information in mere moments, and without the need of an implant."

"What would happen if I were normal?"

"Nothing. If you don't possess an implant you can't send or receive information direct from the brain."

"Can *I* send as well as receive?"

"Of course. It may take a little practice, but like everything you do, Alicia, you'll master it quickly."

Alicia considered everything she'd experienced as Garianne. Underneath it all there was something about the woman herself which she kept hidden away, yet Alicia knew it was there.

Garianne grew sombre as she said, "Now you know what we face. I must ask you not to be a part of it."

"You can't mean that," said Alicia, standing to face Garianne. "After what you've shown me, you expect me to stand by and do nothing?"

"I'm sorry, Alicia, but this is the best way to play this."

"Meaning what?"

"Meaning not only do I want your non-interference, but I want you to leave this universe altogether."

All of Alicia's distrust came to the fore. "Why?"

"I need to have someone who's not a part of this; a player whom our enemies are not aware of and have not accounted for. If you join with the rest of us, you are a known quantity. They will eventually take your measure and defeat you. However, at the moment you are the unknown factor in this struggle and I wish you to remain so — in case the worst should come to pass."

"But you'll have a better chance with me, surely."

"The Adversary's power is limitless. You will be far more effective out of the way. If we fall, then perhaps you can learn from our mistakes and find a solution of some kind."

Alicia rarely needed comfort, though right now she held her arms tightly around herself, feeling very alone.

"I've only just now stopped hiding who and what I truly am. Now you want me to do it again. Lose myself somewhere in the multiverse, pretend to be normal?"

"I know it's asking a lot."

"It's too much," snapped Alicia.

She suddenly regretted her tone. She knew who Garianne was since that, amongst many things, had been imparted to her.

"I don't *believe* you can do it," Garianne looked into Alicia's eyes, "I *know* you can do it. You are so strong, like no other being this planet has ever produced. Even stronger than Jonas."

Alicia looked at her in astonishment.

"I mean it. There is potential in you to be something more than even the super-sentients of the Galacien 'Golden Age'. You need time. You need to survive. That's why you must leave."

"It's too dangerous in this corner of reality, is that it?"

"That pretty much sums it up."

"What about my friends and family? What about everyone else?"

"I already have something set in motion. I'll do my best to protect them."

Alicia shook her head and swore; she knew Garianne was right. Until recently she would have said, without question, she was the smartest person in the world. Garianne was right — it was the best move given the situation. Could she succeed where Garianne and Jonas might fail?

"So I take it you do have a plan?"

"Of course, but be under no illusion — we are desperate. As you've seen from my memories, I've been trying to build an army of super-sentients from other universes, due to the considerable lack of them here. Utilised in the correct manner, there may be a way."

Alicia looked at her, unconvinced.

"Jonas is on the hunt for the elusive Kinsmen. He is convinced that they may represent a power beyond our experience. If they no longer exist, he may find something of them left behind which may help."

Alicia winced. "Now that does sound desperate. That's a bit of a long shot, isn't it?"

"It's all we have. Imagine the Adversary is a rock the size of London and we are a group of ants trying to destroy that rock. You get the idea."

"If we knew exactly what this thing is, maybe that would help us to fight it?"

"Jonas is the only being to have encountered a part of it, and he's the one you describe as desperate. You, Alicia, are our third and, perhaps, final solution."

"Only after the rest of you are dead. That's not much of a solution, if you ask me," said Alicia.

"It is possible the Adversary may not restrict itself to this part of reality. It may continue its rampage across the rest of the multiverse. Something which would take an eternity, and one might argue that life on such a scale becomes inconsequential because it never ends. The Adversary's horrifying task to destroy life would also be never-ending, yet I don't think this would deter it. I myself would argue that all life is precious. It may seem as if the multiverse is infinite, yet if one day it came to your Earth, wouldn't you want something done?"

Garianne was right. There was so much more to this than her Earth and her universe. A multitude awaited out there, all prey for the Adversary. She felt her resolve harden and it seemed as if her path was clearly laid out for her.

"How do we proceed?" said Alicia in a business-like manner.

The corner of Garianne's mouth twitched. "No-one else could have done what you've just done. The assimilation of all that information and already you're taking those first steps."

"Thank you. Now, you were saying?" replied Alicia with grim determination.

Garianne paused for a brief moment as something flashed upon her face that Alicia didn't quite understand.

"You must leave immediately. An Alex I've already recruited will be here shortly to take you to a universe far from here. Everything else you'll need for your new life has been taken care of. Is there anything I can do for you before you go?"

Alicia thought for a moment and slowly shook her head.

"Remember, should we fall, if this part of reality should perish, you must somehow find a way."

Thirteen. Nicola

Earth[4]

Nicola snoozed peacefully in her prison, wearing nothing but the scuba mask they had given her. The sound of her own rhythmic breathing in this cylinder of strange liquid comforted her from the usual nightmares — nightmares of a time unremembered, images her mind recoiled from. Yet, she wanted to know, see and understand who and what she was, where she came from.

She was more than a little annoyed when the door slid open and the man came in, taking a seat and peering at her as though she was an exotic fish in a tank. Not that her nudity bothered her, she had far more important things to consider than that.

"Hello, my name is Dr Tiron Jacobian. I'm here to evaluate you," she heard the man say, this stupid, small man who emphasised the word doctor before his name. This pathetic man who thought he was so clever. "Whatever your mission here was, it seems to have failed."

She remained impassive.

"We, of course, must interrogate you." Dr Jacobian's face expressed regret, but it was for show. It was all for show. Just softening her up for the main event. She knew how these things went. They would see what effect the mere threat of torture would have on her. Would she crack straight away or when they were about to begin? They would be disappointed. "Perhaps if you co-operate now we can avoid such unpleasantries," he said.

The only sound in the room was Nicola's breathing.

"Hmmm... Well, let's make a start anyway, shall we?" She watched, from with the tank, his slightly distorted hands open up a file revealing a number of papers inside. He set them meticulously on the desk and brought out a pen. "Now, full name please?"

Nicola stared at him defiantly. Dr Jacobian sighed. His hand danced upon a touch pad on the desk and finally gave it a decisive tap. The liquid transformed into pain personified and every muscle in her body contracted. She did not scream and could not breathe. As quickly as it had come, it was gone. Her breathing, having lost its calm rhythm, instead had increased as if she had been running at a sprint. She now perceived the liquid around her as having the potential to transform into something horrific at the touch of a button.

"Let's try that one again, shall we? Name please?"

She didn't reply; she merely looked at his watch.

He let out a long sigh before hitting the button again. The pain racked her body, the seconds stretching out into infinity. When it finally stopped, she found herself facing away from him.

"This is your last chance, then I'm going to have to start getting tough with you, my dear. You should take this a little more seriously, after all this is your future. Whether it ends in pain is up to you."

Nicola turned slowly in the liquid, her dark hair seeming to dance in the water. She moved up to the glass, putting her hands against its smooth, cold surface.

"I know my future," she said through the mask, which gave her voice an even more menacing tone. "In a minute I'm going to break out of here and break your neck, but not before I take care of the two guards you have posted outside the door. Finding Aleksandr should prove no problem, thanks to the programs I have placed in your system."

"How did you know about Aleksandr Lethbridge?" enquired Jacobian, nervously.

Nicola smiled. "He's the reason I'm here, you fool. Didn't you question yourselves as to how easy it was to capture me? Why spend days trying to infiltrate this facility when I could simply allow you to bring me to him?"

Jacobian swallowed, considering what she was saying, and then snorted a contemptuous laugh. "Interesting theory, except for the fact that you are trapped."

Nicola looked at the material which contained her more closely.

"What is this, Palmeeos?"

"Yes," said Jacobian.

Nicola looked at him. "Oh dear. Not strong enough." She pushed herself away from the glass and her foot whipped out in a blur against the cylinder. The result was a giant crack

Jacobian slammed his hand down again on the touch pad. Nothing happened. He looked in astonishment at the dead display.

Nicola smiled as she kicked out again and then again against the cylinder. Its contents burst out onto the floor.

Jacobian jumped up, screaming. The door slid open and two heavily armoured guards swung into the room. Naked and wet, Nicola rolled and sprung on the guard to her right. Before he could react, his sidearm was already in Nicola's hand. She found the chink in his armour and shot him several times. The second guard raised his rifle. Nicola swung the first guard round, using him to protect herself. When the shots stopped, she dived to the side, taking out the second guard. She quickly vaulted the table and brought Jacobian down with her arm tightly around his neck.

Nicola tore off the mask, revealing her face.

"Amateurs," she said, referring to the guards. "Some clothes would be nice," she hinted to Jacobian. He gasped for air. "Never mind."

She looked up at the control panel on the desk. It came to life. As maps sprung up, she found where she needed to go.

Jacobian struggled to speak.

"What's that?" She released her grip ever so slightly.

"What you did... That's impossible..." he gasped.

"Well, dear, that's what I do. Never send a man in to do a girl's job." Nicola drew closer to him and whispered in his ear, "And now, as promised."

A swift move of her hands and Jacobian went limp.

The guards were everywhere, armed to the teeth and well-coordinated. Despite this, she avoided them easily. She was patched into their communications and was always aware of their movements. However, she did bump into a few who were not disciplined enough to update their progress to their command. One just stood there staring at her. She took them down quickly and quietly, not even stopping long enough to finish them off. They would probably wake up later wondering how a naked girl had knocked them both out cold. She hadn't even used the butts of her weapons; she didn't need to.

Nicola was completely dry by the time she found her clothes. The cold didn't bother her, it never did. She quickly changed, listening through the door for any other unexpected visitors. Now that they had no idea of her whereabouts, she felt more comfortable using the ventilation shafts. She moved through them silently, stopping when she knew they were nearby.

Eventually she approached the cell where Aleksandr was. It was more like a hospital ward. She could see him, obviously heavily dosed with drugs. Two guards stood by him. She punched off the opening of the ventilation shaft and dropped into the cell. The guards reacted quickly, one even managing to get a round off to her shoulder, but she kept coming. Within seconds they were down. She pushed a wardrobe and the cabinets against the door. It wouldn't hold them long but she could pick them off as they tried to get in.

Running over to Aleksandr, she pulled out his drip and lifted him from the bed to the back of the room. He would wake up almost immediately. Drugs had little or no effect on him, so to induce such a state they would have to constantly pump them in, or he would come to.

She waited a moment, then slapped him hard. "Wake up!"

There was a bang at the door and she drew her pistols.

Aleksandr stirred.

She kicked his leg. "Time to wake up and get us out of here, Aleksandr. You hear me?"

The banging on the door grew louder.

"Now would be a good time!"

Aleksandr looked up at her, blinking, not seeming to focus. He rubbed his head while she hoisted him up, one of her guns still trained on the door which strained against the obstacles. "Aleksandr, there's about twenty heavily-armed guards about to break through those doors. You need to do your thing and get us to safety."

Aleksandr looked at her. "Who are you?"

The door finally broke open and at the forefront were five men. Nicola sunk to one knee with her arm around Aleksandr and fired five shots in quick succession. The five men fell, each with a hole perfectly placed between the eyes. She dragged Aleksandr behind some cover, her gun ready to drop anyone else foolish enough to come in. Nicola knew they had only seconds before the cursory flash grenade and rush.

She looked into his eyes; they were clear.

"Aleksandr, we're out of time. Teleport."

They did, but not far enough. They reappeared still within the complex, outside in the deep snow. Aleksandr's legs shook, but Nicola kept him up.

"Aleksandr, you need to get us at least ten kilometres away, probably further."

They were too exposed; they would be noticed soon. She lifted him up in both arms and carried him towards a giant snowdrift in an effort to stay hidden. She saw a searchlight swing towards them and quickly shot out the glass. They knew she was here, but at least the light wouldn't be on them. It might buy them a few more seconds. She looked around in despair. She could hear them shouting all around her.

"You have to get us out of here," urged Nicola.

"I can't," said Aleksandr hopelessly.

The guards surrounded them and closed in, guns trained. Nicola held Aleksandr and slowed to a stop. She looked around, her breath like burning smoke in the cold night.

"Here..." said a voice behind them.

Nicola spun around, her weapon ready, but her arm was caught mid-arc.

"... let me." And suddenly it was daylight.

Despite the sudden change in surroundings, Nicola followed up with a lethal kick to her assailant's shins but, surprisingly, she missed. Her arm was released and she turned to see a tall, striking woman. Nicola's arm chopped towards the woman's temple but she blocked it. She also intercepted three more expertly thrown punches.

"That's not very nice," said the woman, "I just saved your lives."

In an instant, Nicola's guns were out. She briefly looked at Aleksandr sitting on the floor, regarding them both, then checked out their surroundings. They were in a field; she could hear a river running close by but nothing else. They seemed to be alone.

The strange woman gave her a quizzical look.

"You're not from here, are you?" Nicola enquired.

The woman smiled and shook her head.

"Who are you?" said Nicola.

"Call me Garianne. I'm here to talk to Aleksandr."

"Well, that's too bad because he's with me." Nicola inclined her head towards Aleksandr.

Aleksandr stood. "Excuse me! Listen, I'm grateful to you for saving my life, but I'm not an idiot."

"So you say," said Nicola.

Aleksandr snorted. "Well, clearly you must be if you can't see that if it wasn't for... Garianne, then we'd still be back at the facility."

"How did you do that anyway?" said Nicola to Garianne. "Are you like him?"

"Please, lower your guns, Nicola. It's difficult to talk with them in my face," said Garianne.

"How do you know my name?"

"I know a great many things. Lower your weapons and I'll enlighten you."

Nicola did so, though slowly.

"Just so you know, I've been paid a great deal to retrieve this one. So once we're done here, we'll be on our way," said Nicola.

"Interesting. A gun for hire. It just so happens I have a proposition for Aleksandr and yourself, which I think may supersede all other agendas."

"I doubt that. I just want to get paid, and get back to my life," said Nicola.

"My dear, if 'your' Alex doesn't come with me, you might not have a life or a world to get back to," declared Garianne firmly.

"What do you mean?" asked Aleksandr.

"I have come here from another Earth in a parallel universe. I'm seeking alternate versions of yourself, Alex. Every Earth I visit is a variation of the same story. Something is seeking to destroy the human race, including you. I have seen world-wide plagues and alien invasions. It will happen here as well."

"That's a pretty outlandish claim," said Aleksandr.

"It's preposterous!" exclaimed Nicola.

Suddenly the trio were surrounded.

"It's true," said another Alex, who must have been in his seventies, or possibly older.

Nicola's pistols were already drawn and swinging about. "You've got to be kidding me?"

"No, she's not," said an Alex wearing a military uniform, with a prominent scar down his left cheek. "I come from one such alternate Earth, a world very different from this one, yet something they do have in common is me."

Garianne looked sternly from Aleksandr to Nicola. "Our only hope of surviving what is coming is to work together. Aleksandr, you can sense the truth of my words. You can sense that they are you from alternate Earths. The threat posed to your world may be unseen, but I assure you it is very real. I can prove it to you. Come with us and save all of our worlds."

Aleksandr thought for a moment, considering those who looked so much like him but had been changed by a lifetime in a different environment, an alternative past. He nodded his head. "I'm not saying yes, not yet. But I'll certainly hear you out."

Nicola was on him in a fraction of a second, the muzzle of her gun firmly on his temple. The others didn't move.

"They did prefer him alive," she said, "however, dead is better than not at all. I don't care about what you want. I'm taking him back, one way or another."

Garianne merely shook her head.

Nicola looked in disbelief as her pistols broke up into their component parts before her eyes. Her legs buckled and she was unconscious before she even hit the ground.

"I don't think she wanted to go with us," said Al.

"I'll persuade her," said Garianne assuredly, looking down at Nicola's limp body.

Fourteen. Kallon

The depths of space

Min smiled as Kallon's eyes slowly opened. Apparently his injuries had been even more traumatic than her own and so he was brought directly to Lom's medical bay. Here, bathed in gentle white light, surrounded by technologies which to Min seemed even more advanced than anything she'd experienced on Galacien Prime, miracles were performed.

"How do you feel?" she asked, his hands enclosed by hers.

"Perfectly fine," said Kallon looking around, bemused by his surroundings "Care to enlighten me as to what happened and where we are?"

She gave him a gentle kiss. Her brow furrowed as she recounted how Jonas had saved them from their attackers who were under the influence of something far more sinister and deadly. Kallon took this in with far less surprise than

Min thought he would. He, of course, would believe her. However, this was the word of Jonas. They had discussed him from time to time. Naturally, Kallon was more than happy to. With Min, on the other hand, it always brought out the worst in her. After all these years she still felt anger towards Garianne's deception during the Galacien/Nauerian war. But why was she so angry with Jonas? He could be so infuriating, yet he had always been good to her, and now he had saved her life. Again.

Kallon swung his legs over the bed and stood up.

"I don't understand why they came after you?"

Min found she could not look him in the face. "It appears that they believe he still cares deeply for me. Enough for him to come, even though he knew it was a trap."

There was a moment where Min didn't know what to say.

Kallon broke the silence. "Well, this is going to be interesting."

They left the medical bay and made their way through Lom's corridors towards the command deck. Despite Kallon's effort to make light of it, she sensed he was anxious. He hid it well, so as not to worry her. To protect her. It was one of the reasons she loved him. Yet she could tell there was something profoundly wrong.

"I'm sorry you've got involved in this," she said

"It's not your fault, Min, or his. It sounds like he's doing his best to help us, and even though they sought to lure him out, he did save our lives."

Min shuddered again at the thought of being mortal: she'd never felt so vulnerable. Every breath felt precious, and she thought about death all the time now. Having never made its acquaintance before, the spectre of death seemed to follow in her footsteps wherever she trod. She must create a copy of her mind on the ship as soon as possible, now that the Galacien harboured agents of this Adversary. Were everyone's copies destroyed? Was the entire GCW mortal now? She didn't think even Jonas knew for sure. If this was indeed the case, it changed everything.

They emerged from one of the many anti-gravity shafts onto the command deck. Jonas waited for them expectantly. Min's heart was in her mouth, although she was not sure why. Did she expect there would be some kind of confrontation between the two of them? She did know one thing though: as soon as Kallon walked onto the command deck, something did not seem right. She was sure Kallon felt it too, for he walked nervously towards Jonas.

Kallon looked at Min for a moment and then at Jonas. "Thank you for saving our lives."

Jonas nodded. "You know I could not leave you there. She would never have forgiven me."

Min looked at them both, the silence between the three of them stretching out. She couldn't bear it. "What's our status?" she blurted.

Jonas seemed to relax a little as he looked at the holographic display. "We've cleared the Galacien system. I'm not sure if you are aware, but the inner-system defence platforms inhibit any ship from jumping in or out of hyperspace. The outer one only monitors such jumps. I thought it best we cleared both before we made any kind of jump."

Kallon reached for Min's hand and she took it. Jonas glanced at their interlocked hands and Min shuffled uncomfortably.

"So now what?" she asked, a little more shortly than she had intended.

"We seek out the Kinsmen," said Jonas.

Min regarded Jonas, her mouth agape. "Not this again. You're not still holding onto something that is, at best, a myth? This is your plan?"

"I am sure they exist," he said, full of certainty.

"Are you? You've been on that planet of yours now for over two thousand years and this is it? When I think of how far you came during the war in such a short space of time," Min shook her head, "it seems that we are at odds with a being who processes power without limit and this is our best hope, why?"

"I've known this has been coming since my final encounter with the Nacuerians. Garianne and I have been searching for a way to prevent the extinction of all our species. Every idea, no matter how incredible it may seem at first, fails miserably. We both agree that searching for the Kinsmen may be the only way."

Min felt the old anger burning, yet it had faded somewhat. "Garianne approves of this?"

Jonas nodded.

"Jonas, don't trust her. I believed in her once. Remember the last time?"

He did. No one except Garianne, Min and himself knew that it was Garianne's secret manipulations of the events during the Galacien/Nacuerian war which had allowed him to evolve so quickly, and thus win them the war and continue their current existence.

"How do we find these Kinsmen?" asked Kallon.

Min let go of his hand. She was surprised he'd not enquired further about her accusations against Garianne since she was one of the most respected citizens of the GCW. "Not you too?"

"It seems to be the best idea we have on the table," shrugged Kallon.

"I don't believe this! He's been cooped up on Terra for two eons. It seems desperate." She looked at them both for emphasis. "A dead end, Jonas." She turned to Kallon.

"Where does he get the idea to suddenly go off looking for these Kinsmen again?"

"I get around. Have you forgotten my ability to go anywhere in the universe? Distances are meaningless to me."

"Metaphysical, you mean?"

Min was used to the idea of being observed. Being part of the Galacien, your every movement was tracked, but such devices themselves could be detected. Jonas in his metaphysical form could not. Had he been watching her, she wondered?

"I've spent a great deal of time searching through the Galacien archives and walking amongst the stars. That was when I discovered the Entrophier on the lost world of Tren-dos — lost because it is in another galaxy far out of reach of the Galacien. During the Galacien Golden Age, when super-sentients were common, a number of colonies were established in other galaxies, unreachable except by super-sentient universal or multiversal teleporters. When those super-sentients died out, Galacien worlds such as Tren-dos were cut off from the rest of the GCW."

"Jonas, that was well over four thousand years ago. Who knows what has happened to the people of Tren-dos," Min pointed out.

"I know, because I have been there."

Min considered this. Had he really been that far out? It seemed unbelievable, yet she had seen first-hand that his abilities were easily underestimated.

"What is this Entrophier?" asked Kallon.

Jonas smiled, something he didn't do often. Min so wished he was more like this, like Kallon. "The Entrophier is a truly wondrous device. It was built with the help of three super-sentients over many years."

"Yes, but what does it do?" prompted Min.

"If used correctly, it sees through time, into the past."

Min looked at Kallon, who merely seemed intrigued, and back at Jonas again. "Is that even possible?"

"Some would say not. Yet, where super-sentients are concerned, I would say most definitely," Jonas replied.

"How does this help us find the Kinsmen?" asked Kallon.

Min noticed he was resigned to the task at hand. Kallon's usual questioning nature seemed to dissipate so easily in Jonas' presence.

"During the war I had a personal encounter with one aspect of the Kinsmen. I do not know if it was some form of sentient program or merely a lesser part of something which used to be Kinsmen. However, I do believe it holds the secret to the true nature of the Kinsmen and how they may be found. If we return to that point in space, I can use the Entrophier to observe that moment over two thousand years ago and scrutinize its true nature. My abilities have grown since that time, so I should be able to memorise the data it holds and unlock its secrets, to find out where they went," said Jonas.

Min was astounded. Could he really do all of that? It was an ambitious plan. Yet he exuded unwavering confidence, not unlike Garianne.

"I'm going to regret asking this, but how far away is this super-sentient Entrophier?" said Min.

Jonas turned to the holographics depicting their position just outside the Galacien System. The view receded at an impossible speed, and within seconds the Milky Way galaxy sat there amongst a dozen others. Most noticeable, apart from the Milky Way and a cluster of small satellite galaxies, was the large Andromeda galaxy, 2.2 million light years away. However, Jonas now highlighted a small galaxy on the opposite end of the local group, sparsely populated with only three others.

"The planet Tren-dos is located in the Antlia Dwarf galaxy," declared Jonas.

Min quickly consulted her implant. "Jonas, that's 4.3 million light years away! It would take a ship hundreds, perhaps thousands of years to get there through hyperspace."

"We're not travelling through hyperspace."

"Then how...?" began Min.

"I've built a drive, of sorts, which can traverse the distance in seconds."

Kallon let out a laugh. "Wow, you really did it then?"

Jonas grinned now. "Yes. I'll admit it was no easy feat and I can see why even the great minds of the Galacien are still no closer to discovering the trick behind that one."

Min wasn't sure if she liked how friendly they were being. They barely knew one another. Surely Kallon didn't secretly idolise Jonas the way many in the GCW still did? She wasn't sure she could handle this.

"How does it work?" she asked apprehensively.

"The drive transforms all matter on the ship, including ourselves, into an exotic form of energy and incorporates it into the drive's energy matrices. It then does the same to the drive itself, which allows it to finally drop from normal space and teleport itself unhindered to anywhere in the universe. The process is reversed when we arrive at our destination."

"I've never heard of anything like it. Is it safe?" gasped Min.

"Completely. Mind you, this is the first time anyone has ever attempted a trans-galactic journey using this technique," said Jonas.

"You've never field-tested this thing?"

"No. Min, it will work. Trust me. The drive is perfected. The hard part will be on me."

"What do you mean?" asked Min.

"It's millions of light years away. Our sensors are seeing the Antlia Dwarf galaxy as it was in the distant past and we will be travelling there almost instantaneously. There's no data coming from there to help us navigate. Even Lom's simulations can't predict everything from millions of years in the past to its current state. We would essentially be jumping in blind. I'm going to have to travel there metaphysically and calculate a safe jump point."

"I can't imagine how you'd do that," exclaimed Min.

"As I said, it will be difficult."

"A private moment, please," Min said to Jonas.

Jonas moved to another area of the command deck, manipulating holographics. Min shook her head, taking Kallon by the hand again.

"I'm not sure about this. What do you think?"

Kallon considered Jonas and then turned to Min. His eyes looked sad.

What's wrong with him? she wondered.

"Jonas knows what he's doing. He's right. We need to trust him," said Kallon.

Min switched to communicating through a secure channel using their implants.

What is it? Ever since you came in here you haven't been yourself, Min thought to Kallon.

Kallon seemed at an impasse, not knowing what to say. *You know I love you.*

Of course. He seemed so timid all of a sudden. *We don't have to do this if you don't want to. I'm sure he can manage fine without us. After all, he's been on his own all this time, so a little longer won't kill him.* She tried not to let any bitterness lace her thoughts.

I don't want to lose you.

And you won't. I love you, I'm not letting you go.

She could see that Jonas had chosen to approach them.

"Excuse me! I know your interpersonal skills aren't as finally tuned as others, but this is a private conversation," frowned Min.

Beneath his seriousness, underneath his focus, Jonas appeared genuinely sorry. "I know that, Min, but there is something you need to know."

She was beginning to lose her patience and the old anger boiled inside her again. "Is now really the time? Can't it wait a little longer?"

"I think we've waited long enough, don't you?" he said, referring to Kallon, who slowly nodded.

Heat rushed through her body, her face reddened.

"You leave him out of this. He doesn't want to go, all right? We don't all want to take it upon ourselves to save the galaxy. There's nothing wrong with that."

Jonas put his hands on Kallon, who looked up.

"No, he's not *like* me, Min. He *is* me."

Min couldn't understand what she'd just heard. But one thing she did know: Jonas hadn't meant it in any metaphorical manner. She let go of Kallon's hand and slowly said, "What do you mean, he is you?"

Jonas was usually like a rock, unfazed by almost anything, yet now, to Min, he appeared to be expressing something bordering on shame. Just like everything, he tried to hide it, but it was there.

"Perhaps you had better sit down," said Jonas.

"I don't want to sit down."

"Perhaps you should…" began Kallon.

"Just tell me!" shouted Min. She took a slow breath. "Tell me what you've done, Jonas."

Jonas was again his usual composed self. "I've known since the end of the war that agents of the Adversary may be coming. I did not know if it was aware I was the cause of the destruction of the Nacuerian force here. But if it did, it might well threaten the people I knew and... had befriended."

"I still don't understand. Get to the point," hissed Min.

"I have been very busy, immersed in my work. I could not be everywhere or watch everyone I needed to watch, such as you. I have evolved in ways you may find it difficult to comprehend. I have mastered skills and abilities not dreamt of, even by the Galacien."

Min was both annoyed and fascinated. "Then you must be able stop the Adversary."

"Despite everything I have learnt, the incredible things I can do, I am as nothing when compared to the Adversary. Its merest thought becomes reality with no effort of will and no counterforce to resist it. Even a super-sentient is nothing compared to that, for even though a super-sentient's capabilities may seem miraculous, his or her will and capacity is limited," said Jonas.

"I was right — your social skills are terrible. You're not making me feel any better, you know," said Min.

Jonas continued solemnly. "Some time ago now I discovered how to replicate my being and place it into the empty body of another."

Arms folded, Min shook her head furiously. "Jonas, the Galacien have been doing that for thousands of years — downloading a copy of your mind into a custom-made body."

"Not quite like this. This is more fundamental. The copy you speak of is a copy. I would describe this as more a part of my essence and, as such, I know what it knows."

Min looked at Kallon: he no longer appeared to be the man she loved.

"Is this what you are, a part of him?"

Kallon nodded.

"As long as he was by your side, I knew where you were and that you would be safe," said Jonas.

"Is that how you knew I was in trouble back on Galacien Prime?" asked Min.

"I could sense it through Kallon," confirmed Jonas.

"You deceived me?"

"I could not let them know who Kallon really was."

Min looked at them both and abruptly walked away.

"Min…" Kallon started, reaching for her.

"Leave her. She needs time to think, alone," said Jonas.

Kallon watched her go.

"What happens to me now?" he said.

"When you first opened your eyes in that body on Galacien Prime, you were me, in almost every sense of the word. In a way, it was as if I was there and my duty was to safeguard Min. You always knew that a time would come when your essence would again become one with mine," said Jonas.

"But I'm not you anymore. I've grown in my own way. I'm my own person. I've made a life with Min. We love one another." Kallon gave Jonas a distasteful smirk. "You simply wish to be rid of me now I've outlived my usefulness. That's pretty low."

"Your life is literally mine. Do not believe for one moment that you are anything other than that. You are not my offspring or a slave. You are me. I may as well argue with an elaborate train of thought. That is all you are: thought given form."

"I would have thought exactly the same before, but I have individuality. Don't kid yourself that despite assimilating all that I am, you wouldn't still be killing me."

Kallon set off after Min, leaving Jonas alone.

Well, not quite, as he was never entirely alone.

"I'm sure you have some thoughts on the matter."

"Always," said Lom.

"Go on then."

"You have a point."

"I know."

"But so does he," said Lom.

Kallon found Min sitting on the bed in the quarters Lom had assigned them. He did not go to her, but stood against the wall and waited, watching her back. She had not told him to get out and he thought this was a good sign.

"You must have known you'd have to tell me the truth, at some point. Why didn't you tell me before?" Min said, still facing away from him.

"I'm so sorry," he answered. "To do so may have put your life at risk."

"He's just like Garianne — controlling, manipulative."

"He was trying to take care of you the only way he could."

"Stop... defending him. Just stop.

There was silence between them.

"Do you want me to leave?" said Kallon.

She said nothing. He turned and the door slid open for him.

"No, stay," she said.

Kallon covered half the distance towards her and stopped. "When I first came into this world, I was to all intents and purposes Jonas. But since then I have become my own man. I am not him. Those experiences unique to me, such as our time together, have shaped me into a distinctive being. Don't take that away from me. Jonas has already written my life off. Please don't do the same. Otherwise, what was it all for? And what am I? Nothing."

"You're not nothing to me," she said, turning on the bed. She got up and went to him quickly. Holding him tight, she whispered, "I won't let him take you away from me." She reached up and kissed him tenderly, tears welling in her eyes.

Fifteen. Intersections in time

**The Galacien Institute for Technological Advancement,
Earth**

It was dark and the stars were out, looking more amazing than Alex had ever seen them before. He followed Garianne down the gentle slope of the small valley. Having teleported only moments before, he was confused because, even through the dim starlight, he could see and hear his surroundings. He knew this was not real.

"Where are we?" asked Alex as he followed Garianne towards a distant light at the bottom of the valley floor.

"Assyria, the year 327 BC," replied Garianne.

"What is this?"

"It's a simulation, not a very good one by our standards. We were able to extrapolate this data from the network of satellites, and the few micro-wormhole sensors we put here soon after the time of these events. As well as testimony I gave. These are the oldest virtual records we have of your planet. Pre-dating this event was a lone satellite on an endless orbit making only the most basic of observations, though still far more advanced than your current technology."

The valley levelled out and they made their way towards the small dwelling.

"How long ago did you begin these basic observations, as you put it?"

"The first ever observations of your world commenced precisely 8,032 years ago," stated Garianne.

Alex stopped and looked at her in wonder. "Earth years?"

"Obviously. Here we always convert to Earth years when necessary."

Alex shook his head in disbelief. "Your records go that far back? That's astounding."

"Our simulations of the past two thousand years are far more sophisticated. With the use of an implant, we can realistically recreate any recorded time period."

Alex's jaw hung open at the implications. "My God, it's a virtual time machine. That's... unbelievable."

"In a sense, yes. The re-creation is perfect, right down to the molecular level," said Garianne.

"But the amount of data storage… how is that possible?"

"The Galacien are capable of many things which may seem impossible from your point of view. Suffice it to say, it is not a problem."

Alex looked away, imagining everything he'd ever done or said being watched by the Galacien.

Garianne said, "We all have our secrets, Alex, those things we don't wish to talk of. The machines that analyse your world and its inhabitants do not judge."

Before Alex could reply, the door of the house opened and a large young man headed to the nearby fence regarding the stars above. Garianne joined him and Alex followed warily.

Garianne smiled at Alex. "It's all right, he can't see, hear or interact with us."

"Then why are we here?" asked Alex.

"To illustrate a point," replied Garianne.

Neither Alex nor the man noticed the old woman approaching until she stood next to them. "Who's this?" said Alex.

"Me, in another guise," said Garianne.

"Admiring the view," said the older-looking version of Garianne from the past.

"Yes," replied the young man, seeming uncomfortable. Alex could see the marks of frustration so ready to etch themselves upon his face.

"Could you not sleep either?" asked the old woman.

"No."

"Do you not feel tired?"

"No," he repeated simply. "I am never truly tired."

"Then why do you sleep?" she asked.

"Because everyone has to sleep."

"People sleep when they're tired. But if you are never truly tired, then why do you go to sleep? Maybe you do it because you have always done it. Perhaps it's a habit," she suggested.

Alex turned to Garianne and the conversation seemed to sink into the background.

"That's Jonas," stated Alex.

Garianne nodded. "I've brought you here because, in a way, this is where our fight began. We face two threats. The first is the destruction of civilisation, as you know it, from an impending collision of an asteroid we have dubbed Sol 9173 with this planet. An event I believe has been carefully orchestrated."

"Why do you believe that?"

"Because, even though the methods are different, I have witnessed similar attacks on your world in parallel universes. This is the real cause behind everything. Jonas and I believe a malevolent godlike being we call the Adversary is the true enemy behind these attacks. This is the second and far more significant threat, which we face."

The simulation continued to run as Jonas and the other Garianne made their way into the small house.

"Why can't you simply destroy the asteroid?" asked Alex.

"The Galacien have a strict policy of non-interference concerning barbaric, immature species and, unfortunately, humanity is in that category."

Alex took a step away from her, his face contorted. "But that's horrific! You're going to simply stand back and allow the destruction of humankind. What does that say about you?"

The Assyrian night vanished and in its place played out scene after scene of humanity's worst and most recent atrocities. The micro-wormhole sensors had recorded, stored and were able to recreate them in perfect simulations. Alex flinched as he saw countless men, women and children killed in every way imaginable, by one another. It made him feel sick to his stomach and he had to bite back the tears which threatened to come. The horrors kept coming in uncensored graphic detail, until he felt he could bear it no longer. He felt ashamed to be human.

"The Galacien won't help a species as destructive as yours, and they won't let you continue. If you joined the galactic community it could be disastrous. We've seen how readily you use the weapons you possess. It won't be long until you have access to weapons which can devastate entire worlds or even solar systems. If you can prove you have truly grown and matured as a species, then they will help," said Garianne.

"There must be a way," he appealed.

She reached out and took his hand. He abruptly felt a rush of strength flow through him and he felt the horrors he was witnessing fade a little. He barely noticed the environment wash away as he was suddenly consumed by her presence.

"I do not agree with the majority of Galacien society. I've been trying to convince them that there is hope for your kind. But it's difficult. As you can see, those that work against humanity's continued survival have a very strong case, and it continues to prove that they are right: you need only watch your news on the television to see that. The governments of your world are aware of this threat to their existence, yet they continue to squabble amongst themselves."

Alex looked at her, horrified by this revelation.

Garianne continued, "They've known for months but have kept it secret from the public. At first we observed them come together and try to work on a way to prevent this catastrophe. But, as we predicted, it all fell into chaos and now they work apart on surviving what's coming."

"Do you believe we have the technology to stop Sol 9173 if somehow we do all work together?" asked Alex.

"No," replied Garianne.

"Then what's the point? I mean, that's not fair, if we had sufficient technology," protested Alex.

"It's not about technology," said Garianne. "There comes a time in every species' evolution when they must face something together. If indeed you did work together, whether you succeeded or failed it would not matter. It's the attempt which is significant. For you would have proved yourself to be all those things you should truly aspire to be — A mature race. The Galacien would step in and destroy Sol 9173 and welcome you fully into the galactic community."

Alex thought long and hard about her words.

"As I said, this is the more immediate threat, yet its significance is overshadowed by that of the Adversary," said Garianne.

"Overshadowed? The end of my world?" exclaimed Alex.

"The history of your world over the last eight thousand years has been archived. It will not be lost."

"Is that supposed to make me feel better? If anything, it highlights how important it is that we don't let this happen." Alex found he was struggling with the memory of his planet's history. "I know how bad we must appear, but there are a lot of decent people out there. People who surely must make a difference."

"It's nowhere near enough, I'm afraid. The good of which you speak on this world is too little, too late."

They stood in an all-encompassing whiteness which defied distance. "Is this what is to become of everything

I've ever known? Everything we've ever achieved, created and built? All our loves, passions and dreams? Just tucked away, left to gather dust in the memory of your Galacien archives? It can't end this way," cried Alex.

"There is perhaps a way to argue in Earth's defence. Something unique to this world."

"Which is?"

"You. The appearance of a super-sentient just so happens to be unique to Earth. It may be argued that Earth is worth sparing, in case more manifest themselves, even though it has been over two thousand years since Jonas. However, there have been no others on any other world since."

"Why do I feel like we're grasping at straws?" grumbled Alex, disheartened.

"It isn't much, I grant you." Garianne stroked her chin, her eyes narrowed deep in thought. "It is a shame you are the only one."

Sixteen. Tea and Sympathy

Camden, London, Earth

Alex teleported outside the door to his sister's flat. He'd been practicing using his abilities all day. Now, given a little time to focus, he could sense anywhere on the planet and check if it was free of witnesses before he teleported in. Alex tried to imagine what the media, the public and the governments of the world would make of someone like him. Would his own government try and make him a military asset? What about the average person on the street? Celebrities were idolised these days. Considering what he could do, would he become an overnight sensation and be sought after by every talk show producer, journalist or even advertising company? Or would they simply fear him? Garianne suggested they would expect him to get involved and solve some of the world's biggest problems, to take sides in the current conflicts of the world. He didn't know what side to take. He was relieved the world did not know of his true nature. Yet it pained him to stand idly by.

Aren't you going to knock? said the voice of the implant in his head.

Give me a moment, just gathering my thoughts. Alex was still getting used to the idea of the cerebral implant. His reaction at first had been rather cynical. However, Garianne had finally convinced him of the benefits of having one.

With his head buzzing with questions, Alex knocked. He did not need to wonder whether his sister was in, he could sense her.

The door opened.

"Hey, this is unexpected," smiled Theresa.

"I'm sorry, I should have texted or rung first," acknowledged Alex.

"Don't be daft," she said, giving him a hug, "come in. I'm not going to apologise for the mess. I was about to tidy actually, I've been meaning to all week."

"Really?" Alex smiled. After the last day with Garianne and James, the concepts of a galactic conglomerate of alien space-faring races, the impending arrival of Sol 9173 and the threat to all life in the universe by some crazed god, Alex felt somewhat comforted and grounded by the untidiness of the flat.

The news was on the television. Alex glanced at it, his smile fading.

"Tea?" shouted Theresa from the kitchen.

"Please. Don't get much for your money living this close to the city, do you?" he shouted back.

"Just you wait until you finish Uni."

Yeah right, he thought. *Just have to convince an alien race who don't like us into saving our world from a meteorite. Follow that up with finding a way of stopping a god hell-bent on destroying anything resembling sentient life. If we survive that, I've got this feeling I won't be working a regular day job.*

Probably not, supplied the implant.

Alex moved Theresa's clothes and sat on the sofa. He watched the familiar scenes on television. One side shooting their automatic rifles at the other side, unseen in a building. A close-up of another man launching an RPG from the back of a truck. Lots of machine gunfire, and the odd large bang of an explosion, then smoke in the distance. The injured being dragged off, writhing in agony.

Try not to worry, Garianne is working on a way to help Earth's case, said the implant.

By doing what? How can we prove we're worth saving? thought Alex.

He sensed Theresa watching him.

"Pretty bad, eh?" she said, looking at the TV.

"Yeah," he replied, thinking of what was coming. Something much worse.

They both listened to the reporter in silence, wrapped up in their own thoughts for a moment until the kettle boiled.

Theresa left and returned quickly with two mugs of steaming hot tea.

"Thanks," said Alex.

Theresa sat next to him and took a sip of her tea. "So, what's the problem?"

"I never said there was a problem."

"No, but it's pretty bloody obvious. You're pre-occupied with something, I can tell. What is it?"

Alex sighed, looking at the television. "Do you think we're fundamentally flawed and self–destructive? The human race, I mean?"

Theresa raised her eyebrows in surprise. "Wow, that's pretty heavy for a Saturday afternoon. What's brought this on?"

"I know, sorry. Forget it," said Alex, drinking his tea.

"No, it's okay." Theresa thought for a moment. "I'd like to think we're getting better, despite the evidence to the contrary though," she said, indicating the TV. "A friend of mine had a theory about this."

Alex sat up, listening intently. "What theory?"

"He reckoned that the only way we'd stop fighting amongst one other, that we'd forget our differences, would be if aliens attacked." Theresa laughed, "Then we'd all realise we're not that different after all, because we're all human, and those differences don't matter that much. We'd all come together to fight the aliens."

Alex tried to laugh but nothing happened. The aliens were here, but they weren't attacking — they were standing by, ready to let humanity die.

"What do you think?" he asked.

Theresa shook her head. "Nah, it would never happen. The politicians would still be arguing as the aliens burned the Earth to ash around them." She laughed and Alex tried to. "Surely this isn't what's bothering you?"

Alex tried an unconvincing smile. "Well, there was something else. This is going to sound pretty... strange."

"What, stranger than that?"

"Yeah." He stood up, knowing now he was committed. "She said I could tell one person if I felt I really had to."

"Who?" Theresa's face was a picture of curiosity.

"Garianne."

"Who's that?"

"The person I work for."

"You've got a job? Aren't you staying on at Uni?" She was confused.

"No. I've been asked to do some important work for, erm... the powers that be."

Theresa shook her head, "Who? The government?"

Alex struggled. He didn't want to lie to her, but Garianne had predicted her answers and reactions so far. He knew what to say, what not to say, and how it would end.

"I have unique abilities," he explained, neither confirming nor denying her last question.

"What kind of abilities?"

This was it: his heart was pounding away and he felt a little nauseous.

"I have... this ability to teleport; to travel anywhere almost instantaneously," he said slowly, wincing as he did so, like a boy admitting to doing something naughty.

Theresa stared at him. "I don't understand."

Alex took a deep breath. "I am what my employers would refer to as a super-sentient being. I have many unexplained abilities. I can sense what others are feeling or, on a rudimentary level, thinking. I can't be hurt easily. I can conjure and manipulate force-fields. But my most significant power is being able to teleport anywhere — well, anywhere on Earth so far — but my employers believe I'll soon be able to traverse a lot further."

"Alex what are you talking about?" Theresa rolled her eyes. He could sense her annoyance.

"Listen. Can you remember me ever being ill or injured, when we were growing up, ever!" Alex demanded, exasperated.

Theresa thought for a while "No, but..." she laughed.

"I'm not joking."

"Clearly you are. I thought zombies and vampires were all the rage. Here, pass me your mug."

"I'll take them," he said. She passed him her mug.

Alex looked her in the eye and suddenly teleported, vanishing before Theresa's eyes.

Theresa screamed as she fell off the sofa. Her breathing quickened as she scrambled to her feet, looking around the room.

Alex slowly came in from the kitchen. "See, told you."

"My God!" She walked over to him, extended a finger and prodded him.

"What's that for?"

"Just making sure you're real and I'm not crazy," she said, her eyes like saucers. "In fact, pinch me."

He did.

"Owww!" She slapped him on the arm.

"You told me to pinch you."

"Not that hard," complained Theresa, rubbing her arm. "You don't know your own strength."

"I thought perhaps you were in a deep sleep," smirked Alex.

"You thought wrong," she said, her arm still smarting. "This is… incredible. How did this happen?"

"I don't know. Nobody does, it just happens."

"Are there others?"

"Definitely one other," he said. "Possibly another," he said thinking of the girl he had heard in his mind, during the abduction attempt, "but I'm not sure about that one."

At this Alex heard the implant in his head. *You must leave soon. Finish up and be on your way.*

"Look, I must be going."

"You only just got here, and I have so many questions."

"I can't answer them. Top secret, if you know what I mean."

Theresa's mouth opened in astonishment. Garianne had predicted Theresa's assumptions.

"I'm sure you realise the delicacy of the situation. You can't tell anyone about this."

Theresa's head bobbed up and down vigorously. "Okay, I won't."

"Oh, and something else. This is the most important thing I've ever said to you."

"More important than that?" She indicated the spot from where he had teleported only moments before.

"Yes. You'll be receiving a visit from a man named Nemulous. You must trust him as you would me. He will make sure you are safe and taken care of while I'm away working."

"Why, what's going to happen?"

"I can't answer any more questions, sorry sis." He hugged her tight, wondering when he would see her again. "Remember, you must trust him, do whatever he tells you, no matter how crazy it might seem. Take care, I'll see you soon. Love you."

"Love you..."

Alex teleported and was gone, leaving Theresa alone and confused in her Lounge

"...too."

Seventeen. The Trans-Galactic Jump

The depths of space

Jonas focused intently on a holographic image of the newly designed engine core. He mentally commanded the disassembly of a section of components and examined them. Behind him, over thirty metres tall in Lom's engine room, the same happened to the real thing. A multitude of nano-machines and force-fields worked in perfect harmony to recreate his every thought in expediting the final adjustments to the new engine, needed for the trans-galactic jump.

Min approached him, alone. "How's it going?"

Jonas looked up from his work "Nearly there." He dragged himself away from the holographics. Work on the core ceased. "You don't have to come, if you really don't want to."

She considered his words. "Not exactly safe here either, is it?"

"Nowhere is safe, I'm afraid, and I can't say in all honesty whether you will be safer with me."

Min lowered her eyes. "You've managed pretty well so far." Jonas seemed distracted as he fidgeted uncomfortably on the spot. "Are you okay?"

He smiled awkwardly "How did things get so complicated between us?"

Min laughed. "You disassociated yourself from me and everyone else in the galaxy for over two thousand years. I've changed. You've changed. What did you expect?"

Jonas gazed at the engine core. "Sometimes I wish I could go back. Though it's greatly diluted, I can feel what he feels when he is with you. It's like a whisper in my mind, then suddenly it's gone."

Min wanted to empathise with him, but yet again she felt a little violated — that he was there, even just a shade of him, when she and Kallon shared their most private moments.

"You should have asked," she said, her teeth clenched.

"If I had, what would you have said?" he enquired earnestly.

Her jaw relaxed, and she felt a depth of sadness well up inside her. Ever so slowly she reached for his hand. The touch made her so afraid, yet she didn't want to let go, not ever. She opened her mouth.

Then Lom said, "Jonas, we have multiple Galacien ships heading this way."

Jonas looked down at their interlocked hands. "How many?"

"Currently seven. There may be more approaching outside the range of my sensors. ETA twenty-one minutes."

"They're keen," said Min, letting go of Jonas' hand as subtly as she could.

"Indeed."

He turned back to the holographics of the engine core and continued making changes.

"How long until it's ready?" asked Min.

"A little longer than twenty-one minutes. You're going to have to buy me the time I need to finish it and make the jump."

Min ran from the engine room. "I'll do what I can." She sprinted down the corridor and whisked up the anti-grav shaft, alighting expertly onto the deserted command deck. "Lom, display." The ship's holographics gave her a tactical overview. "Take us on a course which gives us the maximum amount of time before we encounter one of their ships," she commanded.

"Yes Min," said Lom.

It had been many years since she had commanded a starship. Even in those days there hadn't been that much use for a crew.

She turned to see Kallon arrive on the command deck.

"Lom's brought me up to speed," he said.

She nodded, feeling more focused and alive than she had in years. She hadn't realised how much she missed being out here in the depths of space. Perhaps she should have joined an exploration vessel to one of the satellite galaxies, instead of staying on Galacien Prime.

"What's the plan?" asked Kallon.

"Follow my lead. We have to buy Jonas as much time as possible."

"Then we're going?"

"Are you all right with that?"

Kallon simply nodded.

In the engine room Jonas finished sliding the final holographic piece of the engine core into place. As he walked towards the real core, the holographics equivalent in reality did the same. Jonas gestured and a seat materialised from the floor and a helmet was lowered on connected wires. Jonas shook his head before taking the seat which moulded itself to his frame.

Inelegant prototype, he thought.

I think it's more important that it works than how it looks, commented Lom via the implant.

You think I should have told them? How I only conceived this weeks ago, and built it in less than a day?

You've only just finished it now.

It will work.

At least you're confident, remarked Lom.

You should have more faith in me, Jonas thought, donning the helmet which came over his eyes. *Garianne does.*

You're not going to remind me yet again that you saved my life?

Actually, on four separate occasions.

You always count the Amelerian system.

Quite rightly so. Jonas smiled. *Now leave me, I must focus. See you on the flip-side.*

And you say you hate humans when you use such terminology.

Jonas didn't hear him, for his metaphysical self was gone.

Galacien weapons fire broke out all around the ship.

"Warning shots," declared Min. "Bring us to a full stop, Lom."

The communication prompt came directly to Min's implant. She relayed it through Lom's systems and a holographic representation of the ship's captain came to life on the command deck.

"Greetings, Melntoria Kendeisa. I am Captain Dermarlaine. We believe you are harbouring the fugitive and super-sentient Jonas."

Min did not hear her official name often — was it meant to catch her off-guard? If so, it would not work. Min felt like her old self when she was a competent warrior working closely with the legendary Cieshella Garianne Phulum. She'd checked the files on Dermarlaine. As she suspected, despite the fact she looked a little older than Min, she was young. Only a few hundred years old. By this age they had usually gained enough experience to be cocky, regarding the first-lifers to be ignorant and the older generation, such as herself at 3,652 years (but who's counting), to be stagnant.

"I won't deny he's here. The fact that he's a fugitive is debatable."

"It is common knowledge, since he attacked a company of the council's guards and then went on the run. Do you expect me to believe you were unaware of this?" said Captain Dermarlaine.

"I was unaware, since I myself was cut off from the Galacien grid and subsequently attacked shortly after. What do you make of that?" Min noticed the final ship had dropped from hyperspace. They were now completely surrounded, but she paid it no heed.

"Some of the species on the outer rim have been causing a lot of trouble, to the extent of attacking Galacien vessels and citizens. We're aware of the attack upon your person and your home. We believe they are the cause."

"My assailants were augmented in a way I'm unfamiliar with. Very strong, impervious to pain and mentally aloof to any damage I could inflict," Min said, her brow furrowed.

Then another figure stepped into view, his appearance perfectly represented by Lom as if he were there on the command deck.

"Lytpniuph," Min whispered.

"It is good to see you again, old friend. The captain is quite correct: these rebel factions have been arming themselves and their soldiers with some unconventional tech. It is not you we want. We believe you are innocent in all of this. Jonas is the one we must take into custody. We will not harm him," said Lytpniuph.

Min felt her resolve waver for a second.

As if sensing this, Lytpniuph smiled. "Can you really trust him, Melntoria? He has been exiled on Terra now for thousands of years. There's no telling what his mental state is. He could be paranoid, or worse. It may be wise to at least question anything he has said to you. The Galacien, on the other hand, have always been here for you. The Galacien are the ground you stand on and the air you breathe. If you doubt us, if you can doubt me, then you are truly lost."

Min looked at him, unsure.

Metaspace

Jonas' metaphysical self left the galaxy at a speed that would have dwarfed that of light, accelerating ten-fold. The physical laws of space-time meant nothing here in metaphysical space, for he existed outside them. To say he travelled through space or even hyperspace would be wrong. He existed outside both and yet he sensed them clearly around him as they were still there, inextricably linked. As before, he headed for the Large Magellanic Cloud, which orbited his own galaxy nearly 200,000 light years from his physical position. From his point of view, it looked like a ghost of what it truly was in space-time.

It always fascinated him how time quickened as he moved at such relative speeds. He was now 50,000 light years out, seeing it as it was all those thousands of years ago. In moments he would be there. Stars abruptly burst forth in brilliant supernovae, some creating spectacular nebulae, which spread out in seconds rather than thousands of years. Surely no being from his own galaxy had ever witnessed such a thing. The only other who perhaps had, was the Adversary. Jonas shivered. If it should be out here, it could easily pluck him from this metaspace and end his existence with a thought. He wondered where it truly was at this moment. Would he face it one day?

Jonas refocused on the task at hand. The Large Magellanic Cloud spread out before him. Now that he had his bearings, he turned and headed for his true destination — the Antlia Dwarf galaxy, a little over four million light years away. He reasserted his will and accelerated. The Large Magellanic Cloud quickly became just another point of light as he plunged his being into the great void. The emptiness which he sensed around him threatened to strike fear into his core, but it was an old feeling and one he had habitually used to further strengthen his will to achieve his goals. He only flew that bit faster towards his destination. His sole thought, achieving what normal sentient beings would deem impossible.

Just as it seemed as if Jonas was locked into the darkness, that he was stuck in an unchanging universe, Antlia Dwarf grew. As before, he was strangely drawn to the planet of Tren-dos and was soon heading into the galaxy itself. In moments he was there in the Tren-dos system, the planet itself a dark sphere no bigger than his hand. He could still sense his physical self all that mind-boggling distance away. Even *he* found it hard to understand how this was possible. How ironic, that the super-sentients had achieved and understood so much, yet could never comprehend their own existence. Jonas concentrated on the staggeringly complex calculations involved in making the first trans-galactic jump.

Normal space

"Lower your shields, please," said Lytpniuph.

"And if I don't?" replied Min.

"I have my orders and I always see them carried out. Jonas is far too dangerous to have running around the galaxy."

"The Galacien preferred him in exile, didn't they?" said Min.

"Lower them now!"

"I'm sorry, I..." Min was astonished to see she had suddenly been enveloped in beautiful white light.

"It's begun," said Kallon.

Min's world faded away as she was transformed and incorporated into the engine's energy matrices.

Lytpniuph and the crews of the surrounding vessels stood awestruck as the sentient starship that was Lom was also enveloped in light. Its structure deconstructed and withdrew into the sphere of energy which stood in its place. Gravitational waves pulsed from its epicentre, shaking Lytpniuph's ships, growing in strength, until Captain Dermarlaine was unsure whether they could take the strain for much longer.

"Destroy it!" she bellowed over the din of her straining ship and the scream of its alarms.

"Weapons unresponsive," came the reply.

All their systems were fluctuating out of control.

The energy readouts of what had once been Lom surged exponentially, until, in a blinding flash of light, they were gone.

Eighteen. Lorusia

Lorusia, Earth

Newly appointed President of Lorusia, Nemulous Handerrel, entered his office and dismissed his aides. Only his two bodyguards remained, and he wished he could be rid of them too. He could insist on being left entirely alone, but it would make them feel uncomfortable. He reached his desk, looking down at the appointment which stood out amongst all others: his 7pm meeting with Garianne.

He opened communication with her and she accepted.

I see you're travelling the old-fashioned way.

His implant superimposed her location on the island, heading his way by car, relaying a multitude of sensor readings from the Galacien observation network.

I teleported from London and checked in while you were doing your inauguration speech; it was very moving.

He sensed her amusement. *Thank you. I think we've made quite an impact on the rest of the world for such a small island.*

You've done very well, thought Garianne.

Nemulous smiled and walked out onto the second-floor veranda. The island vista was beautiful. From here he could see the rows of palm trees which lined the streets. Golden beaches flanked his view to the east and west and, in the distance to the north, lay Lorusia's mountains. Indeed, they had done well. In the last one hundred years this small island country off the west coast of Africa had prospered under his guiding hand, whether in his past incarnations or his present one. He'd continue to see it flourish, until it was time.

Looking down he saw her car pull up. The driver opened the door for her. As ever she was impeccably dressed, wearing a close-cut business suit. His escort staff seemed taken aback momentarily.

You are a tease.

Don't be silly. This is my way, it always has been.

He was in her line of sight, but she chose not to look up.

Another person followed close behind. She was armed, and his men tensed, their hands on their weapons.

Tell your men it's all right.

He walked back into his office and pressed a button on his desk and addressed his men through their earpieces to stand down.

Who is she? he asked.

My new bodyguard.

Nemulous laughed. *Come on.*

Her name is Nicola. I found her with an Alex on an alternate Earth.

Why bring her here?

Wouldn't you like to know?

Yes, I would. And by the way, those men should have their minds on their work. Instead, they're going to be thinking about you all day.

If this were anywhere else in the world, I'd say that could be a problem. However, seeing as this is Lorusia, I believe the effect can only be beneficial.

Nemulous shrugged. She was probably right — she usually was. He waited patiently until his chief of staff knocked and entered.

"Ms Cieshella Garianne Phulum to see you sir."

Nemulous quickly glanced at the clock above as it hit 7pm precisely.

"Thank you. Please show her in."

He did so trying not to stare as Garianne passed him; she was almost a foot taller than he was.

Nicola entered looking sultry, like a hunter waiting for its prey. He could sense that this was a very dangerous woman indeed. She seemed to take in the room in an instant. Her eyes darted around for only a moment and then looked to the floor. He felt as if she'd instantly assessed her surroundings. She gave him the same quick cursory glance.

"I must insist that we be left alone," said Nemulous.

The chief of staff paused for just a moment, looking nervously at Nicola, then gestured to the two bodyguards.

The door closed behind them. Garianne, Nicola and Nemulous remained.

Garianne looked into an apparent empty corner of the room. "Complete privacy, if you please."

Nemulous' implant sensed the miniature wormholes close. Now they were truly unobserved.

"Nicola, this is Nemulous, an old friend of mine."

"Pleasure," said Nemulous.

Nicola merely looked at him, saying nothing.

"Nicola has agreed to help us in our cause."

"For a price," said Nicola.

"Yes. The girl seems rather fond of money. She doesn't see how our fight is her fight, that there's no use for money if you're not alive and there's nowhere to spend it."

Nicola looked at Garianne stubbornly.

Nemulous sighed heavily. *Garianne, why is she here,* he said to her privately through his implant.

Trust me. She is different. She can help us.

"You did not have to come personally," said Nemulous.

"But I wanted to," she replied quickly. "How is the work going?"

"See for yourself," he said, escorting them to the veranda. "Lorusia is about to become a major player on the world stage."

Garianne nodded. "Very impressive. You are like a tiny seed — so much potential. I take it you are ready for what lies ahead?"

Nemulous looked into her beautiful eyes earnestly. "Don't worry, it will be done, I will make sure of it."

Garianne smiled and, as always, he found himself doing the same. "I know you will."

Nemulous' smile faded. "What of you?"

"The super-sentients are growing in number, yet I am still unsure as to how to apply them."

This admission concerned Nemulous. Surely she had thought this through? But even taking into account the power of a super-sentient army, how could even she still overcome the limitless powers of the Adversary? He found he did not envy her

"Sometimes I think it is I who has drawn the short straw. Then I think of the impossible task which you must accomplish."

"That is why there is the second possibility: Jonas," she reminded him.

"Ah yes, how is the old boy?"

"Chasing after myths," said Garianne.

Nemulous shook his head, unconvinced. "The Kinsmen? Is that really the best use of his talents? They are a legend at best."

"Legends are perhaps all we may have left," shrugged Garianne.

"And the third?"

Garianne took one last look across the island and went inside with Nemulous following close behind. "I will not speak of it."

"Why?"

She really looked concerned this time and Nemulous felt fear stirring deep inside him.

"Because, even though we may believe that nothing can observe what transpires here, nothing is certain where the Adversary is concerned. Jonas is seeking a device which he believes can peer into the past. If Jonas has found a way to see that which was thought lost, then it is quite within the Adversary's power to do so too."

Nemulous made to put his hand on her shoulder but thought better of it. "If made aware of how significant these events are to it, then could it not simply pluck them from your mind?"

She looked at him solemnly. "If that came to pass, I would have little, but enough, warning to erase the memory of the third and final solution from my mind. Concern yourself no further; you must focus on matters here, unless you feel you don't have enough to do."

Nemulous laughed. "No, the fate of the planet is quite enough, thank you."

"Try the multiverse," Garianne replied.

Nineteen. Tren-dos

Planet Tren-dos , in the Antlia Dwarf Galaxy

Three light seconds from the planet Tren-dos, in the darkness of a quiet and long-dead system, light burst forth from seemingly nowhere. It quickly spread out into a large sphere, before fading to reveal a Galacien starship.

Min found herself kneeling on the floor of Lom's command deck, her thoughts a jumbled mess.

Where am I?

A man sat slumped, looking up at her, his jaw hanging in open-mouthed silence. He saw the dark planet there against the stars.

"He did it. Unbelievable," he whispered.

His name was Kallon, she remembered.

"What happened?" said Min.

"We made it. We're in the Tren-dos system. Over four million light years from our own galaxy!"

She had to know for sure.

"Lom?" questioned Min.

"It's true," said Lom.

The holographics sprang to life depicting their current position in the Antlia Dwarf galaxy. In the top right she could see another graphic depicting their previous position relative to their current position. Min noticed there was no trajectory involved. They had not travelled from point A to point B through hyperspace in the traditional sense, but had jumped instantaneously in a manner she could not quite comprehend.

"Are you all right?" asked Kallon, helping her to her feet. They looked at one another and embraced.

"Fine. That was... weird," she replied. "I've never felt anything like that."

"I'm not surprised; it has never been done before," said a voice.

She turned to see Jonas walk purposefully onto the command deck.

"I'm sorry if the experience was a little unnerving. It's a prototype and doesn't work quite as eloquently as I would have liked. With a few minor alterations to the drive, the jumps will be barely noticeable."

Min suddenly felt self-conscious about holding Kallon so close to her. *Why should I?* she thought.

"How was the experience for you?" she asked, curiously.

"As they say on Earth, a piece of cake," smiled Jonas confidently.

"He exaggerates," commented Lom.

"I believe it is you who are exaggerating," said Jonas to Lom.

"It took him longer than expected to make the journey through metaspace," declared Lom.

"Mere seconds."

"For you, that is a gross miscalculation," Lom pointed out.

Jonas' face hardened.

"It could not have been easy out there, traversing the intergalactic void," said Min, loosening herself from Kallon.

"I'm used to the feeling of isolation. It wasn't a problem," said Jonas. Yet something disturbed him deeply. She could see it in his face, in the way he stood.

"That's not it," she said.

Jonas regarded them both. "You don't understand the significance of what we face. It does not matter where we are or what we do. If our number comes up on the roll of the dice and the Adversary notices us, then we can be snuffed out of existence with but a thought. The only reason it hasn't already done so is either that it is curious and sees us as no threat, or that it is simply too busy to notice us at all. I hope for the latter. Suffice it to say, out there in the void I felt... an echo of its presence imprinted across reality, reverberating through space-time. It was... a distraction."

Min wanted to reach out to him, let him know that he was not alone. He always seemed supremely confident and he had overcome every challenge he'd met. She wondered, though. Garianne believed that Jonas' ability would always allow his mind and abilities to evolve to defeat his enemies, and it had worked so far. But their enemy's capacity was limitless. How could even Jonas attain such abilities?

Then, suddenly, she realised something shocking. He was actually afraid. She could see it in his eyes. She felt a mere fraction of the overwhelming dread which must have haunted him all these years. She had an almost irresistible urge to run over and hold him. Only Kallon's presence stopped her. All that responsibility on his shoulders just because of what he was. It wasn't fair.

Anything which could be discerned as a weakness abruptly faded away from Jonas' face and posture and he seemed his usual assured self. "Lom, bring us in to orbit; let's see what we have."

"What do you know so far?" asked Kallon.

"Not much. When I discovered this place, it was only to confirm its existence with the Galacien archives. Here are the files," said Jonas.

Min and Kallon both accessed the files they received through their implants.

"So you have no idea what's down there now?" said Min.

"No," admitted Jonas.

Min smiled and walked up to the planet on the viewscreen that encompassed the front half of the command deck. "Fantastic."

"Min?" said Kallon.

"This is such a rare opportunity and something I haven't done for so long. The Galacien already explored all the worlds in our own galaxy before I was even born. Supersentients went out into the universe and even to parallel ones. To discover something new, we must join a deep space vessel to one of our satellite galaxies. But here, we don't have a clue what's down there, do we?"

Jonas shook his head.

Min put her hands together and up to her lips, smiling. "I for one can't wait to find out."

"I was going to go alone. It could be dangerous," frowned Jonas.

"Oh come on! I haven't felt like this in so long," she exclaimed.

Kallon was downcast, but Min didn't notice.

"You have to let me go. Look, we'll back me up before we go, if you're that worried," she suggested.

"But if Lom is destroyed as well, somehow," protested Kallon.

"If Lom is destroyed then I'm dead anyway, whether I go or stay," she said smartly.

Kallon seemed crestfallen, yet she found she did not care. It was true she felt more alive now than she had in years, perhaps more than ever, and she knew why. Contemplating the risk of the unknown was both terrifying and thrilling. The prospect of death made life that much more precious. Every waking moment seemed magical again, like those decades of her first life. Before she'd grown accustomed to the fact that she could not die, and then there was no immediacy: nothing mattered that much. It seemed like she had forever and, in a way, she did. But now things were different. Was this how the mortal species felt? The humans didn't seem to realise this, she noticed, and spent most of their lives on wasteful activities. Being faced with mortality she saw how they lived their lives with their eyes closed to this revelation. For if they fully realised the true gift of life, they would be a very different race.

"We'll all go," said Jonas.

Shortly after, Lom teleported two of his complement of SIBATs to the command deck. The white, featureless humanoid shapes stood as still as statues opposite Min and Kallon. Min approached hers, grinning, as if greeting an old friend. Her implant connected to the SIBAT's quasi sentient mind and she felt its thoughts superimposed on her own. Now it would obey her mental commands and automatically defend her if the circumstances called for it.

"Why aren't you downloading yourself into the SIBAT?" asked Kallon.

"No way. When I said I want to go down there, I meant it. You can if you want," she said, stripping off her clothes until she was naked. She stepped backwards into the SIBAT's opening shape; it moulded over her body, leaving only her face uncovered.

She saw that Jonas had chosen that moment to look away. Was he still immature about nakedness? Or was it something else?

Grumpily Kallon did the same.

"We're ready Jonas," she announced.

Jonas turned around. "Have you checked your weapon systems?"

"The SIBATs do that automatically. Don't worry," said Min

"More importantly, have you checked your back-up in Lom's system?" asked Kallon.

"Yes. Again, why would Lom let me down there unless he was sure of it? Relax, both of you."

Jonas and Kallon looked at one another.

"The probes we've sent down have secured us a good location to start from, at the centre of what used to be the planet's only city, Kelsuur. Ready?"

They both nodded, and in an instant were on the planet's surface.

Min took in her surroundings. The dead city of Kelsuur was a dark and broken place. What used to be buildings now lay in ruins — huge chunks of rubble strewn across the landscape. The dark clouds above them seemed unending and the wind blew dust particles into her face. The SIBAT, sensing her discomfort, created a transparent faceplate. A subtle deflector field repelled the particles, keeping her vision clear. She gave a cursory mental thank you.

"Delightful," said Kallon.

"The storm's interfering with my sensors," announced Min.

Jonas stood, transfixed by the huge broken pyramid-shaped building before him.

"This way," he said, making his way towards it.

What's the matter with him? enquired Min on the private channel.

Kallon shrugged as they both followed.

Min consulted the last known contact with the colony. During those last desperate days of what had been the Golden Age, only a handful of universal and multiversal teleporters remained. These teleporters worked tirelessly to return Galacien citizens, established on hundreds of worlds across reality, back home to the Galacien. But time had simply run out. There were too many people and not enough super-sentients to finish what they had begun. Tren-dos was one of many worlds left cut off from the rest of the GCW. The super-sentient Nemulous was the last contact they had. The report said he died returning from a mission from another universe. His archived mind was downloaded into another body. Yet as everyone knew, when this happened, the person in question lost all their abilities and was no longer super-sentient.

"What happened to everyone?" questioned Min.

Kallon looked around. "It's well over four thousand years since they were cut off. An awfully long time to be alone."

"The probes should be able to give us a hypothesis based on the data they've collected soon enough," said Jonas.

They approached the giant pyramid which stretched off above them, disappearing into the dark skies. Lom teleported over a dozen anti-grav light globes to illuminate the vast dark interior.

"The probes ahead are picking up some very faint life signs," said Jonas, sounding intrigued.

Min's heart beat a little faster. Strangely, she found she liked it too.

"Any idea what it is?" she said, checking the readings herself.

Jonas didn't reply.

She walked over to him and grabbed him gently by the arm. With no SIBAT his face was easy to read. "What's wrong?"

"I'm not sure," he muttered, distractedly.

"What can you tell us about those life signs, Lom?" asked Kallon.

"Very faint, I would describe them as dormant."

"Could the colonists have gone into hiber-sleep, in the hope that one day the Galacien would come back for them?" suggested Kallon.

"The readings we're receiving are unlike those of hiber-sleep," said Lom.

"Unless they developed something sufficiently different to appear that way," proposed Min.

"Let's find out," said Jonas, nodding to Min to assure her he was all right.

They worked their way through the wide avenues of the pyramid until it opened up again into what were once the gardens. The light globes sped out in an attempt to cover the vast space. The trio walked slowly down the steps into the eerie gloom, towards what must have been a beautiful landscape. It now seemed to be covered in a lumpy mass of unidentifiable brown moss.

"What is that?" wondered Min.

"I'm not sure," said Kallon, "but whatever it is, the life-signs are beneath it. And, I might add, they happen to be getting stronger."

"Of course they are," said Min, stopping in her tracks. "Jonas, you're the genius. Care to venture an idea of what we're dealing with here?"

Jonas seemed only partially with them. He slowly looked up at Min and said, "Nacuerians."

Twenty. Ruth

London, Earth

The report on the television showed yet another scene of the current fighting in the middle-east. Men and women cried openly in the street besides the covered corpses of their friends and families. The camera followed a stretcher carrying the small body of a little girl. She was covered with a white sheet, yet her dirty bloodstained arms and a leg hung lifeless over the sides.

Alex gritted his teeth and threw the remote against the wall. It shattered into tiny pieces and, surprisingly, the television switched off.

Was that you? he thought, his head in hands.

I thought it might be best, considering the stress it was causing you, replied his implant in its melodic feminine voice.

Alex stared at the blank screen in which his faint reflection appeared, yet all he could really see was the child's body being carried away to the back of the ambulance, again and again in a horrendous loop. He went to the fridge and cracked open a cold beer. He needed it.

What a joke. The human race. That's what we are, a joke. In the worst possible taste. Alex took a mouthful of beer.

Are you wanting an opinion? asked his implant.

Can't you tell?

Usually. That was a bit unambiguous.

I never considered us that bad. Sure, I can see the evil in the world, but I always believed that the good outbalanced it.

What you refer to as evil, we consider immaturity. It cannot be measured in the way you imagine. You are just beginning to realise how imbalanced it truly is. Soon you will see yourselves as we do. Most of you live a blinkered existence. You ignore the reality around you and rarely take responsibility, unless it is for personal gain.

Alex took another drink of his beer.

I can't keep thinking or referring to you as my implant. I think we should give you a name. How about Ruth?

I'm sensing strong emotions attached to this name. An ex-girlfriend?

Alex walked over to the window and looked out over the city lights, as far as the eye could see.

I wish. Let's just say we all have an unrequited love in our lives.

Ah, her? said the implant.

Hey! Have you been spying on me?

A ridiculous statement he realised as there were no secrets with the Galacien. How Garianne had convinced him to put one of these implants into his head he'd never know. She was unstoppable. Somehow he'd found himself agreeing to it.

I merely checked the Earth simulation records.

Are we getting too weird? he asked.

It makes no difference to me. If it makes you feel more at ease, then Ruth it is, said Ruth.

Alex's mouth almost approached something close to a smile. Strange, he did find it comforting, this new presence in his mind.

Sorry if this appears rude, Ruth, but just how sentient are you?

Sentience isn't about whether you are born or created. It is a measure of complexity of thought, the state of self-awareness and consciousness. I am all these things. In many ways I am more sentient than human beings.

I find that hard to believe. The human mind is very complex and you're... well sorry, but you're tiny. A sliver in my head, as I understand it.

The human brain is underutilised, using only a fraction of its full potential, which I would say limits your level of sentience. Also, what exists in your head is not all that I am. My full resources exist in hyperspace. I'm actually much larger and far more sophisticated than I appear.

Alex's jaw hung open; he was beginning to see what she meant. This wasn't some advanced super-miniaturised computer in his head giving him merely the illusion of sentience. She was alive, in every respect of the word. He felt his heart beat quicken and a kind of panic rising.

Frankenstein complex.

"What?" cried Alex out loud.

It's a term for what you're feeling. An irrational, and, might I add, unfounded fear.

Alex took another long swig of his beer, and then another.

Chill out, said Ruth.

Alex spluttered and laughed for a full minute. He found himself smiling, feeling much better, and he could sense that Ruth, in a way, was smiling too.

It was past midnight. Alex turned restlessly over in bed. Garianne had insisted that, like Jonas, he would not require sleep. Now he found himself at odds. The habit of years of sleep tugged at his mind and body. He wanted to sleep, to rest, yet now, more than ever, he found it difficult. The image of the child still haunted him.

Would you like to talk about it? asked Ruth.

Alex stared up into the darkness. *There's no way I'll sleep tonight. I can't stop thinking about the news.*

You must trust in Garianne. She is trying to do everything in her power to give your species a chance and prevent the impact of Sol 9173.

Alex turned over again. What could she do? The Galacien seemed adamant that humans could not be allowed to continue in existence unless they could prove they were a mature race. Alex knew that wasn't going to happen. He could think of no other way: he would have to get involved and find some way of stopping it himself. He could not stand idly by and hope that Garianne would come through for them all. There was too much at stake.

Perhaps I could give you something to help you sleep, suggested Ruth.

What do you mean precisely?

Stimulation of specific neurons and brain chemicals should do the trick. Of course, your super-sentient physiology will naturally attempt to counteract the effects, but you can consciously override that.

I'm not sure about this, Ruth. I didn't know you could affect my behaviour; that's a little unnerving, to say the least.

Only if you let it happen. I can't make you do anything you don't want to. You have natural defences against that, in the same way you can never become sick.

Alex always tried to ignore the fact that he never suffered from injury or illness like everyone else did. He only wanted to fit in and be like other people. In his experience, difference distanced you from others and made for a sad and lonely existence.

All right, let's give it a go.

Just relax, Alex.

He tried to imagine the implant interfering with his brain, stimulating the neurons, changing his physiology in a small yet significant manner.

Your body's fighting it. Stop worrying and let go.

Alex took a deep breath. *Sorry, I will.* He began to feel the first waves of drowsiness hit him and made a conscious effort not to fight it. At the last possible moment he nearly came back, then he thought of Ruth and oblivion took him.

Twenty-one. Atonement

Planet Tren-dos , in the Antlia Dwarf Galaxy

"Weapons," ordered Min.

From her SIBAT came a faint high-pitched whistle as its combat systems came online. It soon faded as she took on a defensive stance.

"No!" shouted Jonas, his arm outstretched.

"You have to be kidding me? There's hundreds of these things. Let's get what we came for and get out of here."

For a moment Jonas seemed unsure. "I... I can't," he said with a shake of his head.

He walked over to the nearest moss-covered mound and pushed his hands through.

"What are you doing?" Kallon asked as Jonas felt around inside.

"Trying to save them," said Jonas, looking hard at Kallon.

"This is dumb. We need to get out of here." Min appealed to both of them.

Jonas's eyes were locked with Kallon's. "Though our experiences may be separated by hundreds of years, you and I were once the same being. You know how I feel about this." Tears were coming to Jonas' eyes, "Only you could ever understand what this means to me, brother."

The last word was barely a whisper. Kallon found he was overcome. Despite everything that had happened to him as a distinctly separate being, he remembered.

He nodded. "What can I do?"

"If there is to be any hope, my work must not be interrupted. I need complete focus."

"We'll cover you. How long do you need?" said Kallon.

Jonas paused a moment "I don't know. I've never done anything like this before."

He heaved a huge, black wet mass from the moss.

Min jumped back. "Whoa, slime!"

Jonas ignored her. He clapped his hands together and, upon drawing them apart, revealed a number of glowing objects. Each moved about the dormant Nacuerian. Above it appeared a perfectly realised three-dimensional holographic representation of the creature. Jonas sat cross-legged on the ground, his hands together in thought. Through thought alone he manipulated the nano-machines into the body of the slumbering Nacuerian.

Min grabbed Kallon's arm. "What do you think you're doing?"

"Think about it — he, we murdered billions of innocents..."

"No. They had their hands around our collective throats, if you remember," retorted Min.

Kallon looked down at the Nacuerian. Jonas had sedated it for his study and, hopefully, some kind of solution.

"I do remember. I remember seeing what they truly were: a great and noble race. Something even the Galacien could aspire to. An almost perfectly mature and peaceful people. We had to destroy them to save the Galacien Conglomerate of Worlds. Look how they've repaid his sacrifice — we're on the run."

Min considered Jonas. "Those Galacien are under the influence of the Adversary."

"All of them? Jonas believes it is only a minority in key positions, yet the rest fall into line so easily. The Galacien believe in the test of whether a race is immature or not. Perhaps this is their test."

Min found she couldn't argue. Jonas had been declared an enemy of the Galacien and, without thinking about what he had done in the past, the entire GCW had indeed turned against him. In their own way as fickle as the humans. *We're being tested, all of the time*, she thought.

Jonas opened up another display of the Nacuerian's DNA and its brain. He ran a quick scan, looking for a miniature connection to metaspace, but found none. The Nacuerians had been transformed mind and body, and set upon their new purpose. Unlike the new agents of the Adversary there was no continued influence: the Nacuerians were created and let loose upon the universe. Jonas' goal was to undo that creation and restore them to what they were. It seemed an impossible goal. Already his mind moved at incredible speed, the world around him moving like treacle. He sensed Min reach out to grasp Kallon's arm and he knew it would be minutes for him, rather than seconds, for her to complete this action. He focused fully on the task at hand, learning everything he could. It would not be long before he would know the Nacuerian mind and body intimately. Would this reveal how the Adversary had initiated such a metamorphosis? Would it be a matter of rewriting their DNA, changing their bodies at the molecular level? Or had the Adversary applied some other, as yet undiscovered, technique here?

He finally stumbled across the dreadful way the Adversary had imposed its will on the Nacuerians. The evidence came from this creature's first memories. From there he was able to extrapolate the manner in which it had been transformed. His sense of elation was short-lived, however, as he realised how difficult any possible solution would be.

Min let go of Kallon's arm saying, "I'm sorry. You're right. Jonas told me about it. But perhaps I never wanted to face the truth and think about what had been done to them — what he had to do to save us all. I am sorry for what happened to them. Perhaps we can make up for that now, if only in a small way."

Kallon held her. It still felt intimate despite the SIBATS.

"It counts," he reassured her, "Now be ready, we may have to harm them in order to save them."

"I understand." Min turned and could see the mounds of moss moving. They seemed to her like hundreds of fluffy eggs reaching off into the distance. "Don't use energy weapons unless you feel like your life is at stake. Low-yield kinetic if you must, and make sure it's non-lethal."

She instructed the SIBAT to arm a selection of non-lethal weapons for her primaries and allocated some more lethal ones as secondaries. She hoped she wouldn't have to use them. The more devastating ones were completely off-line. She wouldn't want to destroy the city.

"Lom, we could use some help down here," said Min.

Another two SIBATs teleported down next to them.

"Is that all you have?" exclaimed Kallon.

"I guess Jonas has no need for any more," shrugged Min.

"I could manufacture some more in about twenty minutes," said Lom through Min's SIBAT.

It could all be over by then, she thought.

"I'll take whatever you can give me," she said.

Kallon looked at her as she sent over a weapons selection list to him and instructions to the two new SIBATs. She could see the Nacuerians breaking out of their mossy shells, slowly picking themselves up. They seemed to be as she remembered them: big, black, tentacled creatures, yet somehow they seemed bigger than she remembered. She did a quick scan and matched them with the SIBAT's records. Indeed, they were almost twice as big, around fourteen feet tall. She held out her hand and the SIBAT produced three tiny spheres from its own structure, dropping its mass less than one percent. They flew far off to the ceiling.

Kallon watched them go.

"Real-time map," said Min. "Watch for it. Nothing must get through and reach Jonas. Now, create a perimeter."

The two other quasi-sentient SIBATs strode purposefully over to cover the back, while Min and Kallon stayed at the front. They quickly glanced back at Jonas, who sat there eyes closed, unmoving.

How can it be done? From elation to despair, upon discovering the Adversary's technique on transforming the Nacuerians into their current form, Jonas desperately sought a solution to reverse the effect. He now ventured into uncharted waters of knowledge beyond that of the Galacien. But he was used to this: for many years he had left the forefront of their science behind. However, that had always been at a pace he set for himself. Now he had a pressing deadline upon which lives depended, including Min's, Kallon's and his own. The only way he could give himself more time was to push his mind harder. To slow the world around him down even further, yet to do so could kill him. He committed himself to the solution, not knowing if it would work or if there would be any side-effects. There was no time to check his theories and no time for simulations. He would be lucky if he could complete his task in time and hoped that he did not do more harm than good.

The first Nacuerian charged and launched itself at Min. In response she raised her hand and let loose a huge concussive force at the creature. The shockwave pushed it over ten metres away. She might have used a higher yield, but to have done so could have mortally wounded it, or, further up the scale, obliterated it completely. Her heart was pounding and her adrenaline rushed through her system. Her implant insisted it subdue the effect, but she declined. She checked the overhead map. There were now over a hundred Nacuerians moving towards them and hundreds more coming to their senses, realising there were sentients to kill.

Where the one had fallen, four more took its place and charged at her. Again she blasted them back. One of them managed to recover since another had taken the brunt of the force before it. It pushed over its unconscious comrade and fired two focused energy beams. Min's shield absorbed it easily, yet several more had joined it and together they fired on her. The shield was holding but it was an unacceptable drain on her systems. She blasted the ground at their feet and the beams moved away as the shockwaves carried the Nacuerians off.

Through the dust she fired miniature darts. Each one homed in on its target and anaesthetised it. They would be unconscious in seconds, yet they did not have enough ammunition to anaesthetise them all.

Now scores of them came through the settling dust. It was an unnerving sight to behold and, for the briefest of moments, Min wanted to switch to her lethal weapons and cut loose. Instead, she began blasting them back with both hands, the darts flying from her shoulders now to keep them down. So many had fallen all around them, yet they kept coming, climbing over the bodies of their kin. She repeatedly brought them down, but the ranks showed no sign of diminishing.

"They're getting closer!" she shouted to Kallon, forgetting there was no need to when he could simply hear her thoughts. *It's the adrenaline*, she thought to herself. *I can't remember feeling so scared and yet so excited at the same time.*

"We need line of sight. They're using each other as shields."

"I'm going to try something." Min flew directly up until she got a clearer view, while continuing to blast back the Nacuerians. Min realised her error just before it was too late. Hundreds of energy weapons were directed upon her suit. She instantly teleported to the ground. Her SIBAT's shields almost overwhelmed, she fell to one knee, her systems desperately attempting to stay online.

"Min!" shouted Kallon.

"Stay in formation!" she growled back at him and shifted all her SIBAT's defence energy into attacking until it could recover. *If they get the drop on me, I'm dead, but I won't give them a chance,* she thought, as she blasted back the Nacuerians who came over the rise. "We're stuck down here. This is going to get up close and personal, I'm afraid."

"Min, the map!" cried Kallon.

She looked at it and her heart sank. Hundreds more Nacuerians were pouring through the entrances around them.

"What!? Where are they coming from?" They both instinctively backed up.

"Any ideas?" he asked.

"Only one." Her eyes fell on her secondary weapons. "Remember, only use them when you feel you have to. You'll know when."

It wasn't long until they felt the need. There were too many of the Nacuerians, and they were too close. Min and Kallon were mere paces away from Jonas. It was impossible to defend him and themselves. She desperately blasted one assault away, when, before she knew it the next was upon her.

This was exactly what happened to him over two thousand years ago, she thought.

No choice.

She quickly flipped over to her secondary, lethal weapons. She locked onto her targets, then there was a flash of overwhelming light and energy.

Min awoke. All was still and silent. She slowly stood up. Fog hung in the air, making her surroundings even darker. Switching to infra-red she saw them all laying about, unconscious. No longer coming for her. She breathed a sigh of relief as she got up and approached the nearest form. It was different, no longer a mass of limbs. This form before her was quite eloquent.

"It is a Nacuerian," said a voice.

She spun round to see Jonas covered in sweat, breathing hard.

"Are you all right?"

He nodded, "It was... difficult." He stumbled towards her and she found herself catching him.

Kallon ran in from the fog, "You don't seem all right," he said, concern etched across his face. "My SIBAT informs me you're exhausted. Sit down before you fall down."

Through dark eyes, Jonas looked as though he might protest, but he sat nonetheless.

He's so pale, thought Min to Kallon.

He forgets he has limits. He must have pushed himself hard to accomplish the task and it looks as though it almost killed him.

"I can hear you, you know," said Jonas with his head down, "despite my current state."

"I thought you cherished privacy," replied Min.

Jonas either agreed or was too tired, for he didn't reply.

Min and Kallon looked at one another and then at the Nacuerians all around them. In no way did they resemble what they'd been fighting.

Their bodies were milky in colour and hairless rather than dark and featureless. They had no tentacles. More humanoid. Two arms and legs and an oval head with small eyes and mouth. They were quite the most non-threatening sentient creatures she had ever seen.

"Please scan its brain and cellular structure for abnormalities," croaked Jonas.

Min did so. "Nothing obvious. Everything seems normal."

Jonas collapsed completely and they were both at his side in a heartbeat.

"He's fainted," said Kallon, after a quick scan. "He'll be fine."

Min could only stare down at him, a deep sadness poking at her heart. She forced it to one side, and looked out across at the hundreds of Nacuerians. "What are we going to do with them all?"

Twenty-two. Dislocation

Earth

Alex dreams. He dreams of other parallel worlds, of alternative possibilities. Yet Alex is not a normal person and these are not normal dreams. He can see his world being destroyed again and again, levels of horror beyond what he witnessed with Garianne. He stirs, he struggles and in the next moment, he is gone.

Earth³

Something hard slammed against him and broke.

Alex, wake up! said Ruth

With a snap, Alex did.

"There's no need to shout," grumbled Alex. He slowly pulled himself to his feet, looking down at the smashed concrete. "Did I do that?"

Yes, it seems that the ground isn't quite as durable as you. I would perhaps stick to non-verbal communication. We have company.

Alex rubbed his head, bewildered. Looking around he could see a number of soldiers staring at him in astonishment. They wore uniforms which looked as though they should be in a museum. It was dark and he was on a train station platform. Alex could see a sign which stuck out from one of the many pillars along the platform. It read, 'York No. 7 Platform'.

York. I've teleported to York?

His eyes were then drawn to the most gigantic steam locomotive he'd ever seen. Granted he'd not seen many, but this was almost ridiculously large.

"Wow!"

Ruth, what the hell is that?

It's a steam train, dear.

Alex rolled his eyes. *Yes, but it's so large. I didn't think they made them that big?*

They don't. Or should I say, you *don't.*

What?

This train is far wider than anything on your home-world; the gauge is over twice the size, said Ruth.

Gauge?

The spacing between the rails able to accommodate such a large locomotive.

A soldier walked up to Alex and slowly saluted him.

Alex took a short step back. "Hello?"

"General?" said the soldier.

Perhaps you should play along. Agree with everything. Be secretive. They obviously think you're their commanding officer.

He looks like me? queried Alex.

Obviously.

"Erm... yes that's me. Sorry about that," said Alex, referring to the ground. "I've been up to general's business. Right, where were we?"

Smooth, commented Ruth.

He ignored her. The soldier looked him up and down, uncertain. Alex followed his gaze. He still wore the t-shirt and shorts he'd been wearing in bed.

"My attire is of no consequence," he said, flapping his hands around. "I have been on a special mission, by order of... of... erm..."

"Me?" came a voice.

Alex spun round and saw what looked like a queen from the nineteenth century, and a young princess. The soldiers bowed.

"Yes. That's right, you," and he bowed too, somewhat awkwardly.

The queen looked uncertain, her eyebrows raised in disapproval. Alex felt distinctly underdressed.

Is this an anxiety dream? he thought.

You're not dreaming, Alex.

"Join me. I believe we have much to discuss, and... get dressed."

She turned without waiting for his response. The little princess flashed him a quick smile and also turned.

"Okay," Alex said, trotting up to the locomotive and following the disappearing princess up the ramp.

Try and sound more formal. She's the queen.

The queen of what? I've never seen her before, and I could do with some help, you know.

The queen's soldiers fell in beside him, one of them handing him a uniform. He paused for only a moment and then fumbled it on; it fitted perfectly. Alex felt strange wearing a military uniform, like an interloper.

They walked through the conduit passageway of the train.

Wow! Look at this place. It's huge. Look how ornate everything is, he thought, tucking in his tunic

It must be the royal locomotive.

The queen and her entourage entered the most elaborate room Alex had ever been in. There was deep red fabric and gold everywhere which was polished to perfection. Was he somehow in the Victorian era? He glanced at a group of officers to his left. They stood by a table, on which sat a strategic map of Britain, sporting a scattering of symbolic figurines.

The queen sat; her unblinking eyes bored into Alex.

The silence stretched out, expectation weighing upon him. He squirmed and fidgeted, eyes darting over every single one of them, willing one of them to speak.

"It is good to see you again," blurted out the little princess. Her hand went immediately to her mouth, as if she'd said a naughty word.

He smiled at her. He could sense amusement in this one, a need to make light of everything. But it was partially a defence mechanism — she had learned to protect herself from the evils of the world. It was unnecessary. Underneath it all he sensed a steely strength about her.

The queen looked at her. "You are mistaken, Victoria. Despite similarities in appearances, you have never met this 'man' before. Notice his youth and the absence of the scar. Isn't this true?"

Alex nodded.

"Then why did you deceive us a moment ago?"

"Sorry... Your Majesty. I didn't want to get in trouble."

The queen tapped her finger tips together lightly, her eyes narrowed.

"It seems to me, as incredible as it may be, the most likely explanation is that you are another Alexander Lethbridge from another universe."

"Another universe?" echoed Alex.

"Yes, Lady Garianne has spoken of such things."

Garianne? thought Ruth.

"Garianne?" cried Alex. "You know Garianne?" The queen nodded. "Hold on a moment. Are we talking about the same person? You have an Alex here, like me. And you also have a Garianne in this universe?"

"She said she was from another universe. A universe where the British Empire did not rule half the globe in the twenty-first century."

"That could be my universe, but how could we know? There are so many."

"Indeed," said the queen.

One of the officers coughed and drew the queen's attention.

"Your Majesty," he said. "We are ready. Perhaps we'd best be on our way?"

"Very well, Captain," said the queen.

He went over to the wall and took hold of a small brass horn-like device, connected to a tube

"Immediate departure," ordered the captain.

Alex heard a faint but prompt reply come from the horn.

Slowly, the great engine pulled away from the station. Alex found himself staring out of the window, hoping for more of a glimpse of this other world, but after the station all he saw was darkness and only the faintest of lights, which he guessed must be distant houses. The rhythm of the train began to build in conjunction with its speed, until settling to a racing heartbeat.

I don't believe it. A new world, a new universe. How did we get here?

Isn't it obvious? said Ruth.

Me?

By your physiology. I think you were having some pretty strange nightmares only moments before you teleported.

Why didn't you wake me?

I tried. But it was taking a while to counter the effects of putting you to sleep in the first place.

He sensed her guilt. *Don't worry about it,* he reassured her.

The queen and the princess approached him. This time the monarch smiled warmly. "Shall we start again Alexander? I am Queen Marina, Monarch of the British Empire. And this is Victoria, Princess Royal of the House of Hanover."

"Alexander, are you a general, like our Alexander?" asked the Princess, beaming at him.

"It's Alex, not Alexander, and, no. I'm a student. Sorry."

"Oh," said the princess, seemingly disappointed by this.

"Do you possess the same abilities as our general?" said the queen.

Alex gave a nervous laugh "Why, what kind of things can he do?"

"He can teleport great distances, he's unusually strong and resistant to illness or injury," said the queen. The princess nodded vigorously. "He can sense how we feel, what we are thinking to a lesser degree. He is aware of his environment in a manner I do not quite understand."

Sounds quite a man, remarked Ruth.

Yes, doesn't he?

"Well, that's quite a list. But, yeah, that about covers it. I can do all those things," he said, smiling at the princess.

The princess tried not to laugh.

"Then would you do us a small favour and provide some intelligence. Use your extraordinary senses to fill the captain in on our current surroundings." Alex wasn't sure what to make of this but he agreed nonetheless. "Would you be so kind?" She gestured towards the map.

Alex joined the captain and his officers. The queen and the princess stood close by.

"Here is our current position," said the captain, pointing to the tiny model of the train on the map of the United Kingdom. "Travelling north." Alex saw their position heading towards the Scottish border.

"Okay," he nodded.

"Could you sense the land around us for about, say, one hundred kilometres?" The captain looked at the queen, who nodded her approval.

"How far?" exclaimed Alex.

"One hundred kilometres," repeated the captain.

Alex breathed out heavily. "That's far."

"Can you do it?" asked the queen.

"I'll give it a try. Anything in particular you want me to keep an eye out for."

"Martians," said the captain.

"Excuse me?"

"Martians," repeated the captain.

Alex looked at him as if he wasn't sure. "Really? Martians... from Mars?"

That's a dumb question, where else would they be from? chastised Ruth.

Well, I'm sorry, but the last time I checked there weren't any Martians. Mars was lifeless.

Apparently not here.

"Yes," confirmed the captain.

Alex looked at the train on the map again, which a female officer pushed a little further away from where York station was marked. He reached out his senses and could almost see the train speeding along, the land flashing by. It was all in darkness, yet with little effort he could see the trees and, beyond, the English countryside. He reached out further and the huge steam locomotive diminished to nothing more than a bold line surrounded by kilometres of countryside and an intricate, almost chaotic, network of roads, streets and lanes. Dotted here and there were villages and hamlets where the faintest of lights could be seen. Most remained dark. Were they hiding from these Martians? He focused on each settlement in turn. They were still occupied, the inhabitants unmistakably anxious. Alex's awareness continued spreading out across the landscape until he came across something unusual.

"What is it, Alex?" came the queen's voice, noticing his change in expression.

"Something... something different."

"Describe it," urged the captain.

Alex's attention focused on the anomaly. "There's a huge metallic, green sphere, actually more like an egg. It's in a smoking crater which must be at least a mile across. My God, look at the devastation it's caused."

The queen and captain looked at one another. "Yes, we know. One landed in London, pretty much on top of Crystal Palace," said the captain.

Alex was shocked. It must have destroyed half the city.

"Is the sphere open or unopened?" the queen wanted to know.

"Unopened." Alex looked at the map to indicate its position. "There," he pointed. The female officer immediately placed a red pin where his finger had been. He noticed there were five other pins on the map south of their position. He looked up to the map of the world on the wall. There were scores of red pins, each representing a Martian landing site.

It's an invasion.

It appears so, agreed Ruth.

The captain measured the distance between the train and the Martian crater Alex had indicted for them, north east of their position. "We might be able to make it."

The queen nodded back. "Best speed, Captain."

The captain raced over to the horn, to relay the orders to the driver on the footplate of the steam engine.

"Alex, can you keep an eye on it and let us know if you can sense any change."

"Of course, Your Majesty."

He could feel the locomotive picking up speed now, its heart hammering away. The atmosphere in the room was tense; even Princess Victoria looked worried.

Alex, Garianne has been here. Find out why.

Don't you know?

Would I be asking if I did?

"Your Majesty, can you tell me what Garianne said and did while she was here please?" asked Alex, as graciously as he could.

The queen said, "Lady Garianne saved our lives during our escape from London. It was terrible. Almost half the city was either destroyed or in flames. We heard reports that it was occupied by at least two, perhaps three, Martian war machines. With Lady Garianne's help we were able to find a safe route to Kings Cross and out of London. With technology far in advance of our own, Lady Garianne illustrated our current plight — the Martian invasion. However, she told us of a peril far more grave. Something which threatens other worlds parallel to our own. She said she needed our Alex to help what she calls the multiverse. This in turn would save our world. Apparently, all of this is the work of one Adversary."

Alex could feel Ruth thinking.

"Lady Garianne said we need only hold out long enough for her to send help if she could, but with so many worlds in peril?" The queen left that hanging a moment. "We should consider ourselves lucky you are here."

Alex realised what she was saying. "Your Majesty, I'm here purely by accident," he confessed.

"I don't believe in accidents or coincidences. I think you're here to help us."

"Look, I'm not sure about getting involved in a war…"

You have to help them, said Ruth.

How can I fight a war? I'm just one man.

You are super-sentient. Jonas saved the galaxy.

You're not getting a rise out of me, Ruth.

"Please help us," said a small voice, breaking Alex from his inner dialogue.

Alex stared at the young princess and, for a moment, he could not help thinking of that lifeless body of a girl under a dirty white sheet.

"Well, maybe a little," he found himself saying.

She gave him another smile, tinged with worry.

Alex smiled back, but it was short-lived as his expression gave way to concern.

The Martian sphere was opening.

Twenty-Three. The Entrophier

Planet Tren-dos, in the Antlia Dwarf Galaxy.

Jonas stumbled over a rock and held himself up against a vast stone pillar which stretched off into the distant ceiling at the heart of the dead city. Kallon had teleported back to Lom to help accommodate the Nacuerians Jonas had recently liberated

"You should go back and rest," said Min. Her hulking SIBAT loomed over his bent form. "I'll go on ahead and retrieve the Entrophier. You can direct me from the ship."

Jonas shook his head. "No. There may be unknowns ahead, defences set by the super-sentients which only I can deal with."

"Even in your current state?"

Jonas forced himself upright. "I recover quickly. You'll see."

He carried on until they came across a giant metal door twenty metres high. Min walked over to the control panel and, using her SIBAT, interfaced with it remotely.

"There's still power but it's been locked from the inside," she told him. "I can't scan inside — there's a force-field."

"There's no one inside, in case you're wondering."

Min selected something clean and efficient from her weapons manifest with which to cut open the door. As she was using a high-yield laser to slice through the locks, it abruptly opened. Just inside the door was the force-field, which suddenly disappeared.

Min looked at Jonas. "Show off," she said as she walked towards the door, then turned to see that he wasn't following. "What is it?" She came back to him.

He found himself struggling again. He did not want to say it but he had to.

"I'm sorry about Kallon. It is quite clear that he is his own man and that he does have a right to his own life, as every mature sentient being does." He took a deep breath, avoiding her searching eyes. "And if he wants to be with you, then he should."

Min stood there for a long time trying to blink back the tears. "Thank you. I think he's earned it."

She didn't know what else to say. She wanted him to be happy, but circumstances seemed to dictate that he was destined not to be. He carried so much responsibility.

"Jonas..." she began.

He finally looked into her eyes. Time stood still between them and she felt she truly didn't know what to do. Min stepped back. "We should... we should retrieve the Entrophier, and get back before something else unexpected happens."

"Of course," replied Jonas, and he headed for the open door.

Min followed. Nothing more was said between them. Only the empty silence as she followed him through the avenues of a dead city.

It wasn't long before Jonas stopped and looked around at the floor beneath them.

"It's down there, in an underground structure. It may be easiest for me to teleport down there now I know its precise location," said Jonas.

"Take me with you, to be on the safe side," Min replied.

In an instant they were in a vast, dark room, and ahead was another room with transparent walls that emitted a bright white light.

Min noticed there had been no teleportation sequence from Lom. "You can teleport?"

Jonas nodded.

"People and objects, without physical contact?"

"Yes."

"How far?" she enquired, looking right at him.

He looked straight back at her and laughed. "I'm not telling you that."

"Why not?" smiled Min.

"I've learnt that deception is a very useful tool."

Her smile faded slowly. "You sound like Garianne. I thought we were friends."

"Really?" said Jonas.

"Yes, can't you tell?"

"I've sometimes found it hard to read your emotions; they seem rather contrary at times."

She looked at him as if this were a revelation of real significance. She thought back to their conversations and her assumptions.

"Only about a hundred metres, possibly further if pushed, and obviously depending on the mass of the object or person."

She shook her head. "What? Oh, right."

Deep under the city they approached the illuminated room. The circular doorway opened upon their approach and Min felt a little tense. Strewn about the room lay an assortment of scientific apparatus. In the centre was a black box with the appearance of polished stone, which came to waist height.

Min scanned the box using her implant. "My sensors can't get through."

"It's in there," said Jonas circling around the back, his brow furrowed in thought.

"How do we open it?"

Jonas smiled and gently touched the top surface of the box, which quickly disintegrated into the atmosphere. What was left was a plinth, and on the plinth an object consisting of two thin metallic cylinders stuck together.

"That's the Entrophier?" asked Min.

Jonas nodded.

"How did you open the box?"

"I wasn't getting anything either, so the only way was to make physical contact with it. As soon as I did, I knew."

"What?"

He smiled again. "It recognised me. The box was supposed to open only for a super-sentient." He took the device and turned it over, studying it.

"Are you sure that's it?" said Min.

"Only one way to find out."

For a moment Jonas' eyes took on a glazed look. Again the world slowed down for him. Min began to blink, her eyes slowly shutting as if she were falling asleep. They stayed closed as Jonas integrated his consciousness with the Entrophier's system, the majority of which existed in hyperspace. In relative minutes he'd learnt all that was necessary and his consciousness returned to normal. Min completed her single blink and Jonas tossed the Entrophier into the air, where it hung facing the way they had entered. With a mental command from Jonas, the two cylinders flew apart and met together again behind them.

Min spun around. "What was that?"

"The Entrophier has created a field encompassing us, through which we can view the past. Look." Jonas indicated behind her.

She turned and saw herself and Jonas teleport into the room. She saw him laugh and her smile. For some reason it made her feel sad. "Incredible! How far back into the past can the Entrophier see?"

"Apparently no further back than the point of its own creation, over five thousand years ago. Far enough to suit our current needs."

"And then some," said Min.

She could see how her doppelganger had reacted to something he'd said and felt a deep sense of regret. The other Jonas and Min approached them and began studying the box. Behind them, the two cylinders broke apart, coming together in Jonas' hand. The view of the past disappeared.

"I believe we have what we came for. Lom, teleport us back."

Min was barely aware of the transference, she was so lost in thought.

Twenty-Four. Battle

Earth

Alex watched in fascination as the two halves of the Martian meteor shell slowly unscrewed. An eerie green light bled out into the dark, cold English countryside. In the distance, from the south west, the great steam locomotive thundered along in a northerly direction. He could sense the growing anxiety of the passengers permeating the train, especially amongst the officers. It was now a race against time as to whether they could speed by before the Martian war machine emerged from its cocoon and attacked them. The officers continually measured distances on the map and made calculations with some kind of archaic metal sliding device he had never seen before. They continued to shout out orders through the brass horn. Alex could sense the room on the train where they wound up a kind of periscope. Through the magnification of the periscope, in the far distance they could just make out the faint green light on the horizon against the dark sky and the total blackness of the landscape.

"Do you have anything to report, Captain?" asked the queen.

"We can't ascertain when the Martian war machine will emerge." He reached for his pocket watch. "However, we will be due west of its position in twelve minutes... mark. This is when we will be closest. After that point we should be able to get away."

"Are we faster than them?" said Alex.

"Yes," said the captain. "Are you surprised?"

"Yeah. These Martians must be more technologically advanced than my own world by at least a hundred years, perhaps more. And, we're about a hundred years in advance of you. They could take this train out easily."

They looked at him soberly.

I don't think they appreciated that last comment, said Ruth.

"Sorry. What I mean to say is, where's their air-force? Or perhaps something military in orbit?"

The captain frowned, "We have seen no Martian airships."

"Well, it's coming. I can't believe this thing — and no disrespect, this is a cool train you've got here — can outrun anything they've got."

Silence hung in the room as the officers and the queen considered his words.

You have a point, even if put quite so ineloquently, said Ruth.

I've never been accused otherwise.

"You believe these Martian war machines are merely their ground troops?" said the captain.

"Yeah. Scouts, until they bring in the big guns. They're..." Alex stopped.

"What is it?" asked the queen.

He looked at her. "It's emerging from its shell. It's scanning the landscape." Alex focused, trying to make out its shape, trying to get a closer look. "It's heading this way."

You must help these people, said Ruth.

What!?

"Can you help us, Alex?" said the queen.

He took a step back, his hands coming up. All activity in the room stopped and all eyes were on him.

"Listen, I don't know what your Alex could do, but I'm guessing he must have been pretty handy considering he was a general and all. I've got no military experience."

You are super-sentient.

That doesn't make me a hero.

"All I ask is that you try," said the queen.

"But I wouldn't have a clue how to stop it."

I can help.

I'm not sure about that.

"We have no other option," said the captain.

"We?" said Alex, instantly regretting that one word. One word that said, 'I'm not one of you, this isn't my world. Their faces showed that betrayal and Alex realised he was part of the problem; the cruel, selfish side of humanity that he had so recently found so sickening.

The little princess came over to him with such openness, he thought his heart would break.

"Please," she whispered.

He couldn't bear it any longer. Nothing was worth the emotional wrangling he was going through.

"All right... all right, just stop looking at me with those big eyes," he said, shaking his head and glancing at the queen, who was trying not to smile.

Ruth, I need your advice big time. How do I stop that thing?

I am aware that your abilities seem to comprise teleportation and the use of some kind of force-field. All super-sentients have some degree of invulnerability and physical strength, however I have no idea of your full capabilities. I wouldn't rely on any secondary abilities, or trying anything new in a combat situation. We should position ourselves between the Martian and the train and use force-fields, until the queen and company are out of danger.

That's your recommendation? Well, it's better than my plan.

What was your plan?

I didn't have one, said Alex, nodding to the queen before suddenly teleporting.

Alex was now outside in the dark. He could feel the soft mossy ground under the soldier's boots he was wearing, and he could just hear the train approaching from behind. Ahead, he could sense the Martian machine coming towards him. He could not see it, so instead he reached out with his extraordinary senses.

I can almost see it.

I'm sure you can, though let me help.

Crisp graphics sprung to life in front of Alex's field of vision.

What's this?

You're own personal 'head up display'. I built it into your retina using nano-machines. You didn't feel anything, did you?

That's not the point. You could've asked.

Sorry. Anyway, look. As well as obtaining tactical information we can switch to infra-red. Now you can really see it.

The Martian machine was a giant. At over thirty metres tall, it strode towards him either not seeing him, or not caring. Alex could not detect much of a body, just a central structure which seemed to be its head, looking like a giant clam. Two huge shoulders sprung directly from this, each one extending two arms, making four in total. These ended in a bundle of fibres. Were these its hands? It walked on two long metallic legs as easily as any human, and Alex wondered unnervingly how fast it would move if it broke into a sprint. Inside the machine Alex could make out a form of some sort.

Is that a Martian inside the machine? he asked Ruth.

It looks like it.

Reminds me of those Japanese robots.

There was a pause from Ruth and Alex knew she must be checking her vast database. *I see what you mean, but it's definitely not Japanese.*

The Martian was getting closer.

I'm not sure this was a good idea, thought Alex.

Stop gawping and erect a force-field.

I don't have the slightest idea how.

Think back to the meta-humans' attack and reproduce what you did there.

Alex extended his hand and tried to imagine some kind of giant protective force-field between himself and the Martian.

The Martian's movements changed.

It sees me!

I'm detecting an energy spike, said Ruth.

Alex saw it in his HUD.

From what must have been the Martian machine's single cycloptic eye burst forth a focused beam of crimson energy.

It broke across Alex's force-field like hot molten metal. He felt it through his body and a building pressure in his head.

The Martian ceased firing and seemed to pause.

I believe it's confused, said Ruth. *Maintain the force-field and be ready.*

He could hear the queen's royal locomotive fast approaching from behind him as the Martian fired again. Alex poured his will into keeping hold of the force-field against the Martian's energy beam. Alex could hear something, a whirring. The pitch of the whirring became a high whistle.

Alex's HUD identified the weapon's energy signature.

Ruth, I don't know what this thing's trying to tell me. What is that?

Something more devastating than what you're currently holding out against. It's bringing out its big gun. Alex, concentrate on making that force-field as strong as you can possibly imagine, now!

Was it Ruth's intensity of thought or was she intervening more directly? Whatever it was, Alex found he was gritting his teeth as he pushed everything he had into the force-field. For a split second he saw some kind of projectile launch from the Martian machine. It smashed into his force-field and he felt as if he'd been hit by a truck.

For a moment everything was black.

Alex, get up! yelled Ruth in his head.

He opened his eyes and everything was still black.

Oh yes, he thought, *it's night.*

Alex, it's going to kill everyone on that train unless you can stop it Now get up!

He slowly got onto his knees. The wetness of the grass soaked through his trousers. He rubbed the dirt from his eyes and could see the Martian machine watching the train come alongside it. He could sense the terrified passengers on board looking out, the queen and the princess holding one another. His HUD showed him the energy build-up from the machine's weapon systems.

He didn't think, he only acted, teleporting between the Martian and its intended target and bringing up another force-field. Alex's vision was filled with crimson energy. The train thundered past behind him. For a brief moment, he saw himself through the eyes of the passengers standing between them and certain death.

The Martian machine stopped firing and launched itself at the force-field, bringing up its great arms. Alex felt the shock through his body as the towering machine repeatedly brought down its massive arms. The force-field still held, holding his enemy back, but each blow was taking its toll on him.

I can't take this for much longer, he thought desperately.

You must. The train isn't out of weapons' range yet.

Alex's despair deepened, as above the sound of the Martian's attack he again heard the low whirring.

Ruth, it's going to fire its big gun and I can't hold my force-field for much longer. We're screwed.

Excuse me, we are not screwed. You underestimate yourself. Alex, you have a vast reservoir of power to utilise, but you're just not used to accessing it. You were able to travel to a parallel universe — do you realise how difficult that is? No-one can do that. Not even Jonas.

The whirring had increased to a high-pitched whistle.

Help me. Tell me what to do! If you believe I can do it, I'll do it.

Create a force-field as strong as you can possibly imagine, something unbreakable. A small one, mind, right in front of its big gun.

Alex gathered his will and imagined plugging up the Martian's gun with something stronger than any known material, something which could not be broken. He thought the pitch could increase no further when there was a great explosion and he was thrown back into the air, landing next to the train track.

Alex quickly scrambled to his feet to see the Martian machine stumbling about like a drunkard, the top half of its body almost completely destroyed, yet it still tried to maintain its balance.

It's attempting to send a signal of warning to the others, said Ruth.

Then jam it, or something.

Already done.

I've had enough of this, thought Alex.

In a moment he teleported beside it, grabbed hold of its leg and teleported again, hundreds of metres high into the air.

Alex let out a gasp as they both began to fall. He caught a glimpse of the queen's train below with its trailing smoke far off in the distance, then teleported again to the ground, landing softly on the grass.

Nicely done, commented Ruth.

Alex looked up into the night sky, sensing the falling Martian war machine.

I hope it can't fly, he thought.

Even if it can, I'd be surprised if it's still able, given the condition you left it in.

He watched it plummet, hitting the Earth with a satisfying crash. Alex headed over to see what was left. It was a mess of twisted metal. His HUD reported that almost every system was non-functional; it no longer posed a threat. Inside the machine, covered from head to toe in some kind of malleable armour, was the Martian itself. Alex's HUD informed him that its life signs were weak.

I believe it is dying, Alex.

"It brought this on itself," he said grimly. *Is there any way we can retrieve some information on it, Ruth.*

I'm already in its systems.

Any problems?

Of course not. This thing has nothing on Galacien technology. I'm done. What about the occupant? Can you sense anything from it?

Give me a moment, said Alex.

Alex hesitantly reached out to the dying Martian to get a sense of its thoughts and intent. The alien nature of it repulsed him, its emotions so very strange. This being felt so wrong. He turned away,

Uuurgh! That's horrible.

What is it?

Look, I know it's an alien, but God, this thing feels... well, like it's been pulled apart and then stuck back together again into some kind of monstrosity.

There was no response from Ruth.

I'm sorry. That's just how it feels.

We should be getting back to the queen, said Ruth.

Alex popped into existence on board the royal locomotive right in front of the captain, causing him to jump out of his skin.

"Sorry, it's hard not to do that to someone when you teleport into a room full of people," said Alex.

The princess ran to him. "You did it!"

"Piece of cake."

Really? said Ruth.

"I knew you could," said the princess, grinning.

The relief in the room was palpable and he could feel a warm sense of gratitude from everyone there. It felt good.

"Thank you, Alex, you saved us. Are you sure Garianne did not send you here?" said the queen.

"It's just a coincidence I assure you," Alex said, though he was beginning to wonder.

"Are we safe?"

"There is nothing north of here. We should be fine," he said.

"Good, I'm sure you would like some refreshments, and perhaps some rest? You must be tired. Margaret here will see to your needs."

Alex didn't feel hungry or thirsty, and the strain of the battle could have been weeks ago: he felt fine. However, he did feel like he needed some privacy to get his head together.

"Thank you, Your Majesty," he said.

The girl, Margaret, led him to a lavish room of his own. She showed him around, explaining the use of the primitive shower and offering him a selection of books should he wish to read. He smiled encouragingly. Again, the furnishings were all very ornate. He could've killed for a television.

She departed with a curt bow, gently shutting the door behind her.

Alex spun on his foot. *Okay Ruth, what the hell is going on?*

What do you mean?

Oh, cut the crap! There's no way my being here is a coincidence.

Alex, I really don't know anything about this.

Garianne was here. Somehow, she was here. She offered them help against the Martians, and in exchange she 'borrowed' their Alex. So now I'm here, like some kind of stand-in.

If you are, you're doing a very good job.

What did she do?

I don't know, Alex. It's the truth.

Then take a guess. Stop holding out on me, and don't pretend you're not. You know Garianne. Consider all that data you carry around with you in hyperspace and give me your best working hypothesis.

There was silence for a moment as Alex paced around the room, waiting for Ruth's reply.

I was never given orders to withhold information from you.

Well, it sure feels like you have been.

It is logical to assume Garianne would not protest about me divulging my own theories, continued Ruth.

Go on.

Garianne is an exceptionally clever being. Considering recent events, I would conclude that she has somehow had a hand in your arrival in this universe.

Alex shook his head. *How is this possible?*

It is feasible she made suggestions to your subconscious. Something she showed you, perhaps, could have sown the seed. She would have to create a situation where you would teleport to another universe — this particular one.

How did she do that?

I don't know, Alex.

I can imagine how she could insert images into some of the simulations of Earth I was shown. Would this be enough?

I don't believe so. You'd need something a little more fundamental.

You're quite fundamental and right here inside my head, thought Alex, feeling a little uncomfortable with where this was going. *Is this what she does: controls people?*

Alex, I haven't done anything, I promise you.

You put me to sleep, and the next thing I know I'm here. Alex felt a deep well of dread. It had seemed such a cool idea — the implant, having access to the secrets of the universe, being able to do things undreamt of by his kind. Garianne had sold it well. But now he was more than just a little anxious about what he'd done.

You're being paranoid.

Am I? What happens when I upset you, Ruth? Do things start getting a bit dark then?

No wonder you humans struggle so much; you see yourselves in others too easily. Well, you're wrong. I'm not going to 'make' you do anything. This isn't one of your terrible movies.

Martians attacking the Earth? It certainly feels like it.

Ah, that.

Alex sat on the bed. *What do you mean, 'ah that.'*

You said there was something wrong with the Martians, more than merely being alien. Perhaps something else?

Yes. What are you getting at?

Ruth said, *This is something which is not widely known amongst the Galacien, but the Nacuerians weren't originally malevolent creatures. Jonas discovered at the very end that they were altered from their original forms into something bent on our destruction. Jonas was super-sentient, like you. He reported that they felt wrong, unnatural.*

That's it! Unnatural. That's how the Martian felt to me, thought Alex.

It's reasonable to assume the Adversary has been to this universe and has altered these Martians in the same way it altered the Nacuerian species. Then let them loose to attack this Earth. Or, perhaps they were never Martians in the first place.

Why this universe, and why this Earth?

I'm sorry, I've no idea.

Alex scratched at his head in frustration. *I want to help these people, I do. But we have problems back on my own world. Sol 9173 is heading for Earth and I've got to find a way of convincing the Galacien to stop it.*

Don't forget the Adversary.

Thanks for reminding me. Alex sighed. *I don't have the time to help these people.*

Perhaps you do.

What do you mean, Ruth?

Every universe runs at a different time relative to another — similar to planets orbiting around a star. The inner planets move around a star quicker than the outer ones. Earth's year is longer than those planets closer to the Sun, and shorter than those further out. This is also true with the structure of the multiverse. Time itself moves at relatively different rates.

Using Alex's HUD, Ruth superimposed a graphical representation of the multiverse on his vision. It popped into existence in the room.

First, he noticed a bright shining light at the centre like a sun.

That's the singularity, said Ruth.

A fraction out from this was a hypothetical sphere on which billions of universes existed. Ruth informed him that the sphere itself wasn't real: it was only there to illustrate the point that these universes were all the same distance from the singularity. After this set of universes was another layer, then another, and another continuing out from the singularity. The number of of universes was mind-boggling.

Alex smiled. Ruth had even made the illusion intersect the walls — the multiverse just kept on going. No super-sentient had ever discovered or sensed any ending, she informed him.

Garianne showed me this, remembered Alex.

Did she also tell you that the further out you go, relatively speaking, the slower the universes run? If time in this universe runs slower relative to our Earth then we may have more time than you think.

Or less if it's further in, he thought, panicking. It could already be over.

Calm down, it's unlikely we've travelled that far.

But how can we tell?

The multiversal teleporters from the Golden Age could tell by looking at an object which universe it came from. They sometimes used this technique to quickly move from one universe to the next: it gave them something to focus on. Also, they'd use these items to train new recruits in our own universe.

Alex tried to imagine what it must have been like all those thousands of years ago when super-sentients were doing all these incredible things. He would have to study this period of Galacien history from Ruth's files as soon as he got the chance — if he got the chance.

He took off his watch and put it on the dresser. *Does it measure time at my Earth's rate or this one's?* he mused.

This one's, I'm afraid. That would be such a simple solution otherwise. Unfortunately, anything brought over to another universe takes on its rate of time, since the forces and matter in this universe compel it to. However, we are looking for something quite different. Not the way the watch measures time but the watch itself.

Alex went over to the bookshelf and curiously browsed the spines of the books.

"*Victorian England in the 21st Century*, by J.D. Brown." Alex laughed." I'm guessing this book was never published in our world."

No, confirmed Ruth. *There is no such book either published or unpublished of that name.*

Again Alex smiled. Ruth knew everything the Galacien Earth simulation had recorded. Even if a man had written such a book in a hut in a forest in the middle of nowhere, had never shown it to soul and then burnt it immediately after finishing it, the Galacien would still have a perfect record of its contents.

Rather comforting in a way, to think that whatever you did was being noticed and remembered by someone. Or was it *something*? No, the machines were sentient, including Ruth.

Are we doing this? Or are you just going to daydream all day? she said.

Sorry. What do I do?

The records say that those who could travel to other universes could sense a difference in vibration from those objects foreign to ours. Don't mistake it for the oscillation of the molecules: that's something else entirely. Even though the watch from your world is now a part of this universe, the particles are still trying to work at their original rate. I only describe this in partially scientific terms for you are trying to 'feel' this, Alex, not measure it in a quantitative sense. Not at first.

He listened to her words and tried to follow her instructions. He tried to feel the watch and then the book in his mind rather than merely look at them; get a sense of the indivisible particles they were made from and how they differed. It came to him almost unsuspectingly, it was so easy. He wondered how he'd never noticed it before. Perhaps because there was nothing in this world which did not belong, except himself, of course.

I see it, Ruth.

Good. Now does the watch run at a faster or slower rate than the book?

Alex reached out with his senses. *The watch runs slower.*

This is what we hoped for. How much slower? Be as precise as you can.

He took his time, feeling the rhythm of each object. There was a big difference. The more he focused, the more aware he became of it. They were like two separate hearts beating. The watch sounded like a resting heart while the book's beat seemed like that of an insect's wings. Time seemed to be slowing down as the beating of the watch slowed more and more, until there was an appreciable interval between the beats. The book had slowed too: it pounded along, yet now it was slow enough for him to count.

"I've got it," he said excitedly, "for every one beat of my watch the book beats eighty-seven times."

That's fantastic. It will be the same for everything. For every hour here, only forty-one seconds pass on your Earth. Every day, about sixteen minutes.

"Wow! Then only a minute or two has passed back home since we arrived? Can you calculate the arrival of Sol 9173 in this Earth's time?"

Less than a year on your Earth. I predict about seventy years this Earth's time.

A euphoric sense of relief swept over Alex, leaving him feeling better than he had in days. Before he'd had so little time to find a way of convincing Garianne and the Galacien to intervene in the impending impact of Sol 9173, only months. Now he had time in abundance, it seemed: all the time in the world. The question was, what would he do with it?

Twenty-Five. Closure

Planet Tren-dos, in the Antlia Dwarf Galaxy

Jonas, deep in thought, looked down upon the dark, cloud-covered world of Tren-dos. Min entered the command deck with Kallon.

"How long?" he said, not turning around.

"I'd like another hour if possible," replied Lom.

Jonas nodded.

"What's going on?" asked Kallon.

"Lom's down there in a SIBAT. He's using the Entrophier to gather information about what happened."

"We know what happened — the Nacuerians," said Min.

Jonas turned to face them. "I want details. Did they ever send a distress signal? Were there any super-sentients here when they arrived?"

"Probably not. If there had been, this might never have happened," said Kallon.

Min cocked her head and Jonas knew she was consulting her implant's database. "The Galacien never received any distress signal from Tren-dos, and there were no super-sentients to check up on them. They were cut off. The Galacien did make an effort to reach worlds such as this. Some of these missions were successful, but they were a lot closer than this place," Min said, gesturing towards the planet.

"To get this far out would have taken hundreds of years, even longer. It's quite dangerous in the void between galaxies. No planets to land on, not much stellar material at all, and no help. The Galacien are confident in their technology, but it seems they didn't want to risk it. They continued sending messages but nothing came back," said Kallon.

"They couldn't have known about the Entrophier," said Jonas "Otherwise, I'm sure they would have sent a probe to recover it."

"Perhaps not," replied Min, "What would be the point? The Galacien have been observing every nook and cranny of our galaxy for thousands of years. Their records are good enough not to need the Entrophier."

Jonas pondered this a moment. "No. This artefact is more than something functional. Its workings are a mystery to the Galacien. Who knows what secrets it could reveal and where such discoveries could lead? I for one am looking forward to uncovering precisely how it works."

The light on the command deck dimmed, tinted by a slight purple hue.

"What is it, Lom?" asked Min.

"I'm picking up a great number of vessels heading this way."

"Can you identify them?" said Min.

"I believe they're Nacuerian. I'll have a better idea soon enough."

Min looked at Jonas, alarmed.

"Don't worry. They won't be here for a while, and by then we should be long gone," he said.

"When you say a great number, how many, Lom?" asked Min.

"Hundreds."

Jonas raised his hands to calm them. "It stands to reason that this galaxy is swarming with them."

"Do you think they were dormant like the others, until our arrival?" said Min.

"I don't know, but we should begin making preparations to leave, and not be here when they arrive. Lom, you have ten more minutes with the Entrophier then I want it back on-board."

"Yes, Jonas," said the ship.

Jonas went across to Kallon. Min could sense a change between them. Jonas' manner and way of speaking had completely changed towards the other. And, now Kallon knew he was free of Jonas, he was a lot more at ease.

"How are our guests?" asked Jonas.

"Lom has restructured a cargo bay to accommodate them, which isn't a problem yet as most of them are still unconscious." Concern grew on Jonas' face. "It's all right, the ones that have come round don't remember anything about their previous... state, but they are confused and they want answers. They deserve answers."

Jonas nodded. "I will speak to them."

"You don't have to go alone," said Min.

"I know. Thank you, but I feel I must," he said, looking sternly at Kallon as he left the command deck.

Kallon's expression was a mirror of Jonas' sadness.

"He didn't have to go alone," insisted Min.

Kallon's eyes were still on the anti-grav shaft through which Jonas had exited. "Some things we must do alone."

"Why does he still punish himself for something he had no choice in?"

"To protect others."

"Who?"

"In this instance, me. Don't get me wrong. I don't flatter myself in thinking it's the sole reason."

"I don't understand," frowned Min.

"Don't forget we were the same being up until a few hundred years ago. I remember what we did, what *I* did. Discovering what the Nacuerians were at the end of the war, when the Galacien teetered on the edge of extinction. Having no choice but to make that terrible decision and destroy them. I killed them as much as he did." Guilt contorted Kallon's features and Min went to him. "He's going to tell them what happened, what they were and what we did. Can you imagine how that must feel? He's finally going to face the ghosts of our past, so I don't have to."

Jonas approached the closed doors of the cargo bay. He could feel them beyond — those whom he had only seen as a memory over two thousand years ago. If he were a less evolved being, he would have stood outside that door trying to gather the strength he needed. As it was, he paused only a moment before heading to face these 'original Nacuerians', as he thought of them. The doors slid open and the memory filled the entire bay, all too real.

He felt Lom's familiar presence in his mind.

I'm here, he said.

I need to do this alone.

I don't count; we are one, remember?

Hundreds of them lay on medical beds stacked four high, creating avenues barely wide enough to move along. Jonas was glad most of them lay unconscious and not only because he was having to face them: the bay would have been chaos were they all awake.

Are you sure? said Jonas.

Positive.

Thank you. It makes this a little more bearable.

Scores of medical bots drifted silently about the place, efficiently caring for their patients. Jonas saw that most of the conscious Nacuerians congregated at the far end of the cargo bay. He made his way over to them. He would have to face only four of them, but it was enough. A well of emotion threatened to overcome him as they turned. Even though he knew it would be difficult, he was sure he could function, yet now the time was here he found he did not know where to start.

The Nacuerians seemed unsure at his lack of communication but one of them spoke. The translator from Jonas' temporary implant performed its job perfectly.

"The one called Kallon spoke of you, Jonas. He said you saved us… saved us all," said the Nacuerian.

The final words were like a knife in his heart as he realised his jaw was clenched so tight he felt it would break. He somehow managed to open his mouth. "No... not all."

"We do not remember."

Jonas took a deep breath. "I'm going to tell you the truth... because you deserve it. You were something else, something..." Jonas swallowed.

"It is all right. I can sense that you are a good 'man'," the translator stumbled over the word, "otherwise whatever is causing you distress would not do so."

Jonas considered his words. "There is something out there, amongst the stars, between all our worlds. A god-like being, malevolent. I do not know its true name but we have dubbed it 'the Adversary'. It... happened upon your species, changed you from what I see before me now into something terrible. Then unleashed what you had become across the universe to destroy all sentient life. You came to our galaxy. We fought you but your number was too great, our end was inevitable. That is until I..." Jonas took another deep breath, "until I stopped you."

Silence stretched out across the cargo bay. The Nacuerians did not say anything in response to these revelations.

"There was no other way," finished Jonas.

The Nacuerian closest to him looked at the others and considered Jonas a moment. "You speak true. It could not be helped. Even though the act you committed seems abhorrent, you had no choice. It is clear who, or, perhaps we should say, what, is responsible. We are still grateful for what you have done."

Jonas felt unnaturally weak and an unfamiliar emotion still threatened to overwhelm him.

"You have carried this burden for a long time, haven't you?" said the Nacuerian.

Jonas only stared at the floor and nodded. He couldn't speak.

"Perhaps it is time you forgave yourself?"

"Perhaps," said Jonas.

"Then let go. Your guilt accomplishes nothing."

"It drove me to risk my friends' lives to save you today."

"Would you have not tried anyway?"

Jonas looked at the Nacuerian. He did not know.

Another newly-recovered Nacuerian joined the group.

"When can we go home?"

Again, all heads turned to Jonas.

Jonas sighed. "Your home galaxy is far from here. It would take eons to get there, and if you did finally reach your destination you would find it occupied by... your altered kin."

"Similar to what we were?"

"Yes. The first thing they did was destroy all other life in your native galaxy."

They looked appalled by this. Jonas remembered vague details of the other species which co-existed peacefully with these original Nacuerians before their unfortunate meeting with the Adversary. How their galaxy was plunged into chaos as the other space-faring species found themselves hunted down by this once peaceful and benevolent race.

"When did this happen?"

"A long time ago," said Jonas.

The atmosphere in the room had gone from grim to an almost palpable despair. He could sense their grief. It was one of his talents and, at this moment, an uncomfortable one.

"There are vague impressions of what you speak. But they are like forgotten dreams," said one of the Nacuerians.

"That's probably for the best," Jonas told him.

"However, there is one thing I do remember. A name. This... thing does have a name, of sorts."

Jonas was intrigued. He had never heard of the Adversary referred to as anything other than that.

"What is it?" he asked, holding his breath.

The Nacuerian looked around the room, thinking, until finally it said, "Rhea-hotut."

Jonas considered it, comparing the name with his vast wealth of knowledge.

"Have you heard this name before?" the Nacuerian asked him.

Jonas came up with hundreds of possibilities, but they were all inconsequential. "Unfortunately not. I don't believe there is any meaningful reference to this name in our galaxy."

"How can we help?" ventured one of the Nacuerians.

"My companions and I must return to our own galaxy. We are searching for a race known as the Kinsmen in the hope that they can help us stop the Adversary. Also, your altered kin who have overrun this galaxy are on their way. We should not be here when they arrive."

"If they are indeed our kin, can we not reason with them?"

"No. Believe me, I have looked deep into their being. There is no way you can reach them. They will kill you. We must leave and you must come with us."

"Can you do to them what you did to us?"

"No. There are too many of them, far too many. I don't think you realise how difficult it was to undo what was done to you. For the Adversary, it simply wishes and it becomes reality. I had to do so much, learn so much. We were lucky it even worked. No, there are simply too many," repeated Jonas.

"Is there no alternative?" queried the Nacuerian who had spoken first.

"There isn't. The majority of you still need medical care. We cannot leave you here in such condition, and so you must come."

The Nacuerians looked at one another making odd movements of their heads and subtle expression changes. He could tell they were debating, and, interestingly enough, all of it was non-verbal — not telepathy of any kind, only culturally-agreed gestures. He could see from their short exchanges that there were hundreds more than in any other species he'd encountered before.

Finally the self-appointed spokesman looked at Jonas. "We will go with you, Jonas, and help you find your Kinsmen, if you wish. We owe you our lives."

"Thank you but there's no need," said Jonas. "The best way you could honour me is by living and flourishing as you once did. There would be no greater gift."

Their feelings of gratitude and respect were almost too much for him to bear. Jonas found he had to leave for fear that he would break down.

“Please excuse me, I must prepare myself and the ship for our trans-galactic jump.”

Twenty-Six. Counter-strike

Earth[3]

Alex crept cautiously across the rubble of the abandoned streets of Bangkok, the humid air making his clothes stick uncomfortably to his skin. Over months of fighting the Martian war machines, Ruth had told him all about super-sentients. He didn't believe it at first.

You mean I don't have to eat, drink or sleep? he'd questioned her.

Of course not.

But I get thirsty and hungry.

Habit, said Ruth. *You've been taught to drink and sleep. You've seen others do it. You expect it of yourself.*

What happens if I don't do these things?

Nothing.

But...

Super-sentients draw their energy from an unknown power source, said Ruth, anticipating his next question.

She was right, of course. She always was.

Why am I sweating, then, if I haven't had a drink in weeks?

Your body still needs water and nutrients, only it seems to acquire these from...

This unknown power source, yeah, yeah.

No need to be like that, reprimanded Ruth.

Well, what's the use in being super-duper, when I'm still sweating cobs.

Be thankful you don't feel the heat like most sentients.

But I'm all horrible and sticky, said Alex.

Nothing compared to what the people of this planet have had to endure.

Okay, fair point, he conceded.

Alex inched forward, hugging close to the corpse of a stone building, avoiding the glass which might crack through the silence and alert his enemy to his presence. As he approached the open junction, he sneaked a glance and peered down the road. Two hundred yards away stood a silent Martian war machine.

Is this definitely the last one? he thought.

Yes.

Are you still jamming them?

No communications have been getting in or out, confirmed Ruth.

Alex had to admit Galacien technology was impressive. One of the first things Ruth had done was to build nano-machines from her own spare components which existed in hyperspace. Then she built another hyperspace link to bring them here to Earth, where they replicated and churned out all manner of tools and machines from the raw materials around them. It didn't matter whether it was the ground or the very air — the nano-machines could take any kind of matter and reconstruct it into anything they desired. She'd quickly built three satellites which now orbited this Earth, preventing all Martian communications. Another small device was sent to Earth's Moon where it began producing more nano-machines.

Are you going to tell me what you're building up there? he asked, pointing at the Moon.

Later. Focus on the matter in hand.

Alex nodded, and stepped out into the centre of the road.

"Hey!" he shouted at the Martian machine.

It turned slowly, as if it had all the time in the world. It began purposefully walking towards him.

Alex smiled. *It doesn't know it's the last one. Let it call for help.*

Ruth signalled the satellites to drop the jamming field.

The Martian machine abruptly stopped.

It's signalling for the others, said Ruth, *calling for aid. It's receiving nothing from its comrades on the Earth. It's calling Mars for reinforcements.*

I can feel its concern. Where are the others? How could this have happened?

On Alex's HUD he saw the familiar energy spike, but more than that he felt it as, predictably, the Martian fired upon him. And, as had happened so many times now, it broke across his force-field.

Is it relaying this to the others on Mars?

Yes.

Good, let's give them a good show.

The whirring began again as the Martian powered up its big gun. Alex waited until the blast was unleashed on his force-field. He held it easily. After hundreds of encounters across the globe it was always the same, and each time it got a little easier. What would have strained him weeks ago, he now found easy. Finally, the Martian stopped firing and ran towards him, throwing its full weight against his shield. Nothing happened as it continued pounding. Alex still felt each blow, but it didn't bother him nearly as much as it used to. Before it felt like someone pounding his head, now it was as if a child was trying to push him over. The Martian machine once more raised its great arms and brought them smashing down to where Alex had stood only a fraction of a second before, breaking the street into pieces and bringing up a huge cloud of dust.

"You missed," shouted Alex from behind.

The Martian swung round, crimson fire once more erupting from its single eye. Alex teleported and the

Martian succeeded in destroying a car and reducing yet another building to a pile of rubble.

"Up here," called Alex, standing on top of one of the few buildings still intact.

The Martian turned and fired again, hitting only thin air. It spun round looking for its intended target. Nothing, only the silence of the dead. It continued down the street to the nearest junction, looking from left to right, weapons humming in readiness. It stood still a moment, then suddenly fired along the adjoining street. There was no force-field this time, no teleportation. Alex violently swatted the energy blast away with his bare hand, and then the next one. He heard the high-pitched whir and brought both his hands up just in time to block the Martian fire, but the force of it was enough to lift him from his feet. He tumbled over a car and the Martian's energy beam veered off target for a second.

Alex was back upright and gestured out with his hand. The Martian's left arms and primary weapon abruptly came away from its body, sliced off, as by some giant knife. Something shimmered in the air, an empty space, into which the Martian's sliced parts disappeared. The next moment the hole to hyperspace was gone. The Martian stopped, considering this a moment, as Alex vaulted over a car bonnet and sprinted towards it, closing the gap between them. He gestured again taking away the lower part of the right leg. The Martian machine fell forward onto its left knee, supporting itself with its right arms. It pointed its one eye at Alex ready to fire. Alex jumped in the air, teleported and in a split second put his fist through the eye of the Martian machine. He pulled out his hand and backed off.

"Stay away from this planet," warned Alex.

His hand flashed in front of the Martian machine and it was gone.

Where did you send it? asked Ruth.

Floating in space between here and Mars. Hopefully they'll pick up its signal and realise what happened. Do you think the rest of them will understand?

Even if they've made no effort to understand your language, the intent was pretty obvious.

And they definitely got it? thought Alex.

Oh yes. The Martian was relaying everything it saw back to Mars right up until the moment you sent it on its way.

Use the satellites to relay it as well. Keep sending it.

Everyone turned as Alex teleported into the dimly-lit room that served as the queen's base of operations, underground at Balmoral Castle in Scotland. The officers surrounded the central table on which there were numerous maps.

"Captain," said Alex, shaking the man's hand.

He turned to each of them in turn, nodding in acknowledgment, aware of how much he'd changed over such a short space of time.

"It's been almost a week since you were last here. How goes it?" said the captain.

"Alex!" shouted a high-pitched voice as the princess came charging into him.

He could not help breaking into an enormous grin. "Hey, how's it going?" He knew she loved the way he spoke.

She smiled, "It is going well. All things considered."

Alex saw the queen approaching and he bowed, "Your Majesty."

"Alex. You were about to inform us?" suggested the queen.

"Ah yes. As I was about to tell the captain, 'we've' managed to destroy the last Martian machine." (Alex remembered trying to explain that there was someone else here with him, inside his head. That had been an interesting conversation.) "We were able to make quite a show of force which the Martian relayed back to Mars, and with it a warning never to come here again."

"Will it work?" questioned the queen.

Alex gestured to the space above the table where a holographic image of Earth and Mars came to life. Above the surface of Mars was a great mass of tiny white shapes. They reminded Alex of bacteria under a microscope, they looked so small, though he knew they were in fact giant Martian warships already heading out towards Earth at great speed. Of more immediate concern was another cluster of these ships, which had almost covered the distance between Earth and Mars.

"They're still coming," said the captain, the frustration and fatigue in his voice obvious.

Alex felt something touch his hand and looked down to see the princess holding it tightly. She was transfixed by the sight before her, her mouth open in wordless astonishment. It seemed the Martians were still determined to invade the Earth. Their first wave of scouts had already done a pretty good job of decimating Earth's cities and towns, throwing human civilisation, as they knew it here, into utter chaos. Now, from what Ruth's satellites could determine, they were sending in their main force. Giant hulking warships, fighters, more ground attack machines and millions of soldiers. Alex was speechless. He'd honestly expected them to turn back after showing them his abilities. How could he stop them?

"What is that?" asked the queen.

From behind the Moon another shape moved towards the Earth.

"More of them?" asked the captain

"One of ours, a Galacien heavy cruiser," came Ruth's voice, resonating like a calming melody around the room. She seldom spoke to them, and their reaction showed that her lack of physical presence made it easy to forget that she was here.

This is what you've been working on all this time, thought Alex

It took time, but it's finally ready, said Ruth.

The new shape was roughly conical and smooth like a pebble — a simple shape in stark contrast with its sophistication. It positioned itself between the Earth and the massive impending force of the Martian fleet. One ship against hundreds. Within seconds the Martian warships began firing projectiles, travelling at a good fraction of the speed of light. They ate up the distance between the two forces at a terrifying rate. The first projectile exploded on the Galacien ship's shield, quickly followed by over a dozen others. The Galacien ship's shield held. The Martians launched over a hundred more projectiles. The effects of this were a dazzling supernovae of light and fire. Yet the Galacien shield still did not break. The Martian cruisers were on top of the Galacien vessel and filled space with their energy weapons, all focused on one point. Yet nothing happened. The Galacien ship was surrounded by Martians, taking all the punishment they could unleash. It sat there like something eternal and immovable. Then, without any kind of warning, all the Martian ships exploded as one and were gone.

"My God. What was that?" cried Alex in astonishment.

He looked around at the others, who could only gawp at what they had witnessed.

"The Galacien vessel opened up a tiny wormhole inside each ship and delivered a small-yield zero-point energy projectile through each one," announced Ruth.

"How could they defend themselves against that?" said Alex in amazement.

"Martian technology has nothing close to defending against such an attack. Galacien ships, however, emit a dampening field which permeates their ships, preventing the opening of such wormholes."

"I guess the trick is to find a way of suppressing the dampening field."

"Yes. If this were ever to happen, then some new method of defence would be needed."

"Round and round we go," said Alex.

"If you two have finished?" said the queen trying to suppress a smile. "Does this mean we are safe?"

They all regarded the holographics. The second wave of Martian ships had stopped.

"It is over," said Ruth.

"But what if they come back?" asked the princess.

"The Galacien ship will hold its position and defend the Earth for as long as it is needed. It will watch the Martians very closely. If they are ever foolish enough to attack this planet again, the consequences will be dire."

"It is only one vessel though," said the captain. "What if they were to attack from different directions around the globe? This one ship can't be everywhere at once."

"The Galacien ship carries a full complement of smaller craft we call SIBATs, which can protect the entire surface of the planet. Rest assured, nothing will get through. It is over," Ruth promised them.

Alex knelt down and smiled at the little princess, "There's no reason to be afraid ever again."

Without hesitation she threw her arms around him. He could just make out a muffled "thank you" as she buried her face against his chest.

"Thank you from all of us," smiled the queen. "Lady Garianne said she would send someone to help, to save us, and it has come to pass. This day will be remembered throughout history as the day you saved the Earth from the Martian invasion."

Alex stood and bowed to the queen.

It seems all has ended well, said Garianne's voice in his head.

Alex froze.

Alex closed the door to his beautiful room at Balmoral Castle.

"Garianne?" he whispered.

She appeared before him as striking as he'd remembered her, yet he sensed it was merely an illusion: she wasn't real.

"Hello Alex. It seems you and the implant you've curiously named Ruth have successfully defeated the Martian invasion that threatened this Earth."

Garianne watched him patiently as he walked around her. The illusion was perfect. Only his extraordinary senses told him there was nothing actually there.

"What are you?" he said.

"Merely a simple program, by our standards, which I created to inform you of what is going on here."

"What do you mean?"

"It came to my attention that the Galacien dispatched a small fleet of ships to your Earth to collect you."

Alex recoiled. "Collect me? What do you mean?"

"Something is happening amongst the Galacien Conglomerate of Worlds here. Something sinister. They are coming, and they believe that one way or another you are going back to Galacien Prime with them."

"For what reason?"

"I don't know, but I don't trust them. The very fact that they are dismissive of your free will, your basic sentient rights, is a clear indication that we're not dealing with the Galacien that I have known and trusted all my life. Malevolent forces were gathering and I needed to send you away."

Alex nodded as if his suspicions had been confirmed.

Ruth, did you know?

No.

"It's true, your implant was never aware of what was happening," said Garianne.

"How did I get here, and why?"

"You are not the only Alex roaming across the multiverse. Some time ago I happened upon an amazing stroke of luck. Your equivalent from another universe travelled to our Earth. He found the Galacien observation agency and myself — or should I say, we found him. I managed to convince him to help us. It was he who, along with some subtle manipulation of your implant, and again, I apologise," she said, raising her hand, "who brought you to this Earth, to help them win their war against the Martians. I needed their Alex, an experienced super-sentient. In exchange I gave them you."

"Unbelievable. You've got some nerve," said Alex.

Garianne continued unfazed. "I needed you out of harm's way. You have no experience; you were in great danger back home. As you have learned, the further out you are from the multiversal singularity, the slower time moves relative to your own Earth. Your abilities have grown significantly over the weeks you have fought the Martians, yet only minutes have passed back home. With more experience you will be far more able to defend yourself against those who threaten your freedom."

"How do I get home?"

"It is feasible for you to do so now, but I would rather you didn't. When General Krrikant and his forces arrive for you, I don't want you here. If you're not here, they can't take you away."

"They can't force me."

"I wouldn't be too sure. They will be well prepared for you. Don't be overconfident with your recent successes: Martian technology is laughably primitive compared with Galacien, as you have witnessed first-hand."

Alex paced around the room, his hands clasped together in thought.

"What would you suggest?"

"The crisis there is over, however there is always more work to be done. Other Earths out there are in dire jeopardy and these would benefit from someone like you. I have secreted unique objects from these worlds in the structure of your implant in hyperspace. You can study these objects. If you concentrate hard enough, you will learn how to teleport to other Earths. This is what I wish you to do. Stay away from home, for now, and develop your abilities to help those who need it most. And, in turn, you'll be more able to defend yourself."

The Garianne figure faded, leaving Alex deep in thought.

Has she really gone? he asked Ruth.

The Garianne program has deconstructed. Alex, I swear I didn't know of its existence.

It's okay, I believe you. She planned this from the start.

It is her way. She only had your best interests at heart.

Why didn't she just tell me?

Perhaps because she thought you would say no, when the answer would have to be yes. Or perhaps there is another explanation. Garianne always has a reason, though it may not seem obvious at first.

Has anyone ever said no to her? Does she always get her own way? asked Alex.

Ruth paused for a moment. *Not often, and yes, apparently she does. What are you going to do?*

Alex looked down at the watch he wore from his own world, considering it for a moment. *What are these objects she left us?*

Twenty-Seven. Dark Encounter

Metaspace

The Antlia Dwarf galaxy receded from Jonas' viewpoint as he plunged himself yet again into the depths of the void. The feeling of total isolation enveloped his being in its icy grip. Ahead, millions of light years away, lay his own galaxy beckoning him home. He did not like it out here; the sooner he was back, the better. The harder he concentrated, the quicker his metaphysical self would be there, and then he could make the trans-galactic jump.

Something was different this time. Something was wrong. The fear that he had felt before, which would have gripped lesser beings, grew, but again he subdued it, pushed it aside. Yet this feeling was growing at an alarming rate, only held back by his sheer force of will. He realised this could not be normal.

Then he knew.

It had finally found him.

The Tren-dos System, in the Antlia Dwarf galaxy

"Something's wrong," said Min.

Jonas had informed them it wouldn't take as long as before. But as that time had come and gone, Min begun pacing the command deck and Kallon looked deeply concerned.

"What's happening, Lom? Those Nacuerian ships are getting awfully close now," worried Kallon.

"I don't know. Looking at his physiology, he seems extremely anxious."

"But that happened before, right? We know how difficult it must be," said Min.

"This seems different. He's really struggling out there."

Min looked at Kallon.

"Should we pull him out of the machine and get out of here?" Said Kallon.

"No," replied Lom. "Let me try and get through to him somehow."

Metaspace

The Adversary. It was here. It had him. It pinned him down as a lepidopterist pins a moth for study. Fear gripped him utterly and this time there was no evading it. He couldn't push it aside, or use clever psychology to ignore his predicament, for the Adversary did not wish it. It had him and it was over.

Jonas felt its power wash over him and realised his insignificance. It decided to examine his mind and it went through what he thought were his defences as if they didn't exist. All his carefully laid plans were laid bare. His darkest secrets and strategies. How clever he'd thought he was. How he and Garianne believed they could stop, what now knew everything he knew. He searched for the Kinsmen. It did not know of them. This Garianne was mobilising an army of 'super-sentients' and something else — modified memories, which the specimen was not even aware of.

Jonas felt something emanate from the entity.

It was amusement.

The Tren-dos System, in the Antlia Dwarf galaxy
Nacuerian ships jumped out of hyperspace all around them as Lom accelerated away from the planet Tren-dos.

"We should have left sooner!" exclaimed Min in frustration.

Kallon put his hand on her shoulder. "We had every reason to believe Jonas would have made the jump by now. Something is obviously wrong. Lom, report."

"It's like he is going into shock. I'm doing my best, but I can't get through to him."

"What's our tactical situation?" asked Min.

Lom displayed a holographic representation of the Trendos system. "The system is swarming with Nacuerian ships from all directions, with more arriving every minute: we are surrounded. The possibility is that we are the only source of other life in this galaxy and that is what is drawing them from light years around."

"Great. Take whatever action you feel is best, Lom. If we work through the least-densely packed areas, then perhaps we can get past them," said Min.

"Agreed," replied Lom. "However, it is only a matter of time before they close in around us."

Metaspace

Jonas was alone in the void. The overwhelming presence left without warning leaving his metaphysical being unable to move, drifting in the equivalent of the foetal position. Unable to function, his mind floated in the vast gulf of nothingness between those points of light so far away.

Nothing he did mattered. Nothing he could ever do mattered. The Adversary was the master of all creation and Jonas was only allowed to exist because he was no threat. He never had been and never would be. There was no point in looking for the Kinsmen. There was no reason to continue. He saw the universe revolve lazily around him, until one point of light caught his attention.

Antlia Dwarf.

Min.

They were in trouble. In the other direction lay his own galaxy. Slowly, with a grim determination he set off towards it, hoping this time his fragile mind could survive the journey.

The Tren-dos System, in the Antlia Dwarf galaxy

It was hopeless.

Thousands of projectiles homed in slowly but surely towards Lom. He reacted by shooting a volley of interceptors. The SIBATs he'd launched also sped to meet this deadly assault. Their weapons flared wildly, taking down dozens. But there were too many. Like a giant multi-taloned claw, the projectiles closed in on their target, cutting down all hope of escape. But, before they hit, Lom was consumed in light. Space-time scrunched up around the vessel. The path of the Nacuerians' projectiles twisted in all directions, unable to track their prey, destroying one another or veering away from Lom, curving around him completely. The distortions built as did the intensity of light.

The Milky Way Galaxy

Min and Kallon ran into Lom's engine room.

Jonas sat there disengaged from the machine, unconscious.

"Lom, is he all right?" cried Min.

"We need to get him to the medical bay," said Kallon.

Jonas' lips began to move.

"No," he croaked. "There is nothing you can do that can help me."

"Why will you not let me back in?" asked Lom

"What's that?" queried Min to the ship.

"We are a part of one another, but he's put up a barrier round his mind," said the ship. "Jonas, I can't help you if you won't let me in."

Jonas slowly opened his eyes. In them Min could only see fear and despair. She had not seen anything resembling that look since they had first revealed the true nature of the universe to his naïve young mind thousands of years ago.

"You do not want to see what I have seen, know what I know."

"Jonas, what happened?" said Kallon.

Jonas considered him. Seeing a version of himself, blissfully ignorant of the nightmare he'd witnessed, unaware of the truth of what was happening all around them — how could he tell them?

"I... there were some unforeseen complications on the return journey. I am sorry to have worried you all."

"It was a little close back there," said Min.

Jonas didn't hear her as he stared at the floor. He knew he was still in shock.

"Leave me," said Jonas.

"But...." protested Min.

Jonas looked at Kallon, something passing between them.

Kallon took Min's hand. "Come."

They both left, Min turning back as they did.

Jonas sat alone in silence.

"You want in?" he said to Lom.

"I want to help."

"Know one thing, though: if I think you cannot handle it, I will erase your memory of the experience."

"That bad?" observed Lom, without a hint of humour.

"Worse."

Jonas opened up and felt Lom enter his mind, experiencing what he had out there in the void.

It was some time before Lom spoke to him again.

It's more terrifying than anything we imagined, said Lom.

Do you want to forget?

No. We will share this burden.

Jonas could not hide the well of gratitude threatening to overcome him.

Thank you, old friend. I fear if not for you, I would now be contemplating giving up and ending it all. I know that may come as a shock to you since you're aware that I have faced the kind of despair unknown by most mortals. Yet this is so... Jonas struggled. *Planning in secret for two thousand years. My deception. Pretending that I was less than what I truly am, what I am capable of. And for what?*

I know. The Adversary hardly seems an appropriate name any more, for it suggests resistance, which we both know is impossible. Perhaps I should destroy myself, and all of us with me, to save from further pain in the future? suggested Lom.

Are you serious?

A little. However, I think you've overlooked something.

Oh?

Obviously your personal experience has affected you a lot more seriously than my observation of the said events. You have lost a little objectivity. So overwhelmed by this entity's apparent omnipotence, you have missed something which may give us a shred of hope.

Which is?

I know it is painful to go back there, but try and remember. What did you sense from it?

Jonas sighed heavily. *It does not see any of us as a threat. It sees everything and everyone as a game for its own perverse amusement. Super-sentients are no threat. Nothing is.*

I've seen what you've seen and what you sensed, replied Lom. *There was something else: it did not want you to know because it wants you to believe it is truly omnipotent.*

What?

The only true thing which is a mystery to it: the Kinsmen. It does not know who or what they are.

Jonas pondered this for a moment.

There is one more thing — something we must never discuss in front of the others.

Oh? said Lom.

The Adversary discovered modifications to my memories.

When did this happen?

I'm not sure, responded Jonas, *only that it happened during my time on Terra.*

That doesn't narrow the time-scale down much.

I know. I had no inkling of this. Whoever did this managed to implant false memories in my mind to account for the ones erased.

Concern laced Lom's voice. *How long are we talking about? And which memories have been falsified?*

Difficult to tell. Days was the impression I got from the Adversary, no longer.

Who could do such a thing, and why? said Lom.

I don't know, but there must be a reason.

They had spent the last two days settling the Nacuerians onto a new world, devoid of sentient life and perfectly suited for their needs. Jonas told them they could start here all over again and forget the nightmare of their past. Jonas easily infiltrated the Galacien probe which observed this remote world and made sure that the Galacien would receive false readings that this world remained lifeless. No-one visited this world. No-one. Though, if they should attract the attention of the Adversary, then all his good work would be undone. He now saw the Adversary as a force of nature. On Earth, people were at risk of floods, earthquakes and pandemics. The Adversary was yet another natural predator like this: whole species were wiped out, or changed into weapons of chaos and destruction.

It happened.

Shouldn't he just accept that? Yet he knew deep down that the Adversary wasn't natural. Somehow he knew that this entity had once been something else.

He had done all he could for the Nacuerians. They had as much chance on this world as any of them did on any world, and that was enough.

Gone was his confident stride. His gait was almost timid, as Jonas entered the command deck.

Remember, they're here for you, we all are, he heard Lom in his mind.

They both looked at him expectantly.

"We're here," said Jonas.

"Where?" said Min.

"Over two thousand years ago the Nacuerian forces decimated the Amelerian system. You were there Min, we all were. In a desperate attempt to learn more about our foes, I boarded one of their vessels. I was taken captive."

"I remember," nodded Kallon.

This brought the merest hint of a smile to Jonas' lips.

"And?" pushed Jonas.

"You… we learned how to interface with their system and, to some degree, take control. There was something else in the Nacuerian system, however, something old and powerful. It described itself as a remnant."

"Of the Kinsmen?" said Min.

Jonas nodded, "Yes." He held up the Entrophier and placed it in front of them. It kept itself there suspended in the air.

"Lom, darken the command deck."

The room was plunged into darkness and the stars came out all around. Lom had made it appear as if they stood unsupported in the heavens.

"I have calculated the precise point in space where I encountered the Kinsmen entity. Once we are in sync with that time-frame, Lom will keep pace with the Nacuerian ship from over two millennia ago."

With a mental command from Jonas the two parts of the Entrophier broke apart, encircling them with a bright screen.

"And now we look back," said Jonas.

With this they were enveloped in an odd organic landscape of differing shades of grey. Shimmering light darted in all directions like scurrying insects, hard at work.

"What is this?" said Min.

Jonas looked at Kallon.

"It's the Nacuerian system — how we perceived it," said Kallon.

"This is when I decided to confront the entity within the Nacuerian system. My dialogue with it was non-vocal, however I've arranged to have the Entrophier vocalise it for us. Look there," said Jonas, indicating a point of light now in a quiet area of the system.

"My name is Jonas. Who are you?" came Jonas' voice from the past.

"Incredible!" gasped Min.

She looked at Jonas, but could see he was so completely focused, she didn't dare distract him.

"I know you desire to keep your existence unknown. I will tell no other of our encounter if that is your wish, though perhaps an exchange of knowledge may benefit us both?" continued Jonas' past self.

Min then heard another voice, like the rumble of distant thunder.

"Is that what you desire, Jonas, knowledge?"

"Is that...?" said Min.

Kallon nodded.

"Yes, knowledge and solitude," said past Jonas.

"Yes we know of you, Jonas, better than you know yourself."

"It seems then that you have me at a disadvantage, for I know nothing of you."

"Few do."

"Who do?" asked past Jonas.

"The Phalinon know, yet they do not."

"What do you mean?"

"They possess the information, awareness of its significance is another matter."

"Why don't you just tell me?" said past Jonas.

"This is part of the necessary process, Jonas. One day you will understand."

Jonas was taken aback. "No, surely not?"

"What is it?" said Min.

But Jonas didn't reply.

"Who are you?" said the Jonas from the past.

"A remnant."

"A remnant of what?"

"The Kinsmen."

Jonas paused their view of the past. "I've got a lock on their energy signature." The left side of his mouth turned up slightly. "It's elusive, but I've got it."

"Where is it?" said Kallon, equally as curious as Jonas, for he had been there too.

"It jumped into hyperspace." His head cocked to one side as the view from the past slowly played out at a significantly slow speed. They saw the system being enveloped by light as the Nacuerian ship self-destructed. "Now they've slipped into Metaspace."

"I don't think they wanted to be followed, whether in the past or by viewers from another time," commented Min.

"Wait!" shouted Jonas.

They both looked questioningly at him.

"They just left Metaspace."

"Into what?" said Min.

But Jonas was studying the viewer of the Entrophier with a concentration and sense of wonder she had rarely seen before.

"Somewhere we've never been before," said Kallon.

"I don't understand. What else is there?" said Min.

"Just because we have no proof of another facet of reality, that doesn't mean it doesn't exist," explained Jonas.

"But why didn't the super-sentients of the past sense it?" said Min.

"We put too much faith in the legends of times long gone. Despite their incredible abilities and wisdom, there are still some mysteries they never solved," said Kallon.

The Entrophier broke apart and the viewer disappeared. Jonas gestured and it landed neatly in the palm of his hand.

"There is another region of space which exists beyond normal, hyper and metaspace. I saw where they went. I will follow and take the Entrophier with me to track them down. I will find the Kinsmen."

"Then I'm coming with you, brother," said Kallon.

They both looked at Min who, after a moment, nodded in agreement.

Twenty-Eight. The End

Earth[18]

From nowhere something appeared.

A brief flash of light and Alex teleported in. He looked around at the war-torn road which encircled the miraculously still-standing statue of Queen Victoria. Everywhere else was rubble and ruin, including Buckingham Palace. A giant alien ship sat beside it.

"Well, this looks familiar," muttered Alex.

That's not a very precise evaluation," came Ruth's voice from the air around him.

"I'll leave the details to you — you're very good with them."

"Usual protocols?"

"Yeah. Get the boys in the air so we can see what the situation is. I don't want any surprises like the last time," said Alex.

"That was because you were getting overconfident, sloppy and..."

"All right, all right. Are they on their way?"

"Give me a moment to build them... Done. Launching," announced Ruth.

Alex could sense the three invisible probes, each as big as a tennis ball, accelerating hard towards Earth's upper atmosphere. He heard distant screams and explosions from the direction of the Houses of Parliament.

With a thought he was there, in the shadows of the broken buildings, watching.

Getting something from the satellites. Oh dear, he heard Ruth in his mind.

What is it?

This isn't a local invasion we're dealing with here.

Then who...

The giant creature teleported in just behind Alex. Its strong black tentacles reached out enveloping his arms, wrapping themselves around his neck.

Nacuerian, thought Ruth.

With all his strength, Alex threw it against a broken wall. He found himself being dragged along with it as they pirouetted across the desolate road.

It's as strong as an ox. Any suggestions? thought Alex.

He pushed it away. For a fraction of a second he created a flash portal to hyperspace between them, cutting off its tentacles where they intersected. He quickly followed through by decapitating the creature in the same manner.

Never mind.

Several more of the creatures suddenly appeared around him and immediately fired their weapons but Alex already had a force-field up. They continued to teleport in until there were dozens of them, each firing its weapon on his force-field, putting more pressure on it than he'd ever experienced before.

A little help would be nice, thought Alex.

Give me a minute.

A minute?!

I need time to build!

Through gritted teeth, Alex pushed out the boundary of his force-field. The Nacuerians stopped firing and pulled back.

I've just lost the satellite covering this part of the globe. I think we should go. We're bound to draw unwanted attention.

This 'is' unwanted attention, said Alex.

He watched the Nacuerians pacing around the edge of his force-field.

Alex, I mean something worse like... I'm sensing a large body closing on our position from above.

Alex slowly looked up, his senses reaching to the heavens, screaming in warning at what was coming. He felt the pressure build at a terrifying rate and a sickening roar paralysing him with terror.

You've got to be kidding me!

Go! screamed Ruth in his head.

He teleported almost completely blind, south onto a field in France. He landed in a crouched position and braced himself. Would it be far enough or would he have to teleport again? He tensed, poised and ready. He saw a great flash of light.

What the hell just happened?

The Nacuerians are bombarding the Earth with meteors. They must have brought them from the asteroid belt; they're pushing them into Earth's gravity well.

They're pushing them towards us and Earth's gravity does the rest?

I'm afraid so. The original satellite was destroyed by the Nacuerians. My two remaining satellites have informed me that the Earth is being bombarded over its entire surface, and I think it's going to get a lot worse.

I don't understand. Why are they doing this?

The Nacuerians exist to destroy life.

Is it me, or is every Earth we go to getting invaded or on the brink of extinction?

It's not you. Garianne obviously wants us to help.

Something else is going on here, I can feel it, thought Alex, finally standing up and looking north. *Does the*

Adversary exist here, and if so, is it the same one we're dealing with in our own universe or a parallel one?

Garianne believes there is only one working across the multiverse.

Then it travelled to this universe and created these Nacuerians as it did in our own. We also reckon it's been interfering with other species, like our friends the Martians?

Almost certainly, affirmed Ruth.

How many other universes has it been to? How far does this go?

As if in answer, Alex heard the great roar from the explosive impact on London hundreds of kilometres away. Moments later the shockwave reached him, reduced now to a strong gale. It grew dark as the clouds slowly filled the sky, blocking out the sun. Anyone could see this wasn't a natural storm.

It was a big one, Alex. Not enough to threaten the planet, but the Greater London area has been obliterated. The south east of England will be a wasteland. Millions dead. I think we should go — floods will be coming.

My God. It won't come this far in, surely?

Difficult to tell. Perhaps, perhaps not.

This is madness, Ruth. We need to do something, and do it quick, before everyone is dead. Can't you build another ship?

I would need to build at least twenty ships to take on the forces they have in orbit. It would take years.

Alex shook his head. *We simply don't have that long.*

Then I'm afraid it's up to you.

Wait. What about the Galacien in this universe?

"Dead," said a voice.

Alex turned to see a standing figure in some kind of body suit conforming to her tall athletic form, even covering her face. His extraordinary senses seemed to break against her like waves upon the rocks. She stood there regarding him, as still as a stone statue, with the dark, rolling storm behind her.

Who the hell is that? Why can't I read her, Ruth?

"Because I don't want you to," said the woman.

"You're reading my mind. Stop it."

She didn't reply. She didn't move.

Ruth?

Interesting. Her attire is that of Galacien origin, but different. She's obviously human. Can you hear me as well as him?

"I can," said the woman.

There was another flash of light, this time from the south-east.

"Who are you? Are the Galacien really all gone?" said Alex.

"They are," confirmed the woman.

"And the others?" asked Ruth.

The woman shook her head slowly. "All that remains are the primitive worlds such as Earth. Galacien Prime is nothing more than debris in space. All the GCW worlds are gone. Any such life which remains is being hunted down. This galaxy is lost."

The woman looked out across the fields to her left. The wind mercilessly battered the trees in the distance. There was a slow cracking of timber as a tree was torn in two by the force of the gale. Alex maintained his balance by sheer determination. The woman still stood unaffected, almost completely motionless.

"It's coming," she said.

"What is?" asked Alex.

She looked up.

Alex followed her gaze and reached out with his senses. "Oh no."

"It's too late for them," said the woman.

"No," said Alex.

Alex, we need to leave this world now, said Ruth

The woman started walking away from him.

"Wait, wait!" he shouted over the roaring wind.

She ignored him and carried on.

He teleported in front of her and she stopped, yet he had the feeling she was extremely dangerous. He should be careful not to push his luck.

"Wait, please."

"You can't save them all," said the woman.

There was a great flash of light which seemed to be everywhere at once.

"It is already too late," said the mysterious woman. "Only minutes remain until this Earth is utterly destroyed. I suggest you leave now."

Without warning, she disappeared.

Alex pushed out his senses as hard as he could, but she was gone. All he could detect was the impending wave of destruction heading their way. A fountain pen appeared in his hand.

I suggest we go. Here is the next item, appealed Ruth.

With a strange mix of awe and frustration, Alex watched as the Earth tore up around him. The winds had reached terrifying speeds. Were he a normal human being, he would surely have been blown away by this great force. The sky was full of debris, both natural and man-made. Alex felt the pressure from the imminent meteor impact building.

This is the end of the world, he thought.

And with that he teleported.

Twenty-Nine. Confrontation

The Galacien Institute for Technological Advancement, Earth

Garianne didn't move a muscle as holographic images flashed up at lightning speed before her eyes. She absorbed the text instantly, evaluated and confirmed it. To the untrained eye it looked as though there was a problem with the display, such was the speed at which she worked.

"What are you doing?" questioned Nicola.

"Just finishing some 'paperwork', before we proceed."

"About that. Granted, I'm up to speed now with your fight against this Adversary, I'm still not sure whether to believe that one, and the current status quo in this corner of your universe. However, I'd like to know a little more about what happens now? If you want me to protect you, a job which I'm highly dubious about, since you seem quite capable of protecting yourself, then..."

"One can't have too much protection," interrupted Garianne, not looking away from her work. "Someone to cover my back, as it were."

Nicola continued, scowling, "The money is more than enough, but I need a little more information about what's going on. You're not telling me everything."

"We'd be here a very long time if I told you everything, Nicola," said Garianne, her attention still focused on the holographics.

Nicola shook her head in frustration, "Listen, I'm not sure I want to get involved in all of this."

Garianne stopped what she was doing and looked up at Nicola. "Let me give you a little insight into how the universe works. All of life is a series of tests. Some of these tests are easy in which the stakes are relatively small. Others are more difficult, where the stakes are high. Pass the test and reap the benefits, chief among these, some may argue, is the lesson itself. Move onto the next level where you have the potential to grow and reap even greater rewards. Fail the test and suffer. If you fail, the world will just keep throwing it back at you, until you get it right. However be under no illusion, reality was never designed this way, as some may have you believe. It just is. The Adversary, as we call it, is also another test. Another puzzle to solve, with the highest stakes imaginable. Analogous to the test or trial Earth currently faces with Sol 9173. The

Adversary threatens us all, hence we are 'all' involved: we are all a part of it."

There was a knock on the door, and James entered the room. "General Krrikant's fleet has entered Earth's orbit. I informed them you would meet in the main hall."

"Thank you, James, I'll be out in a moment," said Garianne, as James left the room.

Nicola folded her arms, her mouth tightening into a thin line. "This is what I'm talking about."

The holographic images before Garianne disappeared "There, all done." She stood up and turned towards Nicola. "Things may get a little... dramatic very soon. I believe you can help us in the difficult times ahead. I really do, Nicola, that's why I want you here."

"But why me? I've seen your technology and it's way beyond my understanding. I don't belong here," said Nicola.

"No, but there is something different about you."

"What do you mean?" asked Nicola cautiously, fearing the answer.

Garianne paused a moment, as if considering something. "All I ask is that you do what comes naturally and trust your instincts. Come."

Garianne left her office with Nicola in tow, briefly running her hand over her weapons as if for comfort. They walked down the corridor, making their way to the main hall.

"So who is this Krrikant guy? And what does he want?" said Nicola.

"He's not a guy, he's a Galacien general. And I believe he wants Alex," replied Garianne as they reached the main hall's doors. James and Aleksandr from Nicola's universe waited for them.

"But..." began Nicola.

"James, I see we are all here," observed Garianne.

"Yes," said James.

"Then let's not keep the good general waiting," said Garianne, opening the doors and entering the hall.

Awaiting them was Krrikant, Korina and over a dozen Galacien warriors.

Krrikant frowned at Garianne's human attire. "Cieshella Garianne Phulum, Chief Observation Agent of the planet Earth. You are hereby ordered by the Galacien supreme council to hand over the human super-sentient known as Alex Lethbridge."

Garianne took her time walking to the centre of the hall and regarding her visitors. "May I see the order?"

Krrikant gave a slow nod as he sent it to her implant.

The silence was complete as Garianne took her time reading the order. Korina looked nervously at her husband, James, who routinely clenched and unclenched his jaw. All he wanted to do was take her out of here and hold her in his arms.

"Well?" said Krrikant.

"This is an order allowing you to extradite him from his home planet, by force if necessary. This is not our way. What if he doesn't want to go?" demanded Garianne.

"That is of no consequence. The current situation has changed, Garianne. Perhaps you've not noticed because your attention has been focused on this world alone. War has broken out all over the galaxy. The Galacien needs to get a hold of the situation before it gets out of control. We need someone to rally our forces to give us an edge. We need him." Krrikant pointed at Alex.

"Him?" Garianne looked at Aleksandr. "You don't have any authority to take him."

"Perhaps you didn't understand the order..."

"I understood every word." Garianne's eyes glazed over as she considered the message again. "The order was to collect the super-sentient Alex Lethbridge of Earth, this particular planet." She looked at Krrikant. "But this Alex is from another Earth. He is not from this Earth, not of this universe, and thus the order does not apply to him."

Krrikant and the others looked at one another. "We will have to verify this, to make sure there is no deception on your part."

"Of course."

With a wave of his hand, Krrikant ordered one of his people to step forward. The warrior stretched out his hand towards Aleksandr. Light danced around the Galacien warrior's fingertips as he scanned Aleksandr up and down.

The atmosphere in the room was tense. Aleksandr's ire was obvious, and Nicola took in every minute detail of those she viewed as her opponents. James only wanted the situation to resolve itself and to finally be alone with his wife. Garianne, in stark contrast to the others, seemed relaxed and at ease.

The warrior turned back to Krrikant and through his implant sent the results.

Krrikant took a deep breath of annoyance. "How does this creature come to be here?"

"He's a multiversal teleporter. Isn't it obvious how he got here?" said Garianne.

"You expect me to believe this is a coincidence, while this universe's Alex has disappeared?"

"By their very nature you would expect them to travel the multiverse. Not finding this Earth's Alex here is no more unusual than you leaving your home world, Krrikant."

"And you have no idea when our Alex will return, I expect?"

Garianne shook her head. "No, sorry."

Krrikant glanced momentarily at Aleksandr. "Then I must insist you hand over this Alex."

"Don't be ridiculous. The Galacien cannot force him," said Garianne.

"It was not a request," growled Krrikant.

At this his warriors' weapons hummed to life and they took their first steps towards Garianne's group.

Faster than anyone could have expected, Nicola's gun was under Krrikant's jaw. "Stop, or the next thing to happen will be... unfortunate."

Krrikant sneered at her. "You are ill-informed; my kind can't be killed."

"Yes, I know all about your backed-up memories, but it's still going to be a pretty big set-back. I mean, you'll miss the party here for a start, and you'll forget about this lovely encounter. Sure, you'll be told. But it's not quite the same as being here, is it?"

Garianne remained impassive as if nothing had happened, while the others were tense, unmoving, unsure what to do or say.

Krrikant blinked, looking genuinely concerned, while Nicola smiled.

"Garianne, who is this creature?" said Krrikant.

"Why do you ask?"

"She is not human. She is something else," he observed, curiously.

The others looked at one another while Garianne remained silent.

Krrikant continued, "My warriors have been trying to disable her brain with a momentary disruption of the synapses. Unlike our kind, she has no implant to shield against such an attack. Nevertheless, we cannot get through. There is no technology, or link to such technology, which we can perceive. I can only conclude that she is not human. Again I postulate the question, what is she?"

With Nicola's gun still pushed under his jaw, Krrikant looked at each of them.

"Do any of you know? Do you?" he questioned, looking at Garianne.

"I suggest you leave while you still can," said Garianne.

"Not until I have what I came for," snapped Krrikant.

Aleksandra's fists tightened. "Just try it."

"I shall."

With frightening speed three things happened: the Galacien Warriors fired on Aleksandr, he instinctively teleported, and Nicola fired.

Krrikant fell dead on the floor. What had been his head now spread over the floor behind him. His warriors considered this only a moment, then teleported out of the hall, leaving Korina stunned. James gasped at the dead Galacien lying before them. Korina ran to him and they hugged one another tight.

"Korina, what's going on? This is crazy?"

"I don't know," she replied, regarding the body of Krrikant.

If there was any remorse for what Nicola had done, she didn't show it. She turned to Garianne. "I take it you don't approve?"

"He was warned," said Garianne coldly. "However, I suspect he may be carrying another body on his ship and it is only a matter of time before his copy is downloaded into that body. We haven't seen the last of him."

"Garianne, what happened?" said James.

"Krrikant took a chance."

"What chance?" said Korina.

"That his warriors could tag Aleksandr before he teleported out, and they did. Not all of the microscopic projectiles hit their target. Some lay around this room. I've managed to secure one and analyse it," said Garianne.

"What do they do?" said Korina.

"They disrupt his nervous system enough to distract him. I'd be surprised if he got very far. After that, they will attempt to paralyse him. They're very sophisticated. Remember, though, he is super-sentient so it should take some time for them to have a significant effect on him."

"Krrikant's people are no doubt attempting to locate him now," realised Korina.

"What do we do?" asked James.

"We've been ordered by the Supreme Council not to interfere, so apparently there is nothing we can do," said Garianne.

James shook his head in dismay and Nicola's frustration was obvious.

"Nicola, on the other hand, is another matter. She is not a part of the Galacien Observation Agency for Earth."

In a dark alleyway twenty feet in the air, Aleksandr appeared, and fell. He spun chaotically, his arms flailing around, until he landed in a pile of bin bags, their stinking contents scattering all around. For a moment all was still, and, as he realised where he was, he jumped out from the mass of waste.

"That's disgusting!"

Aleksandr looked around. His senses didn't seem quite as keen as they usually were. He didn't feel quite as strong as he usually did.

"This isn't where I'm supposed to be. What happened?" grumbled Aleksandr, looking around in confusion. "It must be what they hit me with."

"It is," said a voice from above.

Aleksandr looked up to see one of Krrikant's warriors floating in mid-air. There was no sound or any indication of how it did this. He was aware of how advanced their technology was, but it was unnerving nonetheless. Was he kidding himself in thinking he could fight this enemy? Was he completely outclassed?

"What did you do to me?"

"What we've introduced into your system is, at this very moment, preventing you from leaving this universe, this world. You will become weaker and weaker until you will no longer be able to teleport. Surrender to us. General Krrikant will be here soon. You can't resist us," boomed the Galacien warrior.

Aleksandr knew this thing was right. He could feel an unnatural exhaustion beginning to tighten its grip on him, but he couldn't give up. With grim determination he teleported once more.

The Galacien warrior calmly watched him go. Time was on their side, and Aleksandr wasn't going far.

Garianne, James, Korina and Nicola entered Garianne's office. As the lights dimmed, an enormous, perfectly-realised, three-dimensional holographic Earth sprang to life.

"Where is he now?" asked Nicola.

James looked at the holographics. "Lost him. He must have teleported again. The good news is that if we can't see him, then neither can they."

Korina frowned. Looking at Garianne she said, "I thought your wormholes covered every nook and cranny of Earth. This should be impossible."

"They do. Perhaps he has found a way to avoid detection," said Garianne simply.

"Do you really believe that?" retorted Korina.

James looked surprised by his wife's choice of words, and even more so by her attitude to Garianne. He felt sure Garianne wouldn't let it slide, yet she only stood there scrutinising the holographics as if the question had never been asked.

Korina turned to James. "Where is the Alex native to this Earth?"

"I don't know. We made contact with him after a group of meta-humans from Galacien Prime tried to abduct him. He received an implant, and since then he has simply disappeared. He was in bed at his home when he teleported. From the residual energy he left when he teleported, we suspect he left this universe entirely. Who knows where he is now."

"Who indeed," said Korina suspiciously.

James looked at her. *What is wrong with you?* he asked her privately through his implant.

What do you mean?

You're questioning me and almost interrogating Garianne.

I'm sorry, but the Galacien are desperate to get their hands on a super-sentient. You must have seen the reports by now. For the first time ever, the Galacien Conglomerate of Worlds is beginning to break apart. We need something to bring it all back together. We need him. I don't understand why Garianne is fighting against that. I don't trust her and I'm not the only one who feels that way.

You've never mentioned this before, thought James.

Well, it's true. Even some of her old allies are questioning both her motives and her decisions of the past, Melntoria Kendeisa being the most notable.

Min? thought James, trying to hide his surprise.

Yes, we became quite good friends back on Galacien Prime. Min never explained why, however she said to me on more than one occasion that she could never completely trust her. That Garianne manipulates those around her to fulfil her own goals.

Min said that? Why? thought James.

She didn't say. Only she had her reasons, which she didn't want to go into.

James sighed as he glanced at Garianne.

Thirty. Galacien48

East of Dungarvan, on the south coast of Ireland, Earth[48]

Alex sat down, a few feet from the sheer drop of the cliff top. The sea stretched out before him. He could hear the waves breaking against the shore far below, feel the grass between his fingers. He couldn't sense a single soul for kilometres around. This was a good thing. He just wanted to sit here and listen to the sea.

Do you want to talk about it? asked Ruth.

He did not reply, merely shrugged his shoulders.

Perhaps a hug? A shoulder to cry on? she suggested.

You don't have shoulders.

Beside him threads of gold light danced in the air while others seemed to trace around unseen objects. He then saw the basic form of a woman, as if sketched out by an invisible artist. The form slowly became more solid and he saw points on its skin blossom into being, spreading like a white fluid as they coalesced together until this being was fully realised. The monochrome face was typically beautiful yet lacked anything unique to a normal person, much like a mannequin. This mannequin looked down at him, its soft skin almost glowing in the sun as it smiled.

"Now I do," said Ruth out loud, mouth unmoving as the rest of her body flowed into being before him.

"How are you doing this?" wondered Alex.

"Basic construction, the same way I've built things in the past. This time, though, I thought you could do with some physical company. This is just a morphic shell, skin only. I haven't the time to build a fully anatomically correct human and there would be no point. This shell can simulate skeletal and muscle movement from the node that exists within," said Ruth, illustrating her point by twisting her torso and articulating the joints in her arms.

She smiled, yet with lifeless eyes it was a little unnerving.

"Would you like that shoulder now?" She sat beside him on the grass.

He looked at her. "It's... okay."

She looked out to the sea. "I know it hasn't been easy for you, this last year. We've seen a lot of death. Things I too would rather forget."

"Can't you simply erase those memories?"

"Then you would have no-one to share them with, no-one who understands what you've gone through. But remember, you have made a difference. Think of all the lives you've saved."

Alex looked at her. "Thanks for being there with me. I don't think I could have done it without you."

"Definitely not," she said.

Alex nodded, "It wasn't just me — it was us."

He looked closely into her eyes; they were changing. Instead of plain white, he could see they were slowly becoming real. The retina, pupil, lens and iris were all being constructed at an incredible speed.

Ruth said, "Blue eyes I think, like the sky. The eye is a beautiful thing; beautiful and complex. You don't fully appreciate how complex until you have to build one. Eyebrows and eyelashes," she continued as Alex watched in fascination as they grew in mere seconds from seemingly nowhere. She touched her still bald, white head. "What colour hair should I have? Perhaps green, like the grass."

"Are you kidding?"

"No, I'm from a conglomerate of sentient alien species of every kind imaginable. Green hair is hardly excessive."

"Whatever you want, Ruth," he said amused.

A thick mane of green hair slowly grew from her head; it was all the shades of the grass they sat on. When it passed her shoulders Alex wondered when it would stop. It slowed and eventually stopped at her lower back. She put her fingers through it and looked at it, slowly nodding her approval.

Ruth stood up and looked down at her plain white mannequin-like body. "Hmmm. Now, what should we do with this?"

"Perhaps we should stop there for now and get this job out of the way? Then we can finally go back home."

She turned to him. "Do you think you can get us back then?"

"I've done enough universe hopping now. After this, we're going home."

She glanced up at the sky.

"What is it?" asked Alex.

"You're not going to like this," said the Ruth mannequin, "but I've got a Galacien warship coming out of hyperspace with orders to destroy the human populace."

Alex stood and looked up as well. He could feel them up there.

"That doesn't make sense. Why would they do that?"

"We are in an alternate universe. Perhaps the Galacien here are not as benign as back home. Their technology seems pretty much as advanced as ours, so I'd better get my satellites out of range, before they're detected. I've managed to get a little data though," said Ruth. Her eyes narrowed and her head cocked to one side. "That's odd."

"What is?"

"They've launched a few guardian-class SIBATs. At this moment they're descending through Earth's lower atmosphere. The warship's jumped out of the system."

"Just a few? That shouldn't be too bad."

"Three guardian-class SIBATs are more than enough to reduce the Earth to ashes."

"Hey, I've got you to watch out for me! Now, where are these things heading?"

"New York, Beijing and London."

"Great. What is it with these guys and London?"

Ruth shrugged.

"Well, I'm tired of it. That's where we're going. Where in London?"

"Trafalgar Square."

"What? Again? Weren't we there just last week?"

"Three weeks ago," Ruth corrected him. "Same place, different universe."

Alex took one long, last look at the peaceful surroundings of the southern coast of Ireland before teleporting to the crowded Trafalgar Square in London. A woman yelped at his sudden appearance and several tourists who had also seen him teleport backed away.

I think you're unique look is attracting attention, thought Alex. He regarded the porcelain white woman with green hair beside him.

"I'm not the one who teleported us into a crowded square," she pointed out.

Alex smiled. She didn't care about what she looked like to them. Why would she?

People were starting to take pictures.

"Anyway," she continued, "I think they're going to have more pressing concerns in just a moment." She looked up at the giant guardian-class SIBAT descending from the sky, only a dark speck in the bright sky, but it was slowly getting larger. True enough, many of the people in the square were now looking up in awe. Then, there was a moment throughout the crowds when there was a sudden realisation that this thing was going to land on top of them.

Alex was about to tell them to move when he saw the masses were already running away in all directions. Only they held their ground as the towering SIBAT descended.

Except, Alex felt something familiar nearby. He turned to see Theresa gazing at him, a look of puzzlement on her face, not ten feet away. Alex froze. He hadn't seen her in ages.

This is not your sister, said Ruth. *She is an alternate version.*

Does she have a brother? Someone like me?

No. I've checked this Earth's data-grid. Alex Lethbridge was never born on this world. She is an only child.

The eyes of his sister's doppelganger broke to the SIBAT above.

"Get away," shouted Alex. "Run and don't stop."

She looked at him, with saucer eyes, like a rabbit caught in the headlights unable to move. Then suddenly, she fled.

Alex watched her go, realising how much he missed his sister and his home. This place was so much like it.

I think we should pay attention to the matter in hand, suggested Ruth.

The giant SIBAT landed surprisingly gently.

Suggestions?

Don't bother teleporting it away because it will only come back. You'll have to cut it apart using your hyperspace portals. Be quick and be ruthless.

Alex gestured at the SIBAT, with the intention of intersecting the giant's midsection and sucking its top half into hyperspace.

Nothing.

"What happened?" he said.

"It must be shielded. Somehow it's able to nullify close proximity wormholes of the type you can create. This is something the Galacien back home can't do. They may be more advanced than I initially thought," concluded Ruth.

The towering SIBAT turned to face them, seeming to notice them for the first time.

"We're being scanned," said Ruth. "No. It's trying to break down my defences. I..."

Ruth fell to her knees.

Alex immediately went to her side.

She looked at him. "It's... no... Help... me... Alex," she pleaded.

He felt rage build inside him.

"Leave her alone!" he shouted at the SIBAT as he lashed out with a force-field stronger than he had ever felt before. The giant SIBAT flew backwards across the square and tore through the National Gallery, disappearing in a mass of rubble. Alex looked back to see Ruth lying on the ground. He sensed that she was no longer under any kind of attack, but she had suffered.

He stood between her and his fallen foe, expecting it back at any moment.

Ruth.

There was no answer.

The SIBAT exploded from the rubble, and as it landed it fired a blue beam of energy at Alex. His force-field held. He could feel wormhole points begin to open inside the force-field and created a secondary field around him to prevent their existence.

The unseen wormholes vanished.

"Not the only one who can do that," he snarled at his opponent.

Alex, he heard her in his mind.

Ruth.

The others are coming! You must end this quickly or they will overwhelm you and we will be finished.

The SIBAT before him unleashed a ridiculous amount of energy against Alex's force-field. Somehow he held it. *If only I could teleport it,* he thought.

The other two SIBATs arrived and immediately fired on them. Alex stood at the centre of an inferno of fire and energy, which lashed relentlessly against his surrounding force-field. The immediate ground around him became molten. The stonework around the square, blasted by the fierce heat, blackened. The people fled in panic, and anything combustible within three hundred metres either began to smoke or burst into flames. A part of Alex's mind searched for the Theresa of this Earth. Had she escaped?

Within moments, Trafalgar Square had been turned into something akin to the centre of a volcano. There was a great explosion behind Alex, possibly a gas pipe. He looked up in astonishment through the fury of energies breaking across his force-field as Nelson's Column itself finally succumbed and crumbled to the ground in a resounding crash of stone and an eruption of dust. The solid ground, on which Alex stood and Ruth lay, were kept safe by Alex's force-field — a perfect sphere sitting on a pool of lava which grew with each passing moment.

With his hands held out in defiance, Alex looked down at Ruth struggling to get on her feet. He had never felt so pushed, so energised, yet behind this he could sense that he was beginning to tire.

"Are you all right?" he said.

"I think so."

"They didn't manage to subvert your... systems."

"No. But it was a close thing."

"I can't keep this up forever."

"Alex, it may be best...."

She was cut short and screamed. Like a puppet with its strings cut, Ruth collapsed. Alex was on his knees, holding her in his arms. He couldn't sense any life from her through the implant. In a moment of horror he realised that Theresa, with many others, had perished in the flames. He looked down in despair at the still form of Ruth, as tears broke from his eyes. The SIBATs intensified their bombardment, putting even more pressure on his strained force-field. He concentrated on each of the SIBATs, their shielding deflecting his focus, denying his wishes. But, he remained determined. His awareness of his surroundings fell away as he focused his entire being into one purpose. Without warning the energies falling upon his force-field ceased.

They were gone.

Alex looked at the broken form of Ruth, trying to pick up any sign of life.

"Ruth?"

Nothing.

Ruth? He thought. Again silence. *Don't be dead. Please. We've been through too much together. You can't leave me alone now.* He ran his fingers through her new hair. *It's over, done. We've saved this one. Come back to me, please... please.*

An eerie silence fell on Trafalgar Square in the aftermath of the battle. Alex sat on a small shielded island of stone floating on red hot lava. The outermost edges of the square lay in ruin. Alex had no idea how many had suffered and died, but it was nothing compared to what it would have been. Right at this moment, Alex honestly didn't know if it was worth losing her over.

As time passed and the people came back, he was numbly aware of the sirens of the emergency services. A helicopter hovered overhead, yet still he found he couldn't move.

It's time to go home, Alex, Ruth whispered in his mind.

He broke into sobs of relief as he tightly held the form of her close to him.

Pulling back and wiping at his face he said, "Don't do that to me!"

"I'm sorry," she replied out loud. "Something overwhelmed me and I had no choice but to shut down. It was there waiting for me. To take over my mind should I come back. I believe it may be the same thing we're sensing in the Martians, the Nacuerians..."

Alex nodded and interrupted. "I sensed it too in the minds that inhabited the SIBATs. They're all controlled by the same thing."

"Agents of the Adversary," stated Ruth. "Once the SIBATs were gone, I was no longer threatened. I'm sorry it took a while for me to come back. I had to be sure."

Alex suddenly felt heat around his neck and face. "No... that's okay." He smiled awkwardly, consciously aware of how he held her in his arms. "When you've been so close, as we have, for the last few months. I mean..." He seemed to struggle to find the words.

"It's a unique relationship. Not one your upbringing has prepared you for."

Alex burst into laughter "No definitely not. I think I can say I never expected to have a... friend like you."

Her strange mannequin face managed to beam at him, and he could not help but mirror her expression.

Alex looked at her in wonder. She was incredible. He was both elated and frightened by the mix of emotions whirling inside of him at that moment.

He was conscious he was staring at her.

"Erm," he tried to find something to say as he stood up, helping her to her feet. "Well, Trafalgar Square's done for."

"Better than the whole world."

"What happened to the SIBATs?"

"Teleported them to the Earth's core. I take it even they couldn't have survived that."

"No," she confirmed in a manner which suggested it was more than sufficient. "You should be proud of yourself."

"Are you proud of me?" he found himself saying, another unexpected burst of emotion lacing his words.

She took his hand in hers. "I have been proud of you for a long time now," she said.

"Then I am too."

She looked around at the destruction. "You do realise that the Galacien here will come back, once they realise their forces have failed in their mission?"

"I know," said Alex. "We'll talk to Garianne about a more permanent solution. The two of us can't hold them off. Time to go home?"

A slow smile spread across her lips. "Time to go home," she confirmed.

Thirty-One. Garianne

Earth. The Mariana Trench in the Pacific Ocean. Thirty-five thousand feet below sea level

Aleksandr Lethbridge hides. He would have never dared attempt such a thing a year ago. The darkness is absolute, but far worse than that is the incredible pressure, which attempts to crush his body. He is what the Galacien call super-sentient, though, and he's realised that this means he is difficult to kill. The incredible force exerted on his body by the weight of the water cannot harm him. He feels no need to breathe, even though he's been down here for almost five minutes. The cold doesn't bother him. Yet despite all this, he still feels threatened. He knows he is running out of time, he knows he must escape. A pin-prick of light in the darkness appears and he knows with a terrible dread that they've found him. Even here he can't escape them. They fire their energy weapons, hitting him with the force of a speeding truck. More lights appear. He knows he must go… to where? He does not know. Again he teleports.

The Galacien Institute for Technological Advancement, Earth

"Quite clever, hiding down there," remarked Garianne as she regarded the playback holographics of the attack on Aleksandr, deep in the Mariana Trench.

"I need to get to him," said Nicola.

"At the moment that's not possible, the way he keeps teleporting around like this," said Garianne. Nicola began pacing around. "Be patient, the time will come for you to intervene, if that's what you want."

"He's my only way of getting back home," said Nicola.

"You wish to use him as much as Krrikant does."

"I would ask him," said Nicola, giving Garianne a forced smile, "nicely."

"Aren't you guilty of the same thing, Garianne?" questioned Korina.

What are you doing? thought James to her.

It has to be said.

Garianne slowly turned on James' wife, her eyebrows raised in expectation.

"You want to use Alex just as much as everyone else. Don't deny it."

"Korina," said James in protest.

Garianne raised her hand at James. "I wouldn't say 'use'. A very poor choice of words, my dear. Apply, utilise. Maybe even those words are a little strong. Present him with beneficial options, perhaps. And when I say beneficial, I mean in a 'his and everyone else's continued existence' kind of way."

"Are you sure? I think you are very clever, Garianne. I think most people around here completely underestimate you. I believe you have them all dancing to your tune and they don't even realise it, and that includes my husband."

Garianne considered this. "And how do I exert such control? Considering this is all true, of course."

"As I've said, you're extremely intelligent."

"She doesn't control me," protested Nicola.

"No? Who brought you here? Who's got you where she wants you, watching you?"

"She's paying me, you idiot. As far as I'm concerned, that's the long and short of it."

"She's controlling you."

"And who's controlling you?" said Nicola.

In a flash Korina struck out at Nicola with the back of her fist. Despite Korina's enhancements, Nicola was faster. She turned under the blow and into Korina, ending up behind her, her left arm around Korina's neck and her right hand holding a gun to the side of Korina's head.

"Korina!" shouted James.

"That was stupid," growled Nicola.

Korina's eyes darted about, looking genuinely frightened.

"Let her go," warned James.

"Please. I don't care about her or you. Remind me, who's in control of this situation?" she said, pressing the gun firmly against the side of Korina's head.

Korina looked around the room. "I know what you want me to say, and I will say it, but only because I came all this way to see my husband, and to be shot now would be extremely annoying."

"Forget what I want to hear. Now tell me, who's in control of this situation?"

Korina looked down as if still considering her answer, then at Garianne. "She is."

Nicola's jaw clenched and unclenched. She released Korina, pushing her into James' arms as she considered Garianne.

A beeping sound came from the holographics.

"They've found him," said Garianne. "It appears he's been trying to hide from Krrikant's ship's sensors above the Earth's magnetic pole."

The holographic view in that area expanded until they could make out a tiny figure just outside Earth's atmosphere. What played out before them was a repeat of the events in the Mariana Trench: Aleksandr was attacked and then finally teleported.

"I believe his time is up," said Garianne.

On the outskirts of Oxford — Wolvercote Cemetery

It had stood there for centuries, weathering everything the elements could throw at it. Tonight something fell onto it from a great height, destroying one half of the tower and breaking through the roof with a great crash. Then, all was silent as the clouds continued to stroll across the night sky. The statues in the graveyard cast dark shadows from the glow of the full moon. Inside the church, something stirred. The main doors of the church broke apart as Aleksandr charged through them, only feeling a little guilty for the damage he'd caused: after all, he was being hunted. He stumbled around the graves like a drunk, going from one to another, using them for support. His breathing laborious, he held his head as fatigue threatened to overcome him.

"And so it comes to this," said a voice.

Aleksandr spun around to see Krrikant standing atop a mausoleum. All around Aleksandr, Krrikant's Galacien warriors teleported in, hovering high above, silent, deadly.

"It is over Aleksandr. You no longer have the ability to teleport and, in a few moments I'd be surprised if you had the strength left in you to remain on your feet. Whether you like it or not, you are coming with us."

Krrikant waited patiently, watching. The only sound was the silent rustle of the wind through the tall, dark shapes of the trees. Aleksandr's legs finally buckled, bringing him to his knees. Three Galacien warriors descended, landing softly on the ground. They were making their way towards Alex when Nicola suddenly teleported between them. The Galacien warriors stopped.

"Garianne was ordered not to interfere," said Krrikant.

"Not directly. I asked her nicely to teleport me here, and she obliged. By the way, how's the new body?"

"You have saved me the chore of seeking you out. It is obvious from our previous encounter that there is far more to you than meets the eye. I'm going to find out what that is. It will give me something amusing to do on our way back to Galacien Prime," said Krrikant.

The Galacien warriors closed in on her. Nicola made no move to stop them. The first Galacien warrior's hand touched her shoulder. There was a blur of movement as she grabbed his arm with one hand and punched him twice in the head before violently twisting his arm. He screamed in pain as his arm broke. The second warrior received a devastating blow to his torso, breaking through his armour as if it didn't exist. He fell, clutching his body in shock and pain. The third warrior backed off as Nicola turned on him as the cries of pain from his two comrades echoed across the graveyard. Krrikant and the Galacien warriors looked at both of them, confused.

"Something wrong?" she questioned as she launched herself at the third warrior, slamming her hand into his face. Blood gushed forth from the impact and he fell back. His moans now joined the duo in pain and anguish.

"This cannot be," protested Krrikant.

"Is there a problem?" said Nicola as she walked over to Aleksandr, ready to protect him.

"You know there is. Why can't those three access their implants and cut off the pain? How are you preventing my warriors from firing on you? And why can't I get any readings from you?"

"Not telling," smiled Nicola.

"You're not super-sentient. You are something else. A mystery. I must know. I must have you," said Krrikant, with a look akin to hunger.

Nicola kissed the air and pouted, "Then come and get me." She was poised, ready to fight.

There were flashes of light everywhere like a giant fireworks display as Galacien warriors popped into existence all around Nicola. They kept coming until there were hundreds of them, on the ground and in the air. They converged on her, and those who approached from the front were a little confused to see that she was smiling.

The fight began in earnest as Krrikant watched in fascination. His warriors were being torn to shreds by this lone woman. It was obvious that her strength and speed were not natural. No blow seemed to faze her, and she was highly resistant to physical injury. Yet what intrigued Krrikant the most was the fact that no technology seemed to work against her. Energy weapons fizzled and died in her presence, personal shields were inoperative and implants could no longer nullify the pain she was dishing out. There was no point in bringing in the SIBATs for they would be rendered useless. Without technology, his people were reduced to barbaric ways of combat. Their strength of numbers should have made the difference, but she continued to break them down systematically without tiring or gaining injury.

He had to admit he had never seen anyone fight this way. His warriors were highly trained, yet Nicola moved around them as if she expected every move they made. She even added unnecessary flair to her moves, as if she had all the time in the world and was filling in this time by adding in a bit of style. Then there was the look on her face, as if she was enjoying herself. What was she? The dark presence in the back of Krrikant's mind was fascinated by this anomaly. Luckily he was far enough away from her that he could just about contact his ships above.

A surgical strike on her position, if you will, said Krrikant.

What about our warriors?

Leave them, I don't want her aware until it's too late.

And the super-sentient?

He will survive it as long as you hit her.

Krrikant's implant fed him the telemetry from the ships' weapons systems as it built and fired. A shaft of crimson broke through the clouds and, an instant later, a hole was blasted into the Earth with Nicola at the centre. More of the church fell apart from the shockwaves of the impact. Graves close to Nicola were broken or simply blown over like dominoes, bringing up the earth around them. At the smoking centre, where the grass and top soil had been burned off, a naked Nicola slowly rose to her feet.

Hit her again, ordered Krrikant.

The shaft of light came down again, bringing Nicola down abruptly to her knees.

Keep firing until she's incapacitated or dead. I'd prefer the former.

The Galacien ship in orbit fired three more times until Nicola finally lay still. Smoke rose from all around her, and Aleksandr had been blown over two hundred feet from her. He barely had enough strength to move and couldn't sense whether Nicola was alive or dead.

Krrikant was pleased to see most of his warriors had survived and that their technology was working again.

"Secure them both quickly. Check if she's alive," said Krrikant.

The warriors hurried over the ruined graveyard. Others made their way towards Aleksandr. As soon as the closest warrior touched Aleksandr, he disappeared. The others froze. Krrikant looked around suspiciously until two figures emerged from the darkness.

"I believe you've been looking for me," said Alex as he walked confidently down the scorched path with Ruth by his side. He looked at his alternate self and the still, smoking form of Nicola.

Krrikant's implant's sensors slid off this being. He had obviously created some kind of force-field around himself.

"I can only deduce that Garianne has informed you of who I am and what I want?" questioned Krrikant.

"Everywhere I go it's the same," muttered Alex to himself. Then he looked up. "I suggest you go now."

"I'm afraid Nicola and both you super-sentients will be coming with me," said Krrikant. "Your implant persona can stay, if you want; I have no interest in... her."

Alex shook his head.

"Have it your way," smirked Krrikant.

Within a few seconds, over a hundred protector class SIBATs teleported in. Some in the sky, others on the ground: they were completely surrounded. Alex could sense their lethal weapon systems were armed and aimed at him and Ruth.

"Perhaps it would be best if you reconsider and come peacefully," suggested Krrikant.

"I have travelled to dozens of Earths, fought and beaten Martians, Nacuerians even the Galacien. And, by the way, their technology was more advanced than yours. So either get off my planet, or, as we say here on Earth, bring it," said Alex, strengthening his force-field.

Krrikant could barely hold his anger in check, yet he did, for it would be over soon enough. "Alex, I have just given my ships the order to target multiple locations across the face of this globe. Come with me, or in mere minutes your planet will be reduced to a wasteland. You cannot prevent this from happening. It is over."

"No!" came a voice.

General Alexander abruptly stood before them. Another Alex appeared from behind. First there were only a handful, but soon enough there were almost as many of them as there were SIBATs. Both sides looked cautiously at one another.

Garianne appeared with yet another Alex, and James, as calm and unflappable as ever.

"It is over, Krrikant."

They both approached one another in what had once been the church graveyard. Krrikant regarded the super-sentients as he walked to her.

"An impressive army you've mobilised here — you have been busy. My orders do extend to any and all super-sentients. You are obligated to obey."

"But they are not," said Garianne.

"We've had this discussion."

"And the result was that you tried to force them. Do you believe you can force all of them if they stand together against you?"

"You interfered."

"Only when you threatened the safety of this world. My mandate is to protect this planet from any threat. Even if that threat comes from the Galacien."

"Will you do the same with Sol 9173?"

"That is a natural event. I cannot intervene directly."

Krrikant looked at those opposing him for what seemed like forever, while Garianne waited patiently.

"Garianne," said James. "We're detecting more ships coming out of hyperspace into orbit above the Earth."

"Ah," replied Garianne in apparent understanding. "You've been playing for time."

"I'm disappointed in you, Garianne. I expected more from the War's supreme strategist."

James became agitated. "Over twenty ships, Garianne. They're launching their full complement of SIBATs."

"They will surround this planet in seconds. I suggest you consider handing over the super-sentients. Perhaps explain to them that not even they can intercept and pre..."

Krrikant stopped in mid-sentence as he watched a SIBAT high above to his left drop like a stone and hit the ground with a crash.

Garianne and everyone else too watched this odd interruption. They all turned to see another, to Krrikant's right this time, fall inert to the ground. A third hit the ground only metres behind him, then a fourth some distance away. Before they knew it they were dropping like giant hailstones. Those on the ground jumped aside, teleported or erected a force-field.

As soon as it had begun, it was over. Krrikant stood bewildered.

Report, demanded Krrikant to his ships above.

There was no reply.

"There will be no aggressive action taken against the Earth or its inhabitants," came a voice which pervaded the air. Jonas stood atop the mausoleum mere feet away from Krrikant and Garianne, with Min and Kallon on either side of him. "I will permit you to leave, this time. If you change your mind, I will know instantly and destroy you before you can even finish issuing a single order. Now, go."

With that, Krrikant and his forces were gone leaving Alex and Ruth, for the first time, considering the gathering of these extraordinary individuals.

Thirty-Two. The Game

London

Nicola awoke wearing only simple underclothes. She could feel the firm yet yielding bed beneath her, and the soft covers against her body. She struggled to remember what had happened. Memories. She always had a problem with remembering her past. Sometimes she saw images so brief, she could only get the barest hint of what they were. Nicola had not told any of them yet about her loss of memory: it was her secret and she did not give her trust easily. She looked around the room to see an assortment of unfamiliar medical machines and equipment.

Galacien?

The door opened and in walked James and who she presumed was Aleksandr. She looked uncertainly at Aleksandr. Was this her Alex, as opposed to one of the others she had seen, from other universes?

"What happened?" she croaked, as she brought herself up to a sitting position.

"Krrikant hit you with a particle beam from orbit."

She stopped moving, "Sounds... lethal."

"It was," said James. "They fired several times."

"What happened?"

"Jonas happened. They're gone for good," said James. He paused for a moment, thinking about his next words. "Have you any idea how you could survive such a bombardment?"

"Can't your fancy machines tell you that?" she said, indicating the equipment around her.

"No," he replied.

She considered them both for a moment. "I don't know how, I only know I can. I'm faster, stronger and far more durable than those around me, and..."

"And?" pushed James.

"Technology works or fails, depending on whether I want it to or not."

"You're super-sentient," stated Aleksandr.

"Garianne says she isn't," said James.

"But it all seems to fit," shrugged Aleksandr.

"If I'm not super-sentient, then what am I?" asked Nicola.

"Something else," said James. "We're not sure yet, but we can find out together. That is, if you want to?"

Nicola thought for a moment. "Yes, I think it's about time I stopped running from my past and finally found out who and what I am."

"You have a place with us here, while we help you look for those answers," smiled James.

"What about you?" she asked Aleksandr.

"If what Garianne says is true then we are all involved in the coming struggle, whether we like it or not. I don't quite understand what my part in all this is yet, but there is something about Garianne. I believe what she says and will do what needs to be done," said Aleksandr.

Nicola felt surprised by his conviction and couldn't help but think about what Korina had said. "Forgive me if I'm a little more cynical. For now, though, I'll play along."

James seemed satisfied with this, but his thoughts too were troubled by his wife.

Alex and Ruth stood together on the roof of the Galacien Institute for Technological Advancement building, looking out as the sun set over the cityscape of London.

It's good to be back, thought Alex.

It certainly is, agreed Ruth.

A cool breeze washed over them bringing up Ruth's long green hair.

"Have you got used to it yet?" she said, not looking at him.

"What?"

"My physicality."

"It's growing on me," said Alex

"I keep adding new aspects to it."

"Yes. I must admit I feel more comfortable now your mouth moves when you speak."

Ruth laughed at this, revealing her teeth and tongue, and he could not help but smile.

"I'm glad to see you two are still getting on," came Garianne's unmistakable voice from behind.

They turned as one.

"I guess we were going to get on either very well, or end up killing each other," said Alex.

"You nearly got us killed on more than one occasion with your recklessness," said Ruth.

"Hey, I thought I did rather well, considering the circumstances."

"Yes dear, you did actually. He did," Ruth said to Garianne. "Have you got a medal for him?"

Garianne smiled and to Alex it seemed like time stretched out and the world was so much brighter. "I am proud of both of you. Alex, I'm sorry for putting you in such circumstances."

"You should have asked," he said, surprising himself with his shortness.

"I know." She stopped a moment. Something flashed across her expression, a little too quick to catch. "It is a habit of mine. We all have our flaws, no matter how infallible we, and others, think we are. Mine has been, and will always be, about control. I believe that if we are to survive the dark days ahead then I must be in control. To some this may seem egotistical or even delusional. However, it is neither: it is a simple fact. Consider the last year of your life; was I wrong to send you away? It delayed Krrikant when he arrived. Helped bring the others together, not to mention Jonas. You've grown so much and in such a short space of time relative to this universe. I did what was best for us and for you. However, you are right: perhaps the way in which I did it was wrong, and for that I hope you can accept my apologies."

Garianne waited for his answer, as Alex found himself completely disarmed. He did not expect her to be so open with him. For a moment he was utterly speechless.

"As much as I may want to, I can't stay angry with you. This last year I've seen things which will haunt me forever. However, I've also seen incredible things and experienced wonders I've never dreamed of. I have become something I'm truly proud of," Alex said looking at Ruth.

"We're both proud of you. Aren't we, Ruth?" said Garianne.

Ruth nodded.

Alex said, "But did it make a difference? The multiverse seems infinite... does any of what I did matter, when dealing with something of that scale?"

"In some ways it may seem as if it doesn't. You could spend the rest of your life continuing the work you started, and it would not count for any appreciable fraction of the alternate Earths out there. If it was your world in particular, though — if it were this world, those you loved and cared for, would it then make a difference?"

He thought of Princess Victoria and others from all those other Earths.

"Yes," he said, finally.

"That can never be taken away from you, Alex."

"I couldn't save them all," he added, thinking of the Nacuerian invasion.

"I know; Ruth has already sent me her report. I know about the ones you saved, the ones you couldn't and the ones which are still in danger."

"What are we to do?" asked Ruth.

"What about Sol 9173?" said Alex.

"We will talk of it soon. Don't worry, I will not allow that to come to pass. Despite humanity's immature ways, I personally feel that it has become an exception to Galacien law, due to it being the only place in the galaxy to give rise to a super-sentient in the last two millennia," said Garianne.

The door to her office opened and Garianne entered, regarding Jonas, Kallon and Min.

"It is good to see you again Jonas, and you too Min," said Garianne pleasantly. Jonas nodded simply, Min merely looked at her defensively. "Kallon, I haven't had the pleasure and yet..."

"I know," he said. "In a way we have, when I was once Jonas."

Garianne nodded in understanding.

Min's discomfort increased. "Can we get on with this?" she said.

"Min," frowned Kallon.

"You're still angry with me, after all this time," stated Garianne.

"Only because you haven't changed."

"Perhaps not. You believe me to be arrogant, manipulative and dismissive of the individual for what I consider to be the greater good," said Garianne, without a hint of ire or objection.

"I didn't say that."

"It's what you think."

Min looked down for a moment. "It is."

Garianne nodded. "Now we have that cleared up, what can I do for you?"

Jonas began to tell Garianne of his conclusion about the Kinsmen, how they had moved from his previous encounter with them over two thousand years ago into an alternate universe. How he wanted the help of a multiversal teleporter to follow the trail. As he continued to speak, his metaphysical self left his body, waiting above them as Garianne did likewise. She was a beautiful creature of light in this form, unseen by the physical world. Here they could speak in private as they had done numerous times in the past. Min and Kallon were unaware that Garianne and Jonas were able to converse simultaneously in metaspace.

How goes the work? spoke Garianne's metaphysical self.

As I have said, I will follow the trail. Yet there are two things which concern me, one significantly more than the other.

The first being?

A mystery which has eluded me for some time. When I encountered the Kinsmen entity over two thousand years ago, it told me that I did not understand, but that one day I would.

I have reviewed the recording the Entrophier made of the encounter, stated Garianne.

It seemed at the time that the Kinsmen were trying to help me, to help us, during the Galacien/Nacuerian war. In a way they did. But I now believe something far more... incredible.

Go on, spurred Garianne.

The Kinsmen were referring to my future self. They were speaking to me now, from the past, said Jonas, galvanised by his own words.

Jonas, they could not sense you in the future; that's impossible.

Is it? The Entrophier can view the past.

That's different. The past in any particular universe is set. The future is fluid. Such are the laws of our multiverse, stated Garianne, with a certainty which left no room for debate.

I am well aware of the laws which govern our reality. That does not mean there isn't a way. The Kinsmen could have calculated within an acceptable amount of certainty that I would seek out the Entrophier and view our encounter in the hope of finding them.

Even after all this time?

They knew, Garianne. During the war, they knew I was watching them from the future, our present.

Garianne's metaphysical self smiled. *I've missed our talks Jonas. I think you could be right. But why? Why not communicate directly?*

I don't know. All I can do is follow, and see where it all leads to.

Garianne said nothing as she thought on this, before finally saying, *What is the second thing which concerns you?*

I am being manipulated.

By whom?

By the Adversary.

How? What is the mechanism of this manipulation, she said.

I don't know. Only at times I can sense its intent. At first I wasn't sure but now I am. The Adversary is quite content to watch and wait for me to discover the secret of the Kinsmen.

Again despair threatened Jonas and he numbly pushed it aside.

If you are so sure, then cease your search.

I cannot. They could still prove helpful.

Jonas, I'm concerned about you. What is it?

He looked at her with haunted eyes. *I don't think you fully appreciate what we face, what this thing is. This being can accomplish anything with a thought, yet it does not. It is aware of us and our plans to end its existence because of the threat it poses to us. Why does it not simply wipe us out? Why!?*

Be calm. You must control yourself and stay with me, said Garianne. *The alternative is madness.*

Jonas nodded, looking at her for an answer to his question.

Garianne said, *This creature is capable of stopping every one of us in a blink of an eye. And you are right to ask such questions. I think the reason is for its own amusement.*

Jonas looked at her curiously.

Think about it. A being that can accomplish anything — if it were to destroy everything, what would be left? Nothing. We give it meaning and a purpose. Any limitations it has are only those it imposes on itself.

So this is just a game for its own entertainment? he said.

Exactly. It's all a game. The Nacuerian/Galacien war, just a war-game for its own recreational pursuit.

How can you be sure?

It's speculation, of course, but it seems to fit with what we know and your encounter, said Garianne. *It's just one of the many games it plays throughout the multiverse, except whole worlds are being destroyed, entire species wiped out. It finds super-sentients particularly interesting pieces in this game because of their abilities. The Kinsmen also interest it for as yet it doesn't know who or what they are.*

Could it find out?

I'm sure it could. But imagine an existence where everything is known, where there are no secrets, no surprises. A rather boring one, wouldn't you say? The Kinsmen are a mystery, and it finds that rather exciting, I think.

It doesn't worry it?

Why should it? It is confident in its place of supremacy.

Garianne, do 'you' not feel the dread which permeates my being? said Jonas.

She smiled at him and he could feel no such thing from her. He couldn't understand it. She fully grasped, as he did, the reality of the situation, yet it didn't seem to faze her. Or was that it? Was this just another mask she wore? One that was so much a part of her, through all those years, that it was now who she truly was. How deep would you have to go underneath all that steely confidence to get any sense of fear?

Jonas, to tell you the truth, I feel relieved.

Relieved? he exclaimed.

Yes. I have carried so many burdens alone for so long now. I am glad that this one, especially, I will not bear alone.

Jonas felt strength flow into him as she continued to smile. *You are not alone, Garianne. And we will face it together.*

She took his hand and her metaphysical touch made him feel even stronger.

Only in spirit, I'm afraid. You must continue your search, while I gather the super-sentients.

He held back the urge to tell her of his falsified memories. No. This one he would keep between himself and Lom.

Thirty-Three. Assembly

The Galacien Institute for Technological Advancement building, twenty-first floor

The doors to the main hall opened. James was the first to enter, immediately followed by an assortment of the super-sentients, each of them, in some sense, a variation of the being known as Alex Lethbridge. Each Alex was essentially the same, yet quite different. Some Alexes wore apparel ranging from the colourful to the plain, from a distinctly armoured Alex to one who wore only the simplest of robes. All manner of other physical aspects set them apart. One Alex had grown his hair down to his shoulders, while another had no hair at all, not even eyebrows. Their builds were different, the ways they walked and spoke: some came from Earths where English was a dead language. Many were armed, from simple swords to kinetic and energy weapons, either slung over their shoulders or hanging on their hips.

The last of them was the Alex native to this Earth, dressed simply in jeans and t-shirt with Ruth by his side.

They look like a bunch of extras taking a break at a film studio, he thought.

Ruth suppressed a laugh. *I'd agree, yet look at them. Each one from an Earth entirely different from yours. Each one has his story of this planet different from the rest. I wish I had a chance to speak to them all, find out those stories.*

I feel like I'm getting it already.

Remember, whatever you're sensing they're feeling more or less the same.

The main hall had been reconfigured into something resembling an amphitheatre. Some of the Alexes began to spread out and sit, while others preferred to stand. Alex found it rather odd to see his face everywhere, despite the wide range of differences.

That one's completely covered in tattoos.

They're not tattoos. Not in the typical sense. It's a Galacien shannroj. He's wearing a translucent skin suit. Keep an eye on it; it moves, she thought, looking amused at his confusion.

I don't understand why that one is armoured. He doesn't need it, he's super-sentient, observed Alex.

Possibly ceremonial, said Ruth.

Alex looked her up and down. *Nice to see you're finally wearing something.*

Like him, she was dressed simply in jeans and a t-shirt. *I've been refining my anatomy to the point where it would be considered perhaps indecent to some if I wasn't dressed.*

Alex found his eyes drawn to her as she continued to scrutinize the other Alexes. He wondered just how far she'd gone.

She caught him looking at her and his face reddened. He was glad that it was at this point that Garianne entered the hall, along with Nicola, Jonas, Min and Kallon. The latter three stood to the side of the room while Nicola sat at the front. Jonas and Alex's eyes met for a moment before Alex looked away. He could not maintain the unwavering gaze of the large man. Even though there were scores of super-sentients in the room, they were the only two of this Earth — of this known universe. Yet Jonas had been born over two thousand years ago. How would he start a conversation with someone like that? Apparently he despised humanity, so did this extend to anyone remotely human? The two Jonas kept company with were human. There seemed to be a constant look of suspicion on his face, or was he just deep in thought? Alex was alarmed to see Jonas suddenly break from the trio and approach him and Ruth.

"You are the Alex of our Earth," stated Jonas.

"Erm... yes?"

"It is good to meet you."

"It is?"

Jonas nodded. "In all of our galaxy, and possibly beyond, we are the only super-sentients."

Jonas extended his big hand and Alex took it.

Alex thought of the girl who tried to help him when the meta-humans came for him.

"What is it?" said Jonas, sensing his confusion.

"Something I've not thought about for a while now. A group of meta-humans attempted to abduct me."

"That is unusual behaviour for their kind."

"Is it? Anyway, I heard a girl's voice in my head. She was trying to help me. She struck me as very capable and clever. She was there, I could sense it, but almost as if in some kind of spirit form." Alex regretted his last comment as it now seemed silly.

Yet Jonas was enthralled by his words and showed no sign of ridiculing his speculations. "Anything else?" said Jonas.

"I told Garianne and she said she'd look into it."

"And?"

"She's not spoken of it since and I've only just remembered it now. What do you make of it?"

Jonas looked at Garianne, as if pondering something. "I am not sure."

It was then that Garianne spoke. "If I may have your attention." Her voice resonated around the hall and all noise abruptly ceased. "Thank you. Most of you have managed to make it here today, but not all. Not surprisingly, for your worlds have been, or are at this very moment, in dire peril. You have been briefed and know of what I speak. The god-like being we call the Adversary threatens all your worlds and many more. It is impossible to know how far this goes or whether there is any potential defence out there in the multiverse against such a being. Yet, if we do not take action then perhaps no-one will, and this entity will be allowed to wreak havoc across reality for all time." There were a few mutterings at this. "For the last year, our time, I have been searching for beings such as yourselves to bring together a force with which we can fight the Adversary and its agents. As individuals your abilities are nothing compared to the limitless power of our enemy. But as a combined, cohesive force, applied in the right manner, we may have a chance."

Alex could feel their hope and a steely resolve, as Garianne spoke: she had a way of inspiring people. It also hadn't escaped his notice that each of them having the ability to feel one another's emotions had a self-perpetuating effect: it created an overwhelmingly positive reaction to her words. He could not help but smile.

Only Jonas, in contrast, felt cynical.

Garianne continued, "Jonas here has also offered to help in his own way, by searching for the elusive Kinsmen. Some of you may feel his talents would be best served with us. It is my experience, however, that we have more chance of success if we have more than one plan of attack. The Galacien and all the worlds in this galaxy survived the Nacuerian invasion over two thousand years ago because we had a wild card. This was something the Nacuerians didn't expect or hadn't taken full measure of. That wild card was Jonas. This time, if they can be found, it may be the Kinsmen."

And if both fail? thought Alex to Ruth.

Ruth heard his thoughts. She looked at him, but couldn't think of a reply.

James and Korina kissed one another long and hard in the bedroom of their rather lavish apartment.

James pulled back. "I missed you," he said.

"I missed you too. It's good to be off that Galacien ship and back on Earth."

"You were giving Garianne a pretty hard time earlier. I know she can be pretty tough sometimes, but believe it or not she's our greatest ally."

"Whose?"

He looked at her for a moment. "The human race. She's one of the few insisting that they make Earth a special case due to the super-sentients it's produced to stop Sol 9173."

"I'm sorry, I don't trust her. She plans and schemes, not letting you know what's going on until it's absolutely necessary. I think she keeps things from you... from all of you who work for her."

"Perhaps." He picked up his drink and walked over to the window. "I figure she knows what she's doing. I mean, she's over six thousand years old. We're mere babes compared to that."

"She's still capable of making mistakes," said Korina.

James put down his glass "Can we talk about something else? This is the first time we've been alone since you got back."

"Well, not quite," she replied, looking around for the unseen wormhole that they both knew was there.

"They don't care. I don't care. Do you?"

"I do, actually. I'd like to have some privacy, just once," she smiled going to him, stroking his chest and kissing him once again. "It has been too long, darling."

James put his hands through her hair as he asked the central observation hub for complete privacy until he contacted them again.

The access was granted and they became unseen to the Galacien.

Korina smiled as she looked up at him. "Completely alone."

James didn't smile back. His face went white as he felt his implant go dead, and in its place something dark and sinister entered his mind. He felt it taking over everything that he was, pushing his remaining faculties into a deep, dark corner. All he could do was watch in horror. It was over in less than a minute as Korina looked on patiently.

"Is it done?" she said.

James nodded, saying, "This one also belongs to us. Tomorrow so will the super-sentients."

Light years away on a Galacien ship, Krrikant smiled.

Alex didn't need to sleep, and yet he did. Alex didn't need to dream, and yet he did. The sun had only just set and the light in the garden in which he found himself was fading fast. He was surrounded by pink and white blossomed trees. He could hear water running somewhere to the back of the garden where shadow seemed to dominate, to the point where he was unsure whether anything existed there at all. He considered the old Japanese house; its shutters were closed with golden light straining to pour out.

"It has been a while, Alex," said a voice.

Alex turned and saw the woman he knew in his dreams.

"Cerise," he said, rushing over and grasping her by the shoulders.

She smiled warmly. "It has been too long."

"Longer than you think. It may seem like only days since we last met, but for me it has been much longer," said Alex.

"I've missed you too," said Cerise.

"Cerise, when I'm awake I never remember any of this, yet here I remember everything you've taught me."

"Good. Because it is high time we continued your training."

He nodded. "I'm ready. What will you be teaching me tonight?"

"Not me," said Cerise looking to the rear of the garden.

From the shadows appeared a girl. Her movements were fluid and precise, her focus as sharp as a knife. He sensed her resolve, harder than diamond.

"Hello Alex," she said, "nice to meet you, again. My name is Alicia."

About the author

Pete Cruickshank lives in Huddersfield, England. When not working, looking after his family, reading, or playing video-games too much, he manages to write in his spare-time.

The Kinsmen Book 1: Between Gods and Mortals is his first novel in the Kinsmen saga. This book is the second. If you have any feedback please don't hesitate to contact him at petecruickshank@thekinsmen.co.uk

If you have enjoyed this book please do spread the word or write a quick review on
www.Amazon.co.uk
or
www.goodreads.com

www.thekinsmen.co.uk

www.ingramcontent.com/pod-product-compliance
Lightning Source LLC
Chambersburg PA
CBHW021223060726

47590CB00005B/1616